Rave Reviews

THE WAY YOU LOVE ME

"Fans of Ray's Grayson and Falcon families will be thrilled with the first installment in the new Grayson Friends series. And this is done very well…told with such grace and affection that this novel is a treat to read." —*Romantic Times BOOKreviews* (4 stars)

UNTIL THERE WAS YOU

"Ms. Ray has given us a great novel again. Did we expect anything less than the best?"
—*Romantic Times BOOKreviews* (4 stars)

"Crisp style, realistic dialogue, likable characters and [a] fast pace." —*Library Journal*

"Francis Ray's graceful writing style and realistically complex characters give her latest contemporary romance its extraordinary emotional richness and depth." —*Chicago Tribune*

"It's a joy to read this always fresh and exciting saga."
—*Romantic Times BOOKreviews* (4 stars)

"The powerful descriptive powers of Francis Ray allow the reader to step into the story and become an active part of the surrender...If you love a great love story, *Only You* should be on your list."
—*Fallen Angel Reviews*

MORE . . .

MAR 09

"Riveting emotion and charismatic scenes that made this book captivating…a beautiful story of love and romance." —*Night Owl Romance*

"A beautiful love story as only Francis Ray can tell it." —*Singletitles.com*

"Readers will find a warm and wonderful contemporary romance with plenty of humor and drama. Adding a fun warmth and reality to these characters and a plot that moves quickly add all the needed incentive to read this fun book." —*Multicultural Romance Writers*

IRRESISTIBLE YOU

"A pleasurable story...a well-developed story and continuous plot." —*Romantic Times BOOKreviews*

"Like the previous titles in this series, *Irresistible You* is another winner…Witty and charming...Author Francis Ray has a true gift for drawing the reader in and never letting them go." —*Multicultural Romance Writers*

DREAMING OF YOU

"A great read from beginning to end, it's even excellent for an immediate re-read." —*Romantic Times BOOKreviews*

"An immensely likable heroine, a sexy man with a heart of gold, and touches of glitz and color, [this] is

as unapologetically escapist as Cinderella. Lots of fun."
—*BookPage*

YOU AND NO OTHER

"The warmth and sincerity of the Graysons bring another book to life....delightfully realistic."
—*Romantic Times*

"Astonishing sequel...the best romance of the new year...the Graysons are sure to leave a smile on your face and a longing in your heart for their next story."
—*ARomanceReview.com*

"There are three more [Grayson] children with great love stories in the future."
—*Booklist*

SOMEONE TO LOVE ME

"Another great romance novel."
—*Booklist*

"The plot moves quickly, and the characters are interesting."
—*Romantic Times*

"The characters give as good as they get, and their romance is very believable."
—*All About Romance*

ALSO BY FRANCIS RAY

GRAYSONS OF NEW MEXICO SERIES
Until There Was You
Only You
Dreaming of You
Irresistible You
You and No Other

The Way You Love Me
Any Rich Man Will Do
Like the First Time
Someone to Love Me
Somebody's Knocking at My Door
I Know Who Holds Tomorrow
Trouble Don't Last Always
Not Even If You Begged
In Another Man's Bed

ANTHOLOGIES
Rosie's Curl and Weave
Della's House of Style
Going to the Chapel
Welcome to Leo's
Gettin' Merry

Nobody But You

FRANCIS RAY

St. Martin's Paperbacks

This is a work of fiction. All of the characters, organizations, and events portrayed in this novel are either products of the author's imagination or are used fictitiously.

NOBODY BUT YOU

Copyright © 2009 by Francis Ray.
Excerpt from *And Mistress Makes Three* copyright © 2009 by Francis Ray.

Cover photograph © Shirley Green

For information address St. Martin's Press, 175 Fifth Avenue, New York, NY 10010.

ISBN: 0-312-94685-6
EAN: 978-0-312-94685-2

Printed in the United States of America

St. Martin's Paperbacks edition / March 2009

St. Martin's Paperbacks are published by St. Martin's Press, 175 Fifth Avenue, New York, NY 10010.

10 9 8 7 6 5 4 3 2 1

To my daughter, Michelle, who went with me to Texas Motor Speedway. You are always in my corner no matter what—even if you have to get up at 5 a.m.

Acknowledgments

This book could not have been written without the tireless and wonderful assistance of Mike Zizzo, Director of Media Relations, at Texas Motor Speedway. Mike invited me to the Dickies 500 and gave me a media and a cold pass that allowed me in the garage and pit area. TMS is one of the top racing tracks in the country. The employees are friendly and knowledgeable. The experience is one I'll never forget.

Mike recommended I read *NASCAR for Dummies* by Mark Martin with Beth Tuschak before I attended the race. The book was invaluable and helped make sense of all the fast-paced action on and off the track. I highly recommend it if you want to know more about NASCAR. NASCAR.com is also a great place to find information.

and

Jim Gaughan, a NASCAR fan, who helped me understand the working of a NASCAR racing team and why all those rows and rows of Goodyear tires were treadless.

Thanks also to the following people:

McClinton Radford Jr., my only brother, and a former drag racer. Thank heaven big brothers don't mind if you call and ask the same question again and again.

Kerry Tharp, NASCAR executive, who was kind enough to give me an interview and discuss diversity. Women and minorities are gaining visibility in NASCAR and making their mark.

and

NASCAR for Dummies by Mark Martin with Beth Tuschak

THE MCBRIDE FAMILY TREE

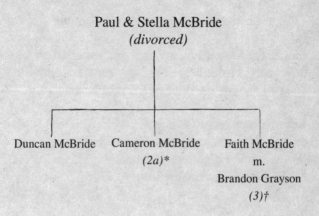

Paul & Stella McBride
(divorced)

Duncan McBride   Cameron McBride   Faith McBride
                 (2a)*   m.
                                    Brandon Grayson
                                        (3)†

GRAYSONS OF NEW MEXICO NOVELS
1. Until There Was You
2. You and No Other
3. Dreaming of You†
4. Irresistible You
5. Only You

GRAYSONS FRIENDS SERIES
1a. The Way You Love Me
2a. Nobody But You*

Prologue

She wasn't responding the way Cameron McBride had anticipated.

He was experienced, not some wide-eyed kid who went for speed over technique. He prided himself on his ability to match his skills against anyone's. Yet, he knew his mind wasn't on what he was doing.

A surefire way to get into trouble going over a hundred and eighty miles per hour with twenty-three other drivers gunning to snag the checkered flag was to let your mind wander. Knowing it and doing something about it were completely different. It had nothing to do with the experimental race car he was driving on the California Speedway. The two-mile racing surface was one of the best tracks in the NASCAR Sprint Cup Series.

He was the problem.

Cameron always had trouble in California. Los Angeles, his last known address for Caitlin, was an hour east of Fontana, the home of the California Speedway.

Caitlin, why did you leave me at the altar?

Firmly pushing her from his mind, he concentrated on the approaching curve. Cars had to slow down or risk spinning out of control. Before he reached the straightaway he had to work his way into position to pass the car ahead of him. He also had to watch the slower, lapped cars.

"Cameron, how is she?"

The soft-spoken voice of his crew chief came over the headphones in his safety helmet just as Cameron accelerated in the straightaway. Michael "Mike" Alvarado was one of the best crew chiefs in the business, and had been with Hilliard Motorsports racing team for the past seven years. "Rough and tight," Cameron answered, his fingers curled around the steering wheel. "She might be the Car of Tomorrow with all the safety features NASCAR has required, but I don't think she's ready for the track."

"Hilliard says different. Might I remind you that's why you're racing in the Busch Series race today, to get her ready for next week's NASCAR Sprint race in Las Vegas," came his crew chief's reply.

"When Hilliard is sitting where I'm sitting he can make that decision. Until then you can tell him—"

"Now, Cameron." Mike chuckled, in a deep drawl reminiscent of his Texas roots. He was a gentleman and peacemaker on and off the track. "Is that any way to talk about the man who signs your checks?"

"Yep," Cameron shot back. He respected Sean Hilliard, was honored to be on one of Hilliard's four-man NASCAR race team, but he wouldn't hesitate to tell Hilliard his honest opinion. Case in point, the car he was driving. "She's too tight, Mike. She doesn't feel right."

"Bring her on in, Cameron," Mike told him. "No sense borrowing trouble. We'll look her over again."

"Not a chance." Cameron shot around a curve, straightened, and managed to muscle his way past another car. "I'm in fifth place now with fifteen laps to go. I can win this ra—" The loud explosion of a blowout negated what Cameron had been about to say.

Muttering a curse, he fought the steering wheel as the car went into a wild spin. Another race car clipped his right rear bumper, sending him in the opposite direction.

Cameron saw the retaining wall looming ahead of him, knew he was going to hit and there wasn't a thing he could do to prevent the crash.

Chapter 1

"It's a miracle you're alive. I caught the crash on the TV in a patient's cubicle," commented Dr. Dan Reems, the chief resident in the emergency room of Mercy Hospital, his long arms folded across his thin chest as he peered at Cameron over the silver wire frames of the eyeglasses perched on his nose.

Cameron agreed wholeheartedly. His car's front end looked like crumpled paper, but thanks to the new safety regulations NASCAR had implemented in the Car of Tomorrow, he had walked away with minor bumps and bruises. "Yeah."

"Will he be able to race tomorrow?" Hilliard asked, his teeth clamped on an unlit cigar. As owner, he had a lot riding on the answer. Sponsors wanted winners. Fans tended to patronize the advertisers on the cars that grabbed the checkered flag. Hilliard was very wealthy on his own after taking his money from a buyout of the computer firm he'd started, but it was nothing for one team's expenses to run from 10 to 15 million dollars a year, and Hilliard had two teams.

Cameron had long ago gotten over the fact that

the race, not the driver, came first. He was only a tool. But he was one of the best.

"I don't see why not." Dr. Reems shook his graying head of hair and peered at Cameron over his eyeglasses again. "The X-rays and EEG checked out. He'll be sore as hell in the morning. He won't be able to take the muscle relaxants and drive. It will depend on him."

"I'm driving." Cameron reached for his black T-shirt and pulled it over his head, wincing as sore muscles protested.

"I'll give you a prescription for tonight." The doctor went to the counter and quickly scribbled on a pad, tore the sheet off and returned. "An autograph for an autograph."

"Sure." Cameron exchanged the prescription for a pad and pen his publicist, Mike's daughter, Hope Alvarado, held out.

The room was crowded with his pit crew chief, the engine specialist, and a couple of reps from his two biggest sponsors. The reps wanted to make sure their investment was protected and Cameron was still racing the next day.

From years of practice, Cameron quickly personalized the autograph, and signed his name with a flourish. "Thanks, Dr. Reems."

"Thank *you*," the middle-aged doctor said, proudly looking at the autograph with a wide grin.

A tall, attractive woman in a black double-breasted business suit and white silk blouse stepped forward, her right hand extended, her left hand wrapped around

a leather folder pressed to her chest. "Mr. McBride,
I'm Ms. Jessup, the hospital spokesperson. There are
quite a few news media representatives outside waiting for you. We've set up a conference room just off
the emergency room for you."

"Thank you," Cameron said, his grin slow and lazy.
"I appreciate it."

The woman blushed. "I'll show you the way."

Cameron eased off the exam table. Mike opened
the door and they all piled out of the cubicle. Conversation in the various patient units scattered around
the open area stopped for a full fifteen seconds.
Since winning the Daytona 500 last week, he'd been
thrust into the limelight more and more. Used to the
stares, Cameron usually didn't pay them any attention. But he was well aware that if things had gone
differently, his life might have been dependent on the
skill of the hospital's staff.

The moment he walked through the double doors,
cameras flashed, the waiting media surged forward.
Questions were fired at him. Several off-duty policemen acting as security moved in front of the boisterous
crowd.

"Please hold your questions and move aside. You're
obstructing the hallway," the hospital spokesperson instructed.

The policemen pushed the crowd back to clear a
path to the patient care area of the emergency cubi-
cles. As they parted, a small group of people, apparently seeing a chance to get past the media, quickly
came through the narrow opening.

Leading the charge were two men in white lab coats. Directly behind them was a young boy on a gurney being pushed by a woman in scrubs. His leg in a splint, he appeared to be in his mid-teens. On the far side of the gurney and away from Cameron was a woman carrying a small child. Her head was bent, her arms clasped securely around the boy, whose face was turned away.

There was something oddly familiar about the woman. She hadn't glanced in his direction, but he'd seen her hunch over further as her hand clutched the child closer to her. Cameron slowed his steps, turning to watch the woman. In a matter of seconds, she had passed them.

He couldn't say why he couldn't take his gaze from her. No woman had ever come close to making him feel even a fraction of the all-consuming desire he'd had for Caitlin.

He was afraid no woman ever would.

Just before she would have rounded the corner, the woman paused, then glanced back. Their gazes met. The jolt to his nervous system was worse than hitting the wall.

Caitlin.

He had finally found her.

Her eyes rounded, her mouth opened, but no sound that he could hear emerged. Quickly turning away, she hurried around the corner and out of sight. His jaw clenched. Without thought, he started after her.

It had been more than five years and she was still running from him. *Why?* He'd asked himself that question too many times to count after she'd shamed him before his family and friends. In all this time, he hadn't figured out the answer.

"Cameron," Mike said, catching his arm. "Where're you going?"

Anger rolled through him. "Let go of me," Cameron hissed, not taking his gaze away from the spot where Caitlin had disappeared.

Frowning, Mike's fingers uncurled. "Cameron, son. You all right? The doc miss something?"

The doctor, the nurse, and the spokesperson who had attached herself to them ten minutes after he'd arrived, converged on him. "Do you have a headache? Blurred vision? Are you in any pain?" Dr. Reems asked, his bushy brows furrowed.

Cameron's head snapped back around. "Hurt" was a mild word for what he felt. He'd tried to dismiss her, forget her, hate her. He had been unable to do any of those things.

The media, sensing something was wrong, pushed closer. The two policemen were able to keep them back. If they sensed the woman who had made him a joke of the NASCAR circuit was nearby, they'd exploit it to the hilt.

He didn't need that. Winning the Daytona, the NASCAR kickoff, last Sunday boded well for him for the rest of the season. He planned to win the NASCAR Sprint Cup Series championship for the second year in a row. Nothing was going to stand in his way.

Firmly, Cameron turned around. Now wasn't the time. He didn't want the media bringing up her jilting him every time they interviewed him this season. He'd had enough of that the season after Caitlin had wrecked his life. The media had had a field day at his expense. NASCAR SPRINT SERIES DRIVER LEFT AT THE ALTAR.

"Cameron, do we need to postpone this?" Hope asked. Even before she finished speaking, some in the media were protesting. Hope kept her eyes on Cameron. She wouldn't be swayed by what the newspeople wanted. Hilliard put winning first, Hope put her clients first. She had several NASCAR drivers as clients and had a reputation as a tough cookie. When pushed, she pushed back. Cameron liked her for that reason.

She might only be twenty-six, reach to the middle of his chest, and weigh a hundred ten pounds soaking wet, but like her father, she had steel in her backbone. And the media knew it. They didn't mess with Hope Alvarado.

She would push him or any of her clients if necessary, but she had a sixth sense for when to back off. Since his first win of the season at Daytona, life had been crazy. She had helped keep it manageable.

"Let's get this over with," Cameron finally answered.

Surrounded by his team members and the media, Cameron started down the hall, still trying to process seeing Caitlin after all these years. He'd looked for her after she'd run away, but she'd made good her escape.

Entering the small conference room, Cameron continued to the front, his mind unable to fully relinquish

Caitlin. What he didn't understand was the fear he'd just seen in her eyes. Was it because of the little boy she held so protectively? Had she moved on while he couldn't erase her memory? Was he that big of a fool, to have kept hoping that one day she'd come back to him despite the McBride curse of being lucky in business but unlucky in love?

Faith, his little sister, had certainly escaped the curse. Married to a man she had loved since high school, she couldn't be happier. Cameron and their older brother, Duncan, thought they had escaped the curse as well, but both had been proven terribly wrong.

"Mr. McBride, please have a seat behind the middle mic," instructed the hospital spokesperson. "Mr. Alvarado and Mr. Hilliard can sit on either side of you."

Cameron did as told, his mind back in the emergency room. Did he want to find the answers to his questions or just move on? He wished he knew.

Caitlin couldn't stop shaking. Wasn't it enough that Joshua had tried to make a trampoline out of the sofa and injured his shoulder on the end table when he'd fallen? She had to calm down and deal with seeing Cameron. The day she'd dreaded and dreamed of had finally happened. And it couldn't have come at a worse possible time.

"Mommy, you're squeezing me too tight."

"Mommy is sorry," Caitlin murmured, making herself release Joshua and set him on the exam table.

"I want to go home," he murmured. "My shoulder doesn't hurt any more."

Caitlin swept her hand over his head, cupped his

soft cheek, glad he was too young to notice that her hand trembled.

"Mommy, you're doing it again." Joshua wiggled in her arms.

Caitlin stared down into her son's face, felt the lump in her throat grow larger. Each time she looked at him she was reminded of his father.

Her smile trembled as she brushed her hand over his head again. "You scared me," she said, an understatement if ever there was one.

Her heart had stopped on hearing Joshua's scream of pain. Her son was too much like his father. He didn't know fear, and that scared her more than anything. She hadn't been sure what she'd find when she rushed from her home office to the den. He'd been on the floor, crying and holding his left shoulder.

It wasn't until after they'd arrived at the emergency room that he'd calmed down enough to tell her and the doctor what had happened. He'd lost his balance while using the sofa as a trampoline. He'd mumbled the explanation with his head down, and for good reason.

They had rules about playing on furniture and about trampolines. Caitlin refused to buy one or allow him on the one belonging to the family of his best friend next door after another neighbor's daughter Joshua's age had broken her arm the week before. That was enough for Caitlin to put it off limits.

Joshua looked up at her. "My arm doesn't hurt anymore."

She kissed him on the cheek. "I'm glad, but we still have to wait until the doctor looks at the pictures."

"You think she'll give me a treat like Dr. Bob?" Joshua asked, his eyes wide and hopeful.

"Probably not," she told him. "But since you were doing something that was against the rules and dangerous, do you think you deserve to get a treat?"

The answer wasn't long in coming. "No, ma'am, but it would make me feel better."

Caitlin had to smile. Joshua had a way of turning things around in his favor. He was a charmer, just like his father.

The smile died on her face. Sitting on the bed, she hugged Joshua to her, careful of his shoulder. She hadn't known about Cameron's accident until she was sitting in the emergency room waiting for Joshua to be seen. Racing was big business, but since NASCAR only had two races a year at the California Speedway racetrack, she managed to endure the madness.

Terrified, she'd watched on TV as his car spun like a top on the racetrack as other cars tried to miss the out-of-control vehicle. One couldn't avoid the contact, clipping his right back bumper and sending the car straight for the wall. She shivered again.

She'd almost lost Cameron today. He still made her body want, her heart race. And today her greatest fear might have come to fruition—she might have lost him.

That was the reason she hadn't been able to resist one last glimpse of him when she unexpectedly passed him in the hall. She'd been sure he wouldn't notice her with all the media and his crew around him.

She'd been wrong. Once, perhaps, her mistake could have been costly, but not after more than five years. She'd hurt him. Deeply. He probably hated her, and she couldn't blame him.

The curtain whooshed back. Caitlin tensed before she could help herself, then relaxed on seeing Dr. Mathis, who had examined Joshua, enter. She was over-reacting. Cameron wanted no part of her. He was probably long gone.

"The X-rays confirmed what I thought," Dr. Mathis said. "Just a deep bruise. You'll be fine, Joshua. Just remember, a sofa is not a trampoline."

Joshua looked sideways at his mother before answering, "Yes, ma'am."

The young doctor chuckled. "I'm betting your mother will help you remember," she said, then turned and spoke to Caitlin. "You can give him Motrin if he complains of discomfort for the next couple of days."

"Thank you, Dr. Mathis." Caitlin stood and took off the hospital gown Joshua wore and helped him put on his shirt, watching his face as he lifted his arm. There was only a slight grimace, unlike the howl of pain he'd given when she removed it after they arrived.

"Thank *you*," Dr. Mathis said with a smile. "Because I was on call, I got a chance to see Cameron McBride."

Caitlin tensed as she buttoned Joshua's shirt. Her gaze snapped up to the grinning young doctor. "He's not still here, is he?"

The pretty woman sighed dramatically. "Afraid not. The press conference lasted only about ten minutes. I understand McBride ended it early, saying he had things to do."

Caitlin tried to tell herself she was glad Cameron had left. Unfortunately, she didn't do a very good job.

"Are you a race fan?" Dr. Mathis asked.

"No," Caitlin quickly said, shaking her head for emphasis.

"My fiancé is nuts about NASCAR." The doctor pulled a sheet of paper from a prescription pad out of the pocket of her lab coat. "I managed to snag his autograph on his way out the door. My fiancé will be ecstatic."

"Thank you for fixing my owie," Joshua said.

"You're welcome." A friendly smile on her face, Dr. Mathis brushed her hand over his head. "Just play safe. A nurse should be here shortly with your discharge orders and you can get out of here."

"Please. I'd like to get Joshua to bed."

Nodding, Dr. Mathis left the cubicle. Almost immediately a male nurse entered with a clipboard and went over the discharge orders again. Caitlin quickly took the pen the nurse handed her and signed. Putting the sheet of paper in her purse, she picked up Joshua and headed for the door.

Quickly she exited the double doors of the emergency room entrance, and headed for the exit straight ahead. She was almost there when a man stepped out of a hallway to block her path.

"What's your hurry, Caitlin?" Cameron asked, as he lifted his shades.

Caitlin gasped and stepped back, clutching Joshua tighter to her. She didn't look around for an escape because she knew there was none.

Time had run out for her.

Chapter 2

Despite how tense the situation was, she couldn't help but be thankful Cameron was unharmed and admire how gorgeous he remained.

Cameron was six feet two of lean, conditioned muscles and elegance. The plain black T-shirt molded his wide chest. Gently faded denim flowed over his thighs, and cupped his impressive rear.

Joshua lifted his head from her shoulder. "Mommy, what's the matter?"

She flushed at being caught ogling Cam, but she now had a more pressing problem. Helplessly she watched anger build in Cameron's face.

"It didn't take you long to forget, did it, Caitlin?"

Joshua turned toward Cameron. "You know my mommy?"

The anger in Cameron's face swiftly gave way to stunned recognition, then fury. Caitlin couldn't recall one thing she had rehearsed all of these years to say when this very moment might come.

Cameron stared in amazement at the little boy's face. He'd know the McBride stamp any place, the startling black eyes, the no-nonsense nose, the dimples that all of them detested. The child was his.

And Caitlin had kept him from Cameron.

There were so many emotions—joy, anger, relief, betrayal—that Cameron had no way to sort them out. So he did what he did on the racetrack where there was no place for any thought except winning the race: he tucked the emotions away and concentrated on the most important thing—his son.

Concern banished Cameron's rage. He closed the distance between them. He had to clench his hands to keep from reaching out and touching his son. *His son.* Looking at the tiny replica of himself, he still found it difficult to believe.

And Caitlin had kept him a secret. He might not have been able to find her, but she would have had no trouble letting him know he was a father. He'd take care of her later. For now, the child was all that mattered.

Cameron's eyes hardened again when he noticed the simple gold band on the third finger of Caitlin's left hand. She had let another man raise and love his child. Had he ever known her?

The woman he knew, loved more than life, wouldn't have kept his son from him. She was one of the most loving, giving people he knew. Family meant a great deal to her since her childhood had been so tragic. Cameron's gaze traveled back to the child who was looking at him with mild curiosity.

Unable to delay the moment any longer, Cameron lifted his hand, gently touched his son's cheek with just a finger so as not to frighten him. "Hello," he said, his voice thick. "My name is Cameron."

"Hello, Cameron," the little boy answered, lifting his head to stare at Cameron. "You get a boo-boo, too?"

Cameron's gaze quickly surveyed his son, looking for an injury. Seeing nothing obvious, he looked at Caitlin. Her frightened gaze told him nothing. "What happened? Is he all right?"

Her arms tightened around their son before answering. "He's fine, just sore. He fell off the sofa and hit his arm on the coffee table."

"Where were you?" Cameron asked, his voice harsh. Caitlin flinched. Cameron clenched his hands to keep from reaching out to her. He hadn't meant the question to sound accusatory.

The little boy tucked his head and laid it back against his mother's shoulder. "I broke a rule."

"I need to get him home and into bed," Caitlin said, the words meant to dismiss Cameron.

Cameron nodded. She'd gotten away from him once, but never again. Not with his son. "Where are you parked?"

She moistened lips he still dreamed about. "In the garage."

Cameron gently grasped her arm. "Let's go." He would have reached for his son, but after being hurt, he needed his mother. But later . . .

She balked. "I can manage."

"If you think—" Cameron bit back what he had been about to say when the little boy raised his head.

In a calmer voice he continued. "Let's get out of here before a reporter decides to come back to interview the staff."

Her golden-brown eyes, slanted and beautiful, widened. She clutched the boy so tightly against her, he squirmed. Her protectiveness of their son was obvious.

"Are we going home, Mommy?"

"Yes, sweetheart," Caitlin answered, but she didn't move.

"Whatever you're thinking, don't. I'm not leaving." This time when he gently took her arm and urged her forward she complied. Outside the temperature was a warm seventy-three. Lights from the security camera lit the area. Neither spoke as they walked to her car on the first floor.

"I need to get my key," she said, her gaze bouncing away from him.

Cameron released her, then reached for his son. "Which arm was hurt?"

"I can hold—"

"Give him to me," he told her, looking at his son who looked back with the same black eyes. "You don't mind, do you—" His gaze flicked to Caitlin, hardened for a fraction of a moment before going back to his son. "What's your name?"

"Cameron Joshua Lawrence," he said, going into Cameron's outstretched arms as if he had done it a hundred times. Cameron gently folded him in his arms, felt the warmth, the slight weight, but there was sturdiness there as well. His uninjured arm went around Cameron's neck.

His body trembled with emotion. The fact that she'd given the boy his name somehow increased his anger. He could have given his son so much more. Because of Caitlin's betrayal, Cameron had missed so much of his son's life. He had to be over four years old.

"You have a lot to atone for, and a lot to explain."

She turned away from him and unlocked the back door of a BMW SUV. A car seat was in the back. Cameron stepped around her when she reached for Joshua and placed the little boy in the car seat. Finished, Cameron climbed inside next to Joshua and closed the door. Caitlin stared at him a long moment, then rounded the car and climbed into the driver's seat.

Cameron's and Caitlin's eyes met in the car's mirror. "I did what I thought was best."

"You—" Cameron broke off abruptly. "We'll talk later."

During the fifteen-minute ride to where Caitlin and Joshua lived, neither she nor Cameron spoke. Joshua had fallen asleep five minutes after they left the hospital. She kept checking to ensure he was all right, and each time she had looked, Cameron had been watching his son.

He'd never forgive her; she accepted that irrefutable certainty. It couldn't be helped. Joshua's safety and well-being were well worth the price she'd have to pay.

The hurtful truth was that Cameron had paid a price as well. She couldn't change that.

Turning on her signal, she passed the unmanned

guardhouse and stopped by the code box. Moments later the eight-foot black iron gates slowly swung back. She pulled through as soon as space permitted. The sooner she and Cameron talked, the quicker he'd leave.

She swallowed, her damp palms clamping and un-clamping on the steering wheel. Who was she trying to fool? There was no way Cameron was leaving his son. They'd never talked about having a family when they dated or after they'd become engaged, but she knew the kind of man Cameron was—dependable, intelligent, loyal. He'd want his child.

Although his parents were divorced, he was close to them and his sister and brother. Family was im-portant to him. And she had kept him from his son.

He might never forgive her. That was his right, but under the same circumstances she'd do it again.

Five houses down she turned into the side drive-way of a single-story stucco house with a red barrel slate roof. For three years she had called the house her sanctuary. That was about to change. Pulling up to the driveway, she activated the gate, waited until it opened, and pulled inside the triple bay. Joshua's bike was in the second bay. By the time she switched off the mo-tor and rounded the SUV, Cameron was lifting Joshua from the car seat.

"I'll take him."

"You'd had him enough."

Fear leaped into her heart, lodged in her throat, making speech impossible. Cameron was a popular NASCAR driver, more so since he'd won the Daytona 500 last week. Even before that he'd been on numerous daytime and late-night talk shows, and had graced the cover of several magazines, including *GQ* and *People*.

If he decided to seek custody of Joshua, she'd have a difficult time winning. Especially when it was learned that he hadn't known he had a son. "I love him."

"I know. You just didn't love me."

Caitlin gasped. The words were so preposterous she just stared at him. She'd loved him with all her heart. She still did.

He stepped around her and headed for the door leading to the kitchen. "Joshua needs to be in bed."

He was right this time. Their son was what mattered now. Their son. Funny, she'd seldom let herself think of Joshua as *their* son. Just hers. She realized it had been easier that way. She hadn't missed Cameron as much if she did . . . at least it worked until she was alone in her big empty bed. The ache was unbearable at times. More times than she cared to remember she'd gone to sleep with tears on her cheeks, hugging a pillow.

Unlocking the back door, she stepped inside and flicked on the light. "This way." She went through the spacious kitchen, family room, then turned down a wide hallway and entered a room at the end of the hall on the right and turned on the light.

The room had built-in bookshelves crammed full of books, favorite objects he'd found at the beach or on vacation, his computer. Joshua was an inquisitive boy, and daring, just like his father.

Going to one of the twin beds, Caitlin bent to pull back the top covers. Straightening, she went to a chest of drawers and pulled out a pair of pajamas. "He can skip a bath tonight."

Without a word, Cameron gently placed Joshua on the bed. Much to Caitlin's discomfort, he didn't step back. "I can manage if you want to wait in the den."

He finally looked at her. His eyes were cold, with none of the playful charm and warmth she remembered. "I'm spending as much time with my son as possible." Cameron began to unlace Joshua's tennis shoes.

Caitlin's hands clenched on the pajamas. She had been afraid of that. The McBrides might be unlucky in love, but perhaps because of it, Cameron and his family were fiercely loyal to one another. His mother divorcing his father had made them even closer.

Cameron knelt by the low bed, unbuttoned Joshua's jeans, and began to slowly pull them off his legs. The sight tore at her heart. Despite knowing the futility of it, she had, at times, imagined Cameron being a part of their lives.

She wanted that for herself as well as for her son, but the risk was too high. She couldn't, wouldn't, allow him to follow in his father's dangerous footsteps. Today proved how right she had been to leave and keep Joshua a secret.

At four and a half, Joshua was beginning to ask questions about his father. So far she had been able to evade them, but she knew her time was running out.

Still on his knees, Cameron looked up at her. "What about his shirt? Will it hurt his arm if I take it off?"

She shook her head. "No, but he can keep it on."

Aware she couldn't keep standing there, she went to the bed. Cameron only moved back a few inches, his gaze on Joshua as if he still couldn't believe he had a son. Used to maneuvering the boneless Joshua into his pajamas, she quickly got him ready for bed. Finished, she pulled the covers up to his chin, a useless act since he kicked them off at night, just like his father.

"He'll be all right if he rolls on his shoulder, won't he?"

The tenderness and concern in Cameron's voice tore at her. For the umpteenth time she wished things might have been different, wished his father hadn't chosen such a dangerous profession.

Nodding her head, she reached over to the lamp and clicked it on to the first and lowest setting. She usually plugged in the night-light, but tonight she wanted to be able to see him more clearly. Bending over, she brushed her hand across Joshua's head, then kissed him.

"Good night, Joshua. Sleep tight." Straightening, without looking at Cameron, she left the room, leaving the bedroom door open.

"Where's your room?" Cameron asked as he followed her into the hall.

She couldn't stop the hot shiver that raced over her. Cameron had been her first and only lover. He had been an excellent teacher. They'd made a shambles of more than one bed. Even broken a few headboards. Her body heated. "Across the hall. I wanted to be able to see him. There's also a monitor in his room."

He glanced at the partially closed door to her

room, then back at a sleeping Joshua. "How could you have kept him from me?"

Guilt and pain splintered through her. The quiet voice didn't fool her. The quieter he was, the angrier he was. He once told her that he had had to learn to control his emotions to race. "I wanted to keep him safe."

His hard gaze snapped up to her. "Make sense, Caitlin."

"Let's discuss this outside." Without waiting, she went into the family room and waved him to a slate-blue leather side chair in front of the matching sofa. She'd wanted the house to be pretty but functional, to not worry if Joshua spilled something or came inside with mud or dirt on him.

She'd made a home, a good home for her son, but the cost had been high. Too nervous to sit, she wrapped her arms around her jittery stomach and made herself not fidget or pace as she so desperately wanted to do.

Cameron didn't even glance in the direction of the chair. "Explain."

Oddly she was reluctant. How could she explain the unexplainable to Cameron? He'd never understand. Never in a million years.

"I'm waiting."

And he wouldn't wait much longer. Cameron was a fair man. He was a patient man on the race circuit, waiting for his chance, the opening to move ahead, then he'd be fearless. He'd be no less aggressive now in finding answers.

"Did you let another man raise my son?"

"No." She wasn't foolish enough to think he was jealous. It was his son's love and affection that concerned him. "I'm not married. I thought it would be better for Joshua if everyone thought I was married."

His jaw clenched. "You didn't want to marry me."

Her nails dug into her arms, which were crossed over her waist. She'd wanted that more than life. Leaving him had almost killed her, but she couldn't stay. Eventually her fear would have driven them apart or made him hate her. "I didn't tell you about him for the same reason I couldn't marry you."

Hurt he couldn't hide flickered briefly in his eyes, then there was nothing. "I was the joke of the NASCAR circuit."

Her hands clenched. She'd read some of the news reports. It hadn't been pretty. She'd cried for both of them. She'd been miserable and lonely until she discovered she was carrying their child. "That wasn't my intention."

He took a step closer, bringing with him the masculine scent that was uniquely his and his barely leashed anger. "You could have fooled me."

Her eyes widened, her nostrils flared at the haunting scent. He was too close, too dangerously tempting. In the past five years he'd lost his youthful handsomeness. His face now had character. He was the only man she had ever loved and the one man she couldn't have.

"Talk, Caitlin. I want to know about Joshua," he told her, his patience obviously strained. She couldn't blame him. She couldn't begin to measure the agony she'd feel if Joshua were taken from her. If she didn't get Cameron to understand, that was exactly what might happen.

"I didn't know I was pregnant when I left. When I discovered it, I didn't want to tell you for fear you'd make our child a part of the racing world I hated."

"You should have told me," Cameron insisted.

"NASCAR racing is your life. You wouldn't be happy doing anything else. On race day, your eyes light up like a kid's on Christmas morning."

"We've been through this before," he said, his impatience evident by the flicker of his gaze down the hallway toward Joshua's bedroom.

"Yes, but that was before I knew Johnny Jenkins. Before I saw his race car hit a wall and explode. Before I sat next to his wife and six-year-old son and watched it happen." Tears clogged her throat. It had been horrible.

"I'll never forget Nan's screams. Their little boy crying for his daddy." Her voice trembled. "After all these years, just thinking about it still makes me physically ill."

Cameron's expression softened. He took the step necessary to pull her into his arms. She considered evading his touch, but it was no more than a passing thought. The comfort and warmth of his body was a lure she couldn't resist. It had been too long; she loved him too much.

"Sometimes I can still hear her scream, hear the car hitting the wall, see it explode seconds later, splintering into pieces, the fire, his son calling for his father." And each time she did, she thought it could have been Cameron, who had been several cars ahead at the time.

Her hands clutched Cameron's T-shirt. "In the blink of an eye, he was gone and there was nothing anyone could do to help him."

"Caitlin, don't. Please." Cameron's large, callused hand swept up and down her back. "Johnny wasn't just a teammate, he was a close friend. His death affected all of us. His tire blew. Safety measures have been initiated in the cars and the equipment since then. Racing is safe."

Her laughter ragged, she pushed out of his arms. "How safe were you when you hit the wall this afternoon?"

He didn't flinch, didn't look away. "Very. I'm here without a scratch and it's because of the car that I'm okay. The safety measures worked."

"How can you be so blasé about it?" she snapped. "Today isn't the first time you've crashed."

His eyes narrowed. "How do you know that?"

She could have bitten off her tongue. She'd let fear overcome caution and said too much.

"How?"

Her mind sought an answer that wouldn't condemn her even more. "NASCAR is a big business and growing. You can't pick up a newspaper or go into a number of major chains during racing season and not see something about NASCAR. That you're one of the few African Americans to race in the NASCAR circuit, and the first to finish in the top ten year after year, puts you even more in the spotlight."

"Which means you could have easily found me to tell me I had a son," he told her, his jaw tight.

"I won't have him sitting in the stands and watch you hit a wall or another car," she told him fiercely. "I won't do that to my son."

"He's my son, too, in case you've forgotten," he reminded her. "You can't make all the decisions. Not anymore."

"I'm his mother," she cried.

"I'm his father," Cameron shot back.

Her chin lifted. "I'm a good mother. I've always done what's best for Joshua."

"That's debatable, but that's about to change," he said.

"What . . . what do you mean?" Her stomach felt leaden.

"You can't possibly think I'm just going to leave and let you have my son." Cameron braced both hands on his hips.

Terror sent a chill through Caitlin. "You race thirty-eight weekends out of the year, live in a motor coach three to four days every week during that time, make public appearances, woo sponsors. You're busy from the moment you get up until you go to bed each night. You don't have time to take care of Joshua."

"I've missed enough of Joshua's life. I don't plan on missing any more." He turned toward the boy's bedroom.

She caught his arm, felt the solid ripple of muscles,

the warmth, the strength that she had once leaned on. "You can't possibly think of taking him."

"You can't possibly think I'll leave him," he told her.

"His life is stable here. He has friends here. His school," she cried, trying to make him understand. "He has everything."

"Except his father. And guess who is to blame?"

The last words slapped her in the face. Her fingers uncurled. Helplessly she watched Cameron walk down the hallway and enter Joshua's room. Fear that she'd never experienced before coursed through her.

Cameron might take her son.

Cameron entered his son's room and went straight to the bed. Joshua had kicked the covers off. Cameron's mouth curved upward. He did the same thing. Replacing the sheet and bedspread with comic-book characters, he wondered what else they had in common.

His mouth hardened. He'd missed enough of his son's life. No more.

Cameron's hand brushed tenderly across Joshua's forehead. The surge of love he felt for his child was staggering.

"You have grandparents who are going to want to spoil you, an aunt and uncle who will do the same, but not as much as I plan to. I want to know what you like, dislike. Know the sound of your laughter, be there to soothe your hurts. Watch you grow up. And I promise you I will be."

Adjusting the covers up to Joshua's neck, Cameron

sat back in his chair and watched his son sleep. A
simple pleasure that Caitlin had deprived him of.
Never again.

   After the race tomorrow he was leaving California
and when he did, he was taking Joshua with him
whether Caitlin agreed or not.

Chapter 3

Silently, Caitlin turned away from Joshua's door and crept across the hall to her room.

She'd heard Cameron talking to Joshua. The softly spoken words had sent a stab of remorse through her. She understood Cameron's anger. He had a right. But with a mother's love, she knew she had a duty to protect Joshua. Her decision had been the only one possible.

Leaving the bedroom door open a few inches, she went to the dresser and pulled out a sweatsuit instead of pajamas. She wouldn't be able to sleep tonight, but more to the point, she didn't want to be in her nightgown if—no, make that when—Cameron wanted to talk to her again.

She didn't think Cameron would come into her room while she showered. He hadn't given any indication that he still cared about her, but she wasn't taking any chances. Whatever there was between them had to stay in the past. It would only make the impossible situation between them more so.

In her bathroom, she changed into the lightweight top and bottom and brushed her teeth, her thoughts still on Cameron. The announcer on the television in the hospital had said Cameron had qualified for the NASCAR Sprint race the next day and was slated to be in the eleventh slot of forty-three drivers.

If he followed his usual routine on race day, he'd want to be at the garage when the crew arrived early in the morning to check the stock car over thoroughly. Before he left in the morning, he'd want to see her. Not because he still loved her, but because of Joshua.

Finished, she stared at herself in the mirror. There were a couple of wrinkles in her forehead that weren't there five years ago, and her black hair was longer, but otherwise she looked the same. There hadn't been a flicker of attraction in Cameron's stern gaze. She'd never let herself dwell on how he'd feel about her if they met again. She'd been more concerned about his reaction to Joshua.

She'd killed any chance for them when she left him at the altar. She understood that. The nail in her coffin was Joshua. He'd never forgive her for that.

Picking up a brush, she pulled it through her hair several times, tossed it on the marble vanity, then walked back into the bedroom. Through the door, she could see Joshua in one of his boneless scrawls, asleep on his stomach. The covers were tucked around his neck.

Cameron's doing.

Joshua kicked the covers off at least twice every night. She regulated his room temperature at seventy because of it.

Caitlin quietly slipped out of her room and went

to Joshua's open door. Cameron remained in almost the same position in the chair with his hands laced across his flat stomach, his long legs stretched out in front of him. He was used to being almost immobile in his race car for hours.

The California Speedway was two miles. The cars went five hundred laps with only absolutely necessary pit stops, and during that time the driver remained in the race car. That ability for stillness always amazed her.

Joshua was the same intent way when he was really interested in what he was doing. His patience at his age astounded her. She caught glimpses of Cameron's personality and quirks in her son, like kicking off the bedcovers, more and more. One thing she would fight tirelessly against was Joshua's following his father into stock car racing.

She'd lost her father to racing, she would not lose her son. Her hands clenched. She'd lost her mother at the same time. She just hadn't known it then.

Before Cameron could notice her, she went back to her room and eased the door partially closed and climbed into bed. Cameron would watch Joshua. There was no need to worry about him tonight. Tomorrow was another story.

Watching Joshua sleep, Cameron pulled out his cell phone and dialed. In seconds he was talking to his older brother, Duncan. He was incredulous that Caitlin had kept their son a secret. Cameron didn't want to discuss Caitlin. He didn't want to think of how wrong he had been about her or recall how much he still wanted her no matter how much he wished otherwise.

"Let me get Faith on the line, and let her know she's an aunt," Cameron suggested.

"You all right?" Duncan asked.

Cameron blew out a breath. His brother wasn't fooled. Both of them had been kicked in the teeth by the McBride curse and lying women. It had taken both of them time, and a lot of brotherly and sisterly love, to pull their lives back together. They loved hard, but not wisely.

"I've got a son. That's all that matters."

"What about his mother?" Duncan asked quietly.

"She didn't want me enough to hang around. Her choice, but she's not taking my son from me one day longer," Cameron said tightly. Too tense to remain still, he paced, his gaze on the sleeping child. He stopped.

"You should see him, Duncan. He looks like pictures of me at that age."

"Hopefully, he'll grow out of it," Duncan said.

"Funny," Cameron said, aware his brother was trying to lighten the mood. "Hold on while I call Faith. At this time she should be in her office." He hit speed dial. The phone was answered on the third ring.

"You're still all right, aren't you?" Faith asked.

"Better than all right." Cameron had called Duncan on the way to the infield infirmary and asked him to call all the family. His mother didn't watch the races, but his father did . . . if he wasn't fishing. Duncan usually watched, but Faith, with a five-star hotel to run, seldom had the four hours to spare.

"You have the pole position for the race tomorrow," she guessed.

The fastest qualifying car gained the pole position and track starting preference. Besides the driver being awarded a check, it brought recognition to him and the sponsor. "Nope, I have a son." There was utter silence.

"What?" Faith asked. She sounded stunned.

Duncan explained everything and finished by saying, "He's there now with him."

"I can't believe Caitlin would do anything so heartless," Faith said.

"What do you call leaving me at the altar with over four hundred guests?" Cameron asked, his voice sharper than intended. "Sorry."

"You have nothing to be sorry for," Faith told him. She had always been a nurturer. "What does my nephew look like? When can we see him? Oh, my." She sniffed. "You have a son, Cameron. Oh, my. I'm an aunt. Brandon and Duncan are uncles. Mom and Dad are grandparents. Do they know?"

"I wanted to call you and Duncan first," Cameron confessed. Through the years the three of them had grown closer after their parents' divorce, and even more so after the debacles concerning his and his older brother's love life.

"Take a picture with your BlackBerry and send it to me. I can't wait until we can see him."

"It might be a couple of weeks. I want Joshua to get used to me first."

"That means you're planning on taking him with you?" Duncan asked.

"Yes." Cameron stared down at Joshua. "I've lost enough time with my son."

"What about Caitlin?" Faith asked quietly.

"Perhaps it's time she knew how it feels to be separated from your child."

"Cameron, I know you're upset and you have a right to be, but you can't separate a child that age from his mother," Faith said. "He has to be a little over four."

He rubbed his hand over his face. "I don't even know his birthday."

"You will, but Joshua comes first," Duncan said. "We were adults when Mom and Dad divorced, and it still took the wind out of us."

They'd hurt for their father who still loved their mother. She, on the other hand, wanted her freedom and had moved to New York. Four months later, she'd married an architect. They'd feared for their father's sanity until he'd taken up competitive bass fishing. "Don't worry. I'll think things through before I make a move."

"I know. You're cool on or off the track," Duncan said.

Except when it came to Caitlin. "Good night. I'm going to call Mom and Dad and let them know they're grandparents."

Cameron hung up the phone and dialed. His father answered his cell on the fourth ring. "Hi, Dad. Christmas came early this year."

Cameron smelled coffee. His eyelids flickered, then opened. He glanced at his wristwatch and frowned. It was 6:05 A.M. Caitlin wasn't an early riser and wasn't much of a coffee drinker. On the other hand, he had to have his shot of caffeine in the morning. One cup loaded with cream and sugar and he was good to go. And on race day he was up by six and in the garage an hour later with his team checking over the car.

Adjusting the covers over Joshua, who was sprawled on his stomach, Cameron brushed a kiss across his forehead and left the room. In the hallway, he paused in front of Caitlin's door. He'd caught a glimpse inside the room last night. Soft peach and beige tones, a wide bed with lots of pillows.

If he let himself think about her in that bed or who might have joined her in it, he'd lose it. Just because he hadn't slept with another woman didn't mean she'd been by herself all these years. He'd let that stay in the past. Joshua was what was important now.

Not wanting to open the door any further, he rapped on the doorframe. He just hoped she wasn't wearing one of those short thin silk gowns she'd preferred when they were living together. Mornings were always tough enough without seeing those long silky legs and recalling them wrapped around his waist as he wrung cries of pleasure from her.

"Cameron."

He whirled. Caitlin stood less than ten feet away dressed in jeans and a soft cotton top. She was covered from her neck to her toes. He tried to tell himself he was pleased. She certainly wasn't. She wore that same weary expression she had last night.

She had good cause.

"I figured you'd want to talk before you left. I made coffee."

She was trying to be civil and he was trying hard to forget the soft, fragrant skin he'd loved to kiss and taste under the slim-fitting jeans and white tee. More than the coffee, he'd liked making love to her in the mornings. His body stirred as if it were yesterday instead of five years since they'd made love.

Moistening her lips, she glanced away. Apparently he wasn't the only one dealing with memories best forgotten. "Thanks."

Nodding, she turned and went back down the hall. He followed, his gaze dropping to the denim cupping her hips, the feminine sway of her body. His hands clenched. He jerked his gaze upward, but not before he recalled his hands cupping her hips as he surged into her moist heat.

In the kitchen, she waved him to the round table for four. He practically dove into the cushioned seat. His jeans were too tight in the wrong place. He looked around the spacious, ultramodern room to clear his mind.

A blue mug trailing tendrils of steam was set in front of him. Instead of sitting at the table, she leaned one hip against the bar stool at the end of the counter. The seat of the stool next to hers was built up five inches higher. The fabric matched. She caught him staring at the stool.

"Joshua likes sitting with me so I had the seat built up."

"You seem to have done very well for yourself." She'd been a struggling travel writer when they'd first met.

"I write a syndicated cartoon script," she said

proudly. "I have a home office so I can spend more time with Joshua. He's on a soccer team, in the children's choir at church."

He folded his arms. He knew she was pointing out how she'd provided for Joshua and how disruptive taking him would be. "He sounds busy."

"Busy and happy. I can provide everything he needs," she said. "You don't have to worry about him."

"You seem to have forgotten one thing."

She eased away from the stool. "I did what I thought best for Joshua. Don't use him to get back at me."

He came out of his seat in one controlled rush. "Use him? If anyone has used him, it's you. You've selfishly kept him from his father because of your fears. You didn't think what was best for him, just what you wanted."

"He's safe with me."

"Then why was he in the emergency room last night?"

She gasped.

He saw the hurt flash in her eyes and clenched his hands to keep from reaching out to comfort her. "You've had your turn, now it's mine."

"You can't take him from me!"

"You mean I can't be as cold and callous as you? What if I took him for four years?"

Her arms circled her waist. "I did what I thought was best."

"So you keep saying."

"Please, Cameron."

"Have Joshua ready by nine in the morning to go

with me. I'll be more generous than you were, but only for Joshua's sake. You can come if you want, but I won't be denied my son."

"You can't just take him!" she cried.

"I can and I will. Defy me or try to run, and you'll regret it," he said, his voice a cold promise. "I'm not without contacts and I'll use every one of them to obtain permanent and total custody."

Caitlin sank down on the bar stool, tears misting her eyes. "Don't do this."

"You've left me no choice. Have my son ready or else." He walked from the room and out the front door. He shut his eyes, but he couldn't get Caitlin's shattered look out of his mind. He'd played hardball, but he didn't have a choice.

Obviously she had the financial means to run. If she did that he might never see his son again. She'd disappeared once. He'd initially tried to find her for about four weeks, then, with his pride in tatters, he'd accepted she didn't want him and tried to put his life back together.

Outside, he started for the entry gate. His car was coming for him. He'd called Frank, his motor coach driver who doubled as his gas man, to come pick him up.

He'd gone only a few feet before he realized he needed a code for the car to enter the gated housing development. Turning around and going back to ask Caitlin was out of the question. The pedestrian access gate was probably coded as well. Scaling the ten foot fence was impossible.

As he pondered the situation, a car leaving the development passed him. Knowing the gate would open, Cameron increased his pace and managed to slip through the gate behind the car just as his driver pulled up in Cameron's black Chevy truck.

On the track Cameron drove a modified Chevrolet Monte Carlo stock race car, one of the four types of stock cars sanctioned by NASCAR. Out of loyalty, and because he liked the way they handled, he'd purchased the same make for his personal use.

Climbing inside the black Silverado, he spoke to the driver. "Morning, Frank. Thanks for picking me up."

"You all right, Cameron?" Frank asked, his questioning gaze on Cameron.

Last night Cameron had had to practically threaten Frank for him to leave Cameron at the hospital. Frank was a good man and a friend. Taking care of Cameron was a responsibility he took very seriously on race weekends. "Nope, but I will be. Wake me when we get to the garage." Leaning his head back against the supple leather, Cameron closed his eyes and tried to concentrate on the coming race, and not the tears in Caitlin's eyes.

Cameron planned on taking her baby away from her. She had to leave before Cameron returned. The sound of the front door closing had barely faded before she rushed to her bedroom and pulled out her suitcase. She had enough money, could do her comic strip from anywhere in the world.

Her hands were trembling as she blindly tossed

undergarments in the direction of the open suitcase on the bed. She was reaching for an armful of clothes when Cameron's ominous words came back to her.

"What if I took him from you for four years?"

Shutting her eyes tightly, she clamped her fists, hung her head. If she ran and was caught, she'd lose Joshua.

Cameron would come after her, and then his fury would know no bounds. Yet, even if by some miracle she did manage not to be found, what kind of life would that be for Joshua?

She couldn't even put him in school, have his friends over. They'd live in secrecy. Joshua was too outgoing for that type of life, and she wasn't about to punish him for her lapse in judgment in loving the wrong man.

Opening her eyes, she went to her son's room and sat on the edge of his bed. No, that wasn't being fair. Cameron was a kind, loving man. It was his profession that she couldn't accept, and he loved racing too much to give it up. They had an impossible situation, one that she didn't see the answer to now any more than she had five years ago when she'd made the most heart-wrenching decision of her life.

She'd noticed him the moment she entered the lobby of the Casa de la Serenidad hotel in Santa Fe. He'd been wearing tobacco-brown slacks, a white shirt, and a wheat-colored sports coat. Since he was behind the desk when she checked in, she thought he was there on business.

She'd been struck by his striking good looks, and

laughing black eyes that sent goose bumps skipping up her arms when he'd introduced himself. He'd offered to show her Santa Fe for the travel article she was writing.

She'd been half in love with him before he took her out to dinner that night at his best friend's restaurant, the Red Cactus. She had no idea he raced stock cars.

By the time she found out, she loved him too much to walk away. She prayed it would work out, but it wasn't to be.

She'd kept track of Cameron through the years. She'd told herself that it was to know where he was at all times. She'd even cut out newspaper clippings, his picture on cereal boxes. When Joshua was an adult in a nice, safe job, she planned to give him the scrapbooks about his father.

That wouldn't be necessary now. He'd have the real thing.

Her lower lip caught between her teeth, she stared down at her son. He was oblivious to the changes about to happen in his life. All she could do was to be there for him. He'd be ecstatic to learn he had a father. His best friend, Stephen, and Stephen's dad were close, and often included Joshua on their outings. Every time afterward Joshua would come home and talk about wanting his own dad.

He now had one.

She brushed her hand over Joshua's head. He wanted a father more than any games or toys on the market. She hadn't wanted to tell him his father was dead or that he didn't want him in his life. So she'd settled for a half-truth: they'd separated and his father didn't know how to find them.

Her lips curved into a sad smile on recalling Joshua's coming to her that very afternoon with her suitcase. He wanted them to pack and go search for his father. It had taken a long time to convince him that that was impossible. She'd never forget the sadness in his face.

He'd be happy to learn his father had found him. The problem was, the father didn't want the mother.

Mike, his crew chief, met Cameron at the side door of the hauler later that afternoon. He took one look at Cameron's tight-lipped face and jerked his head toward the back room of the hauler where everything from a soft drink, to downtime, to a driver being chewed out, was conducted. They wouldn't be disturbed or overheard.

Mike faced Cameron as soon as he closed the door behind them. "You're sure you're all right? What's going on? It's not like you to stay ou—"

"I was with Caitlin."

Shock lifted jet-black eyebrows. There was total, dead silence, then a muttered curse word Mike didn't even try to hold back, which showed his displeasure. NASCAR was a family sport. Profanity brought a hefty fine or suspension. Since no one wanted that to happen they all tended to watch what they said even when off the track or in private."

"You all right?"

"Yes," Cameron answered, and knew it was the

truth. When Caitlin had left him at the altar he'd been hurt, stunned. He hadn't cared what people thought, he just cared about locating Caitlin and fixing whatever the problem was.

He hadn't found her and by the time race season began in February he was neck deep in anger and bordering on depression. He'd lost race after race, went from being the team member with the most wins to having the least. He'd dropped like a rock in the standings.

For the first time since his rookie year, he hadn't had a snowball's chance in hell of finishing in the top ten at the end of the race season, which meant he was out of contention for the NASCAR Sprint Cup Series championship when that was to have been his year. The year before, he'd finished second in the series.

Hilliard had fired him after the fifteenth straight race of not making it into the top twenty. Cameron had understood. In the past, he'd consistently finished in the top ten. When Cameron had come in twenty-ninth at the Dover International Speedway, his worst showing since he began racing, he had known he would be let go.

He couldn't even blame it on the track—concrete and bumpy—four hundred miles of grueling race on the "Monster Mile." He'd won there the year before. Hilliard had been waiting for him when he'd climbed out of the stock car. He didn't even have to say a word, just started walking toward the hauler. Tied and exhausted and angry, Cameron followed.

Hilliard had chewed him out then cut him. "We

don't need dead weight." His being fired had capped off a piss-poor day.

Embarrassed, hurt because Hilliard's voice had been loud and had carried, Cameron had left the hauler and gone to his motor coach, slamming the door. He'd grabbed one of Frank's beers instead of his usual Gatorade. Racing was his life. No, that was Caitlin.

And he'd lost both.

He hadn't even heard the door open, but Duncan and Faith had been there. It hadn't taken much to get the story out of him.

He'd lost Caitlin; he hadn't known how he'd go on if he couldn't race. Duncan had suggested mortgaging his ranch to sponsor him. Faith said the same about the family-owned hotel, Casa de la Serenidad.

He'd vetoed both ideas, thought it was over. But an hour after they'd left Hilliard had knocked on his door, saying he'd changed his mind. He'd give him one more try, but he had to come in no lower than twentieth.

The next race was at Pocono Raceway, one of the most difficult raceways because of the many adjustments of speed needed on the course. Coming down the front straightaway, cars easily reached two hundred miles per hour. Cameron had never won there. His best had been twelfth when he was hitting on all cylinders. The last time he'd been there, he and Caitlin had sneaked away to the Pocono Mountains for a lazy, fun-filled afternoon. He'd be fighting memories *and* fighting for his career.

Hilliard wasn't known for changing his mind. He was fair, but he didn't give second chances.

"Twentieth it is," Cameron said.

Hilliard had looked at him out of eyes blue as a sky but which could turn cold as icicles. Cameron had known that was his last chance. He'd come in nineteenth and hadn't looked back.

Caitlin could never be his. He couldn't make her happy. The truth of that would burn a hole in his stomach if he'd let it.

"Yeah," Cameron repeated to Mike, knowing he wouldn't allow Caitlin to ruin his career again.

A brief knock sounded on the door. "The ceremony starts in ten minutes. You're needed on the field, Cameron," Hope said through the door. Besides Hilliard, she was the only one with enough guts to disturb the two.

Mike eyed Cameron, searched his face. "You ready?"

"Yes." Cameron smiled. "Let's go kick some serious behinds and win this race."

Mike's wide grin split his olive-colored face. "Now, that's what I'm talking about."

Chapter 4

Caitlin never thought she'd do this. Her hand trembled as she pressed the remote. The black screen filled with the color and sounds of two hundred thousand cheering fans at the California Speedway.

Too easily she recalled the smell of gasoline and burned rubber, the revving motors in the garage area trying to get the best out of the race cars, the noise of the frenzied crowd as they cheered their favorite driver or booed the driver who came too near their favorite.

The camera left the grandstand and panned in for a close-up of a driver. Her trembling hand clenched.

"Mommy, that's Cameron," Joshua cried, scrambling out of his seat next to her on the sofa to stand in front of the thirty-six-inch television screen.

"Yes," Caitlin answered. Joshua had only seen Cameron for a short while, yet he'd remembered him, just like his mother had been unable to forget his father.

"Glad to see you're here today after yesterday's crash," the TV announcer said, mic in hand.

Cameron grinned. "That makes two of us."

Off camera, the screams of women could be heard. The newsman chuckled. "I think we can safely say others are just as pleased. How do you feel about today's race, Cameron? This is just the beginning of the NASCAR Sprint Cup Series chase. You won the Chase last year, but you'll have stiff competition from other drivers, including team member Reggie Young."

"The competition is fierce. Reggie, of course, is a fantastic driver," Cameron said. "My team and I will take one race at a time. My Chevy is running great. I have the best crew chief and pit crew in the business. We're ready to win this one."

"California Speedway is one of the five tracks that starts the races in the afternoon and finishes at night. How do you feel about night racing?"

"This is one of the best tracks in the NASCAR Series. The lighting is fantastic." Cameron flashed a grin. "In any case, I love challenges." The smile slid away. "If I don't win, it won't be because I didn't give it my best shot."

"Your best has put you in the top ten for the past four years. You're starting in eleventh place today."

"That means I'm ahead of thirty-two other cars," Cameron said with a chuckle.

The announcer chuckled with him. "Good luck."

"Thanks." Jerking down his baseball cap with HILLIARD MOTORSPORTS on the visor, he walked away.

The reporter faced the camera. "That upbeat personality is why Cameron McBride is one of the most popular drivers today, but he has skills. It's hard to believe he went winless and out of the top twenty for fifteen straight races before pulling out of a slump five years ago."

Caitlin's hand clenched on the remote. After every race she'd gone to the Internet to look up the race stats. Each loss tore at her because she knew how competitive he was, how much he wanted to succeed. He'd been well on his way to winning the Chase Cup, finishing in the top ten ever since his rookie year when he'd been named Rookie of the Year. That year was supposed to be his. He'd told her as much. He had the car, the team, the sponsor, the woman. Nothing could stop him.

Except her betrayal.

The camera switched to Cameron. He grinned lazily. Her heart foolishly fluttered. She was afraid it always would.

Flashing a thumbs-up sign, he climbed into the back of the truck that would take him to his car on the grass of the track. Cars were pushed onto the track by the pit crew. No engines were started until the signal was given. Hopping nimbly out of the bed of the truck, Cameron went to his car. With the ease of long practice, he slid through the window into his regular car, number 23.

Joshua giggled. "He climbed though the window."

"That's how they get into the cars they race. There's no door." There was no speedometer, either, to tell the driver how fast he was going. Often he reached a hundred eighty miles per hour with only inches between the next car at times.

She hadn't wanted Joshua to know anything about

racing until he was older, but that choice had been taken from her. Cameron might be angry with her, but he wasn't vindictive enough to take Joshua completely from her. He'd tolerate the mother for the sake of the child.

"Gentlemen, start your engines."

The rumble of powerful engines was almost deafening. Cars took off around the track waiting for the green flag to come out to signal the start of the race.

"They're going around in circles. It's like on the road with all the cars on the freeway," Joshua commented. "I see Cameron's car. I remember he's number twenty-three."

It was the same number he'd had when she left. He'd wrecked that car two years ago, but apparently it had been repaired. She hadn't been able to stop shaking when she'd seen a picture of the mangled car. He was blessed to walk away with only a fractured collarbone.

Joshua watched the car duck and dive around the track, getting more of a feel for the surface. Caitlin watched her son.

She hadn't been able to watch a race since Johnny died with three races in the season to go. She and Cameron had planned to marry after the racing season ended in November and the banquet in New York to celebrate the winner of the NASCAR Sprint Cup Series. Instead she'd left a note and her wedding gown in the suite of his family-owned hotel.

The green flag came out. "They're off!" shouted the announcer.

"Wow!" Joshua said, awe in his young voice, as he watched the cars race around the track.

The doorbell rang. Instead of running to answer it as he usually did, Joshua stayed in front of the television. "That's probably Stephen and his mother," Caitlin said.

That got his attention. Joshua headed for the door. Tossing the remote aside, Caitlin followed. Joshua went to the glass panel by the door. On the other side was Stephen, grinning and waving. It was a game they played. Caitlin opened the door.

"Hi, Diana and Stephen," Caitlin greeted.

"Hi, Caitlin. Joshua," Diana said, stepping inside with her son. Tall and thin with shoulder-length red hair, she always wore a smile. Today was no exception. She had been the first neighbor to greet them when they moved in.

They'd hit it off immediately and so had their children. Diana was a full-time homemaker and wouldn't have it any other way. After trying for ten years to get pregnant, she said she planned to enjoy and watch every second of Stephen growing up.

"Joshua, why don't you take Stephen out back to play."

Joshua shook his dark head. "Can I show him Cameron racing on television?"

"Cameron McBride?" Diana asked

Caitlin blinked in surprise. Joshua took her silence for permission. Off he and Stephen ran.

"No running in the house," Caitlin and Diana said at the same time. They'd said the same thing dozens of time together. Usually they laughed about it when the boys were out of sight. This time Caitlin wrapped her arms around her churning stomach. She had never felt less like laughing.

Diana studied her closely. "Caitlin, what is it? You said you needed a favor."

"I do. Let me check on the boys first." Going to the family room, she saw Stephen and Joshua shoulder to shoulder, sitting side by side in front of the TV set.

"That's Cameron's car. He climbed through the window," Joshua said, pointing to the television set.

"He came to your house?"

Joshua nodded. "Last night." Joshua turned to his mother. "Is he coming back?"

Caitlin felt the weight of Diana's stare. "Yes."

"Can I meet him?" Stephen asked. "You think he'll let us climb through the window, too?"

"Will he, Mom?" Joshua asked, his young voice gleeful with excitement.

Caitlin moistened her lips. She had wanted to prepare him, had hoped he'd be bored by the cars going around in a circle. "The car is taken back to the home base in Charlotte, a long distance away, after the race."

The boys let out disappointed twin sighs and turned back to the TV.

"Diana and I will be back in a minute. We're going to the kitchen." She'd learned the hard way that it was best to let the two active boys know where she was so that they were aware that they weren't being left alone.

In the kitchen, she folded her arms and leaned

against the countertop. "Do you want anything to drink?"

Diana caught both of Caitlin's arms and nudged her to a nearby stool at the bar. "Sit. What is it, and how can I help?"

"You already have," Caitlin said. "Anyone else would be asking plenty of questions."

"I'm curious as the next person." Diana took a seat next to Caitlin. "But I can tell this is difficult for you. You'll tell me when you're ready."

"Thank you." Caitlin stood and went to a message board and removed a set of keys on a metal ring. "Joshua and I are leaving in the morning for an indefinite period. I don't have time to stop my mail or get someone to house-sit for me."

Diana took the keys and slid them into the pocket of her pants. "I'll take care of everything. You need me to drive you anywhere?"

Caitlin momentarily glanced away. "No, someone is picking us up."

"I know I said I wouldn't ask questions, but would that someone be Cameron McBride?"

Caitlin sidestepped the question. "How do you know Cameron?"

"You know Stephen's father is a sports fanatic. He recently caught the NASCAR bug. If he wasn't on a business trip, he'd be at the racetrack now," Diana explained. "As one of the few African-American drivers in NASCAR history, Cameron stands out. But it's his racing ability that has taken him to the top of his field."

"Racing is dangerous."

"So are other sports, but I think there's more to this."

Caitlin swallowed. "He's Joshua's father."

Cameron strode to the winner's circle with a smile on his face. This time it was to congratulate the winner, Slim Oliver. You couldn't win them all and unless you learned that Lady Luck wasn't always on your shoulder and to appreciate the skills of the other drivers, it would make you a bitter loser.

"Congratulations, Slim. One heck of a race."

The man who'd also won one NASCAR Sprint Cup grinned and shook the hand Cameron offered. "Thanks. You were dogging my tail all afternoon."

But not close enough. His concentration had slipped a couple of times. He'd lost ground and the race. He wouldn't lose his son. "Get you next time."

Slapping the man on the shoulder, Cameron walked away. He'd come in at ninth place, enough to keep him in contention once NASCAR began the process of selecting the top drivers to compete for the Cup. And he would have one of those spots. This was his year.

He grimaced. He'd thought that before, and his life had crumbled. His jaw clenched. That wouldn't happen this year. All he had to do was stay focused. A driver without focus didn't win races and he certainly didn't win championships.

Climbing up the steps of his motor coach, he opened the door and went inside. It was past midnight. If it wasn't so late he'd go pick up his son. Tomorrow. First he needed a shower.

"Cameron. Great race."

"Thanks, Frank," Cameron answered, removing his race boots. "You can head out in the morning anytime you want. I'm staying tonight, but I'm taking a jet back."

Frank frowned. "You're riding with Hilliard?"

Cameron grunted, then stood and unzipped his race suit. Hilliard's niece had made it pretty clear from the day they met two years ago that she wanted Cameron. Once he'd found her naked in his bed. "I'm not suicidal yet."

Frank, whose job as driver included taking care of Cameron's gear, reached for Cameron's boots. "Got it." Cameron grabbed the shoes and pulled the race suit from the crook of the other man's arms.

"Are you going to let me do my job?" Frank asked.

"Force of habit." Cameron tossed his suit over his shoulder. "Mother taught us to be self-sufficient." Cameron frowned as he recalled why. In case the curse that no McBride male would ever be lucky in love was true. Faith was happy, but she was also the first female born in several generations of unlucky McBride males. It was almost as if, because of their financial success, they were doomed never to find lasting love.

"Cameron?"

Cameron looked at Frank. "Yeah?"

"You all right?" his driver asked.

"Yep, and in the morning, I'll be doing even better."

The frown on Frank's lived-in face didn't clear.

"A woman? You never went in for the groupies before."

"Still haven't. This is much more important than a woman." With Frank staring after him, Cameron went to the shower.

There were so many things going on in Cameron's head the next morning that he wasn't surprised that he'd forgotten to call and ask Caitlin for the gate code. Pulling out his cell phone, he shook his head and returned it to his belt loop. Somehow he knew without checking that Caitlin wasn't listed.

"It's the gated development just up ahead to the left," Cameron advised, hoping one of the cars ahead of them was turning into the housing development.

"Yes, sir, Mr. McBride," the driver answered. "I've been out here before to pick up or deliver." The broad-shouldered man pulled up to the gate and punched in a code. "This is a beautiful neighborhood. The houses are spectacular and everyone takes care of their yards."

The gates swung inward and the stretch limo pulled through. One problem solved, and many more to take its place. "Fifth house on the right. Just park at the curb."

"Yes, sir." The driver did as directed, then left the motor running to get out and open Cameron's door. He smiled at Cameron, who was already on the sidewalk. "I could have gotten that."

"No problem, Kerry." Cameron wasn't the kind of man who liked being waited on, but he acknowledged that some of his haste was because he was anxious to see Joshua again. "I'll be back, and we'll head to the airport."

"Do I need to accompany you and get the bags?" the chauffer asked.

"I got it." Cameron started up the multilevel walkway. It was as the driver had said, the yards were well cared for. Despite his anger at Caitlin for not letting him be a part of Joshua's life, he had to admit she had provided a good home for their son.

But now it was his turn.

He rang the doorbell. When seconds ticked by and there was no answer, he rang the bell again. *Be here, Caitlin.*

The door opened. Caitlin stood there, her eyes huge in her face.

"Where's Joshua?" he asked, trying to look behind her into the wide foyer and beyond.

"I—in the study," she answered, moistening her lips. "Cameron, if we could talk about this."

"I've done more than enough talking." He stepped around her, but she caught his arm.

"What do you plan to do?" she cried.

"Take my son," he answered.

She quickly looked behind her. "You can't just blurt it out," she hissed.

"I wouldn't have to, if you had contacted me. You let your fears cheat me and Joshua." He glanced meaningfully at his arm. "I have a plane waiting."

Her fingers tightened. "Please, Cameron."

He refused to let the quiver in her voice, her unsteady hand, sway him. Once he would have gladly laid down his life for her. "You should have thought of this earlier." Flexing his arm, he was free.

She passed him and reached Joshua first. She looked as if she wanted to snatch him up and run. He shook his head. Once. If she disappeared again, he'd come after her and he wouldn't be civil.

Oblivious to the undercurrents, Joshua sat at a child-size built-in desk playing a computer game. Five feet away was another computer with an adult chair. Obviously they shared the office.

He'd shared nothing with his son. Cameron's hands flexed with the need to hold him. Instead he walked over. "Hello, Joshua."

Joshua jerked his head around. When he saw Cameron a wide grin split his young face. "Cameron!" He jumped up from his seat. "I saw you climb through the window."

Cameron couldn't hide his start of surprise. His gaze went to Caitlin, who hovered nearby. "You did?"

Joshua nodded. "Mommy explained how you don't have a door. My best friend and me wanted to ask you if we could get in the car, but Mommy said it was probably on the way back to where you live in Charlotte."

Each innocent word condemned Caitlin more. She could have easily found him, yet chose not to. Instead, she'd chosen to live her life without him. So be it.

"Your mommy's right, but would you like to take a trip with me and see the car? Get inside of it?"

"For real?" Excitement gleamed in the little boy's eyes.

Cameron hunkered down to eye level. "For real. We're going on a little trip this morning."

"Wow," he repeated.

Her eyes huge with apprehension, Caitlin swung Joshua into her arms. Cameron told himself not to let the fear affect him. He couldn't quite do it. His heart squeezed. He started to reassure her that he wouldn't take Joshua from her, then decided to remain quiet.

From the looks of the house she lived in, the expensive SUV she drove, her syndicated comic strip was doing well. If she bolted this time he might not be able find her. As long as she feared him, he could have time with his son.

"Is he packed?"

Her arms tightened. "*We're* packed."

He didn't miss the emphasis on "we." "Unlike some people, I'm not that heartless. Yet!"

Caitlin sucked in a breath. Her arms tightened. Cameron's gaze was focussed on his son. Cameron didn't want her pain to affect him, make him want to take her in his arms.

When he felt there was nothing in his face or eyes to give him away, he looked back at her. "Just remember who is in charge," he said, his voice unbending.

"I understand," she whispered, her voice unsteady.

Slowly he reached out and gently touched Joshua's arm. "How is your shoulder?"

He smiled. "All better."

"Good, because I want you to be able to enjoy the airplane ride we're about to go on."

"For real?"

"For real," Cameron repeated.

Joshua grinned for all he was worth. "I've never been on a plane before. I wanted to go look for my daddy, but I didn't know where he lived." The smile died.

Cameron's hard gaze sliced to Caitlin, but she refused to meet it. She had a lot to answer for.

"I wish I had a daddy like Stephen."

Cameron's chest felt tight. Caitlin's fear had deprived him and his son of so much. "Is Stephen your best friend?"

Joshua nodded. "He lives next door with his mother and father, and they have lots of fun. I get to sleep over sometimes."

"You'll have a sleepover tonight at my house." Cameron leaned closer, tried not to start when he smelled Caitlin's perfume. "I promise it will be an experience you won't soon forget."

Cameron straightened, trying to keep his breathing even, his lower body from responding. "I'll get the luggage." He walked away, telling his usually disciplined body to behave. The only thing between him and Caitlin was their son. Forgetting that would be a mistake he and his silly heart couldn't afford to make.

Cameron lifted a brow at the two suitcases. Caitlin obviously thought the stay would be a lengthy one, and she had no intention of leaving Joshua. She'd been afraid, but she'd stood up to him for Joshua. She'd fight for the son, just not his father.

Picking up one piece of luggage, he grabbed the handle of the large rolling suitcase and left the room. He found Caitlin and Joshua by the door. She held a large leather-bound folder; Joshua held a small wooden case.

"What are those?"

"Mommy's pencils to do her drawing for the comic strip. She has her sketch pad," Joshua explained, and looked up at his mother. "*Being Joshua* is named after me."

"Do you really need that?" he asked.

"My work is important to me," she told him. "And I have a deadline."

"Wouldn't want to interfere with your work." Crossing the room, he opened the door.

"You—" She stopped, pressed her lips together when she saw Joshua closely watching them.

On the porch, Cameron turned. "Did you find someone to look after the place while you're gone?"

She glanced up from locking the front door's double lock. "Yes. My neighbor."

"Mr. McBride, I'll take those and store them in the trunk." The driver quickly came up the walkway and reached for the luggage.

"Wow," Joshua said. "We're gonna ride in that long car?"

"We sure are." Cameron reached for the sketch pad, but Caitlin shook her head.

Pressing his lips together, Cameron took Joshua's hand and started down the walk. "Come on, Joshua."

"Joshua, wait!" cried a little boy's voice.

"Stephen! Here he is!" Joshua pulled away from Cameron and started running toward the little boy heading in his direction. Laughing at his son's enthusiasm, Cameron followed, stopping beside Joshua in the middle of Caitlin's immaculate green lawn.

"This is Cameron," Joshua introduced.

The little boy looked up at him with wide eyes, saying nothing. Cameron had seen that stunned look before. He hunkered down and stuck out his hand. "Hello. I hear you and Joshua are great friends."

Stephen nodded.

"Stephen," a woman called.

Cameron looked in the direction the sound had come from and saw an attractive redheaded woman in her mid-thirties coming from the house next door. "Stephen, you know you're not supposed to leave the house without telling me."

"But Mommy, you were on the phone," Stephen explained, apparently finding his voice. "I'm not supposed to interrupt, and they were leaving."

"It was an emergency, Mrs. Howard," Joshua said.

Smiling, the woman wrinkled her nose. "I guess I'll let it go this time."

Cameron noticed both boys looked relieved and bit back his own smile. He was about to introduce himself when he felt, rather then saw, Caitlin join them.

"Cameron McBride, Diana Howard and her son, Stephen."

"Hello, Mrs. Howard, Stephen," Cameron greeted them. The woman studied him closely, obviously weighing him. There was more than curiosity in her eyes. A quick glance at the flush in Caitlin's cheeks, and he suspected Diana knew he was Joshua's father.

"Mr. McBride." Diana kept her hand on her son's

shoulder. "Caitlin, have a safe trip and don't worry about the house. I'm only a phone call way if you need me."

"Thank you. I'll call."

Joshua had a friend, but it seemed Caitlin did as well. He shouldn't care, but he found himself glad that she had someone she could count on. She just didn't want to count on him.

"Good-bye, Mrs. Howard. Stephen." Catching Joshua's hand, Cameron started back to the limo.

Chapter 5

Neither said anything in the limo or as they boarded the jet. Joshua's excitement and all the questions he asked kept the silence from being obvious or strained.

"My first ride on an airplane!" Joshua exclaimed, his eyes filled with wonder as he boarded the Learjet. "Wait until I tell Stephen."

"Let's get you buckled up," Cameron said, lifting Joshua and settling him in a plush leather seat.

"Can I explore later?" Joshua asked, trying to look around Cameron.

"Just as soon as we level off." Finished buckling Joshua in, Cameron took a seat on the other side of him. He reached for his own seat belt, making a point of not looking at Caitlin, who remained standing. The flight attendant had taken her sketchbook. She looked alone standing there. Since Cameron knew she wasn't afraid of flying since she'd flown so much in her previous line of work as a travel reporter and when they had been together, he reasoned her hesitation was due to not wanting to sit near him.

Joshua strained to look out the window. "Mommy, look at the other planes."

Caitlin finally moved to take the seat beside Joshua. "I see them. It looks as if Joshua in the comic strip will have another adventure."

Joshua turned to her. "Maybe he can find his daddy."

Caitlin's smile faltered, then firmed. "We'll see."

"We'll be taking off in a few minutes, Mr. McBride," the flight attendant announced. "Would you or your guests like anything?"

"Can I have a soda?" Joshua asked.

"You know the rules," Caitlin said to Joshua, then to the woman. "No, thank you."

"I'll check with you again once we're airborne," she said, and moved toward the cockpit.

Cameron watched Caitlin as she sat beside a talk-ative Joshua. Her smile was as fragile as spun glass. Joshua's innocent words had cut her deeply. She might have thought she had done what was best for Joshua, but she was coming to realize she had also hurt him.

He felt the plane begin to move, and caught Joshua's free hand, not wanting him to be afraid. For the time being that also meant Caitlin had to stay with them. The jet picked up speed and lifted from the runway.

"Wow!" Joshua said. "I'm flying! I'm flying, Mommy."

"Yes, you are," she said, holding his other hand. "We'll have to remember and put it in your memory book."

"Memory book?" Cameron asked.

"It's when I do something for the first time so I

won't forget when I get older," Joshua said. "There's lots of stuff in it from when I was a baby."

The way Joshua frowned when he said "baby" made Cameron smile. "I'd like to see it someday."

"You would?" Joshua asked.

"I would," Cameron said, "especially the baby stuff."

The little boy's face saddened. "I left it at the house."

Cameron brushed his hand over Joshua's head. "No matter, we can have your mother's friend mail it to us."

Joshua brightened immediately, turning to his mother as far as the seat belt would allow. "Can we, Mommy? Can we?"

Caitlin's gaze flicked to Cameron, then centered on her son. "Things get lost in the mail. He can look at it when he takes us home." She pointed out the window. "See how tiny everything looks?"

Cameron stared at Caitlin. She might have thought she had outmaneuvered him, but she was wrong. It would be a long, long time before Joshua went home. He planned to talk with Hope about obtaining a tutor for now and a good school in the fall. Caitlin would fight, but she would lose.

And she'd never forgive him. For his son, he could take it. She leaned over to whisper something in Joshua's ear, making him smile, and Cameron couldn't help thinking how beautiful she remained. It was hard to believe she'd been by herself, just as he had, all these years.

As unobtrusively as possible, he twisted in his

seat, glad he'd worn dress slacks as the fit of his pants changed. She was certainly making it hard on him to keep things impersonal.

The problem with that was he was finding that the more he was around her, the more memories surfaced of them together, the more he noticed the softness of her lips, the swell of her breasts, recalled the haunting taste of her heated skin.

Today she wore a simple cotton dress, but it was three inches above her knees and got his mind to thinking of the times he'd slid his hands under the fabric to caress the warm skin beneath.

He twisted uneasily in his seat again and tried to get his mind off Caitlin and on to his son.

"Mr. McBride, would you or your party care for anything to drink, a light snack?"

Cameron looked at Caitlin. She shook her head. "You want some juice or a soft drink, Joshua?"

"Ye—"

"I don't want him to have a lot of sugar," Caitlin interrupted her son. "Do you have milk?"

"Yes, I can also bring out a fruit-and-cheese tray," the stewardess offered.

"That's fine, and bring me a Pepsi," Cameron said. "And please ask the captain whether Joshua can see the cockpit once we land."

"Right away, sir." The woman turned toward the cockpit.

"Can I unbuckle my seat belt, and go look out that other window?" Joshua asked.

"I—"

"Sure," Cameron said. This time she was the one

cut off. She pressed her lips together, but she didn't say anything as he unbuckled Joshua. As soon as he was free of the restraints, the little boy went to the other side of the plane and proceeded to go from window to window.

"There's a grocery store on the way to the house. We can stop and get whatever foods you like," Cameron said.

"Thank you."

Cameron blew out a breath and turned toward her. His voice lowered. "Look, this is difficult for both of us but we both want what's best for Joshua. Pretty soon the excitement is going to wear off and he's going to realize there is something wrong with his mother."

She glanced at him, then away. "You're right, but this isn't easy."

"You think this is for me?"

She faced him, fire in her eyes. "No, but you can't keep snapping at me. I did—"

"What you thought was best," he finished. "I've heard it before. But the fact remains, you considered only what you wanted, not what was best for Joshua or me."

She cut a glance at Joshua, his face and hands pressed to a window on the far end of the cabin. "From the second I knew I was carrying him, all I've thought about is his welfare. I won't have him going though what Johnny's son went through."

"NASCAR is a safe sport, getting safer every year," he told her. "You hear of more career-ending injuries in other professional sports. You used that as an excuse to run out on me and keep my son. No more. If you want to live in fear, fine, but you won't keep my son with you." Pushing up from his seat, he went to sit with Joshua.

Caitlin clamped her hands together in rising fury. He could go on about safety all he wanted, but the facts remained. Accidents happened. You couldn't predict when or where, and some of the racetracks like Talladega were known for the high number of pileups. True, there had been no major injuries, but that didn't mean they wouldn't happen.

Cameron wasn't afraid of anything. He'd never understand the paralyzing fear she felt when she saw him race, knowing a simple act of passing too close could cause a downdraft and the driver to lose control.

She simply could not handle it. Some wives stayed away, some loved the danger and excitement as much as their man. It was safe to assume that not one of the women had lost their father in a racing accident. She knew too well the risk involved. She wouldn't have that for her son or herself.

Charlotte, North Carolina, was the site of the first official NASCAR race in 1949. NASCAR headquarters might be in Daytona Beach, Florida, but a good number of teams, and thus their drivers, resided in Charlotte. After the grueling season with only one weekend off, Cameron appreciated the slow, easy pace of Charlotte.

As Cameron pulled into the long driveway of his house, he had never been more pleased that Pierce

Grayson, his financial advisor and brother of his best friend, Brandon, had urged him to purchase a home for tax purposes. Or that he and Caitlin hadn't purchased a home. After they because engaged, he'd been too busy wooing sponsors, doing public appearances and promotions during the week, for them to look for a house. They planned to do that after they returned from their honeymoon in Switzerland.

He pulled up in front of the two-story house on a half-acre lot backing up to a man-made lake and stopped. "We're here." He tried to be casual as he said it, but out of the corner of his eye he watched Caitlin's face.

He'd thought all he wanted to do was show her he hadn't let her ruin his life or his career. He'd succeeded, just as he'd always planned.

She looked from the two-story white stucco house with a red-tile roof gleaming in the noonday sun to its well-tended lawn and then back to him. "You live here alone?"

"Who else would live here?" he asked, his voice sharper than intended because he realized something. He'd thought of this moment when Caitlin would see the house for the first time and hoped she regretted her decision. To his utter annoyance, he had to accept that he hadn't completely relinquished her memory.

"I—nothing." Opening her door, she got out of the truck and opened the back door. Joshua was already out of his car seat that Cameron had had Hope purchase and put in the truck that had been waiting for them when they arrived at the airport in Charlotte. "Joshua, please wait for me next time."

"I want to see the water," Joshua said.

"You're not to go near the water unless I'm with you." She pulled him into her arms. "Understand?"

"Yes, ma'am," he said.

Cameron came up to them. "You all right, Joshua?"

He nodded. "Is your car here?"

"No, it's at the garage. I'll take you there tomorrow. In the meantime, let's go inside and see if you like your room."

Going up the curved walkway, he opened the massive ten-foot door, then stepped aside for them to enter. He didn't fool himself that this time he wasn't watching Caitlin to gauge her impression.

Caitlin stepped inside the two-story mansion and put Joshua on his feet. She wasn't sure what to expect. Cameron's apartment had been functional and neat. He'd laughingly told her his sister, Faith, was going to decorate it as soon as she had time. He added that he wouldn't need her after all now because Caitlin could decorate his place. She never had.

Standing in the foyer, she was swept away by the warmth and elegance of the house. Wooden floors gleamed beneath her sandaled feet. On either side of the entranceway were two large curio cabinets holding crystal glasses. The walls were covered with yellow silk. Past the entryway she saw the sweeping staircase to the second floor. The railing was black, the spindles white, the runner yellow and trimmed in white and black.

She looked at him with obvious pleasure. "It's beautiful."

Joshua took off for the stairs. She quickly caught up

with him, taking his arm. Their home was one story, but Stephen's was two stories. He and Joshua had tried to imitate an actor sliding down the balustrade. She pulled Joshua protectively to her side. "We can't stay here."

Cameron merely arched a brow.

"My home is childproof, this isn't," she pointed out and told Cameron about the incident on the stairs. "Fortunately, Diana caught them in time."

Cameron's lips twitched. "He ever try it again?"

Her lips pressed together in annoyance that he didn't take the incident more seriously. "No."

Cameron hunkered down in front of Joshua. "Staircases aren't for sliding on. I know you won't forget again."

Joshua solemnly shook his head. "I won't forget."

Cameron brushed his hand over the boy's head, and stood. "He won't forget."

"Your things are too valuable."

"Not as valuable as Joshua." He caught Joshua's small hand and started toward the stairs. "I'll show you to your room and then bring up your luggage. I'll go pick up takeout while your mother unpacks."

Caitlin was left to follow Cameron. Again. Her eyes widened even as she started up the stairs behind them. The yellow runner, edged with white and black, was obviously custom made. At the top of the stairs in an alcove was a beautiful tapestry of a villa perched on the side of the ocean. Unrepentantly, Caitlin felt a pang of jealousy that another woman had probably decorated his house.

Her house was comfortable, but it wasn't fancy.

Certainly not elegant the way Cameron's house was. The curved yellow upholstered sofa near the top of the stairs fit perfectly and had to have been custom made, as well. That one piece probably cost more than most of her furniture together. Any extra money she had was socked away for Joshua's college fund.

Cameron opened a door down a wide hallway to her right. "You can use this room. Joshua's room is across from yours. If you get thirsty or anything, the kitchen is down the stairs at the end of the hall." He turned away and then turned back. "There is a pool pavilion in the back. The door is locked at all times. There's also a small, spouting fountain off the terrace. It's about two feet deep. Do you think I should have it drained?"

"No, one of our neighbors had a fountain," she answered as Joshua wandered around the room. "Just make sure the pool pavilion is kept locked. He can swim a little."

"It has been ever since I came home to find the neighbor's teenager daughters having a party with about fifty kids and not an adult in sight."

"What did you do?"

"Called their parents, for all the good it did," he said. "They offered to pay for damages and basically thought a check would fix things. They didn't seem to get it that their fifteen- and sixteen-year-old daughters were breaking several laws, including underage drinking."

She looked at Joshua, who was trying to look up into the massive white marble fireplace. "I worry about the kind of friends he'll have."

"Temptations are out there. We'll just have to teach him right from wrong."

She caught the "we," but she wasn't fooled. She was on borrowed time. "How long will we be here before we can leave?"

"I thought I made myself clear on that matter," he said, and stepped around her. "Joshua, you want to help me with the luggage? Then we can go get something to eat."

Joshua came to him in a flash. "Can we go to McDonald's?"

Cameron chuckled. "I see the rite of passage is still the same." He placed his hand on the boy's shoulder. "Maybe next time. Why don't we go to another place to get those hamburgers?"

"Do they have a toy?" Joshua asked, as they headed out the door.

"Nope. So I guess that means we'll have to make a visit to the toy store tomorrow to make up for it."

"Wow!"

Caitlin went to the door and watched Cameron and Joshua go down the stairs, their hands linked. They were growing closer. Where did that leave her?

"We need to decide how to tell Joshua I'm his father, that he's mine."

Caitlin had expected the request after they'd put Joshua to bed that night, but something about the way Cameron said "mine" brought to the forefront her fear that once Joshua was comfortable with Cameron there would be no need for her. "Perhaps we should wait."

Unfolding his arms, Cameron pushed away from

the black marble mantel in the living room. Here again the decorator had used yellow, this time adding a mixture of blue and gold. "I've waited long enough. So has he for his father." He stalked over to stand in front of her. "Do you know how hard it was when we went out and a woman asked if he was my son? I just stood there, unable to claim him."

"That's my point, Cameron," she said, getting to her feet from a side chair in front of the sofa and quickly stepping away. "You're famous. What's going to happen when news gets out that you have a son? NASCAR likes its family image."

His dark eyes narrowed. "You can throw NASCAR into the conversation when it's convenient."

"I don't want people questioning him. Why do you think I'm wearing this ring?" The second the words were out she wished she could recall them. She'd left the two-carat pear-shaped diamond engagement ring on the bed with the wedding gown and veil.

"Whose fault is that?" he asked tightly.

"Mine." She thumped her chest with the flat of her hand. "I'm the villain here and you're the good guy. You can crucify me all you want, but this is about Joshua, not us."

He leaned so close she could smell his spicy aftershave, see her own reflection in his mesmerizing eyes. "There is no us."

She flinched mentally, but refused to lower her gaze no matter how much she wanted to. He deserved to take a few swipes at her. "On that we agree." They stood like two adversaries, each waiting for their opponent to show some sign of weakness so they could attack.

Shaking her head, she pushed her hand through her hair. "I can't do this, Cameron. We both want what's best for Joshua, but no matter what we say, it's hard to take the past out of the equation." She started to walk away then turned back. "So, get it off your chest. Tell me all the things you wanted to say and couldn't. Spit it out and then we'll truly move on. The only link we'll have is Joshua."

"That would take more time and energy than I care to expend," he said. "After breakfast, we sit him down and tell him. As for NASCAR, no one in my crew will gossip. And if a reporter does get nosy, you'll show him your ring."

"You never answered my question. How long do you plan for us to stay?"

"You can leave when you're ready, but Joshua stays with me."

Fear chilled her. "No. I'll fight you, Cameron."

"Fathers have rights. I'm sure the judge will be sympathetic since you deliberately kept him from me." He folded his arms. "I plan to use every connection at my disposal, and believe me, I have plenty."

"Just because you're a popular athlete won't help." She was bluffing and hoped he didn't call her on it.

"Maybe, but my association with Blade Navarone will."

She started. Navarone had billions, and he was married to Faith's sister-in-law. "Be reasonable. With your busy schedule, you can't keep him."

"That's where you're wrong, Caitlin. I can and will keep my son, and there is absolutely nothing you can do about it." He walked away.

"We'll see about that." Caitlin hurried to her room, found her cell in her handbag, and called Diana. Caitlin hadn't wanted to go into detail with her best friend, but Cameron's threat now made that necessary. Caitlin needed answers. Diana's experience as a lawyer would help her get them.

"Hello," Diana answered on the third ring.

"Diana, it's Caitlin. I need your help," she blurted. Too tense to sit, she paced in her room.

"I'm here," came Diana's calm reply, showing why she once had been a top prosecutor for the city of Los Angeles.

"I—" Caitlin blew out a breath. "What are a father's rights?"

"Depends on the judge and the state, but in most cases they're seen as equal. Mothers no longer get a free pass."

Caitlin gripped the phone. "That wasn't what I wanted to hear."

"I know, but you need the hard facts," she said. "From your question, I gather that Cameron wants visitation rights."

"He wants full custody." Caitlin felt a knot in her stomach just saying the words.

"Why now? Especially with his race schedule?"

Caitlin hesitated, trying to find the words.

"He did know about Joshua, didn't he?" Diana asked when there was no answer.

Caitlin plopped down on the bed. "No." She answered the question she knew Diana must be wondering about. "My father was killed racing stock cars. I fell in love with Cameron before I knew what he did for a living. Two weeks before we were to be married Cameron's best friend was killed in a race." She swallowed.

"Oh, Caitlin."

"I didn't know I was pregnant when I disappeared the day we were to be married," she said, her voice unsteady. "I didn't notify Cameron once I knew because I didn't want that kind of life for Joshua or to have him see his father injured or worse."

"Caitlin, as a mother I understand, but as a lawyer, I know that you haven't put yourself in a very good position for the court to look favorably upon you," Diana said. "You have deprived a man, a popular sports professional, of his child for over four years."

"Meaning I could lose Joshua?"

"Fathers have rights. The best thing to do is to try and work this out between you," she advised. "Like it or not, there's another person in Joshua's life now, an important person."

Caitlin blew out a breath. "You're right, I don't like it."

"I'll play devil's advocate and ask, how you would feel if you were in Cameron's position?"

Caitlin rested her forehead in the palm of her hand. "He asked me the same thing."

"And what was your answer?"

"I—" She opened her mouth, then closed it because the words would only scratch the surface.

"You're a wonderful mother, a loyal friend.

You're—we're raising two remarkable boys; both deserve the very best we can give them," Diana said.

"And that includes a father who loves them."

"I lost my father when I was young, as well. My mother was wonderful, but she wasn't Daddy."

"Mama never got over my father's death. I lost both of them," Caitlin said. "That won't happen to Joshua. Somehow Cameron and I will work this out. Thank you, Diana."

"Anytime."

"I'd like you to mail Joshua's memory book. Joshua wanted Cameron to see it. Perhaps it will help," Caitlin said. "I'll call tomorrow with the address."

"Now you're thinking. Sharing Joshua is a major step in the right direction."

"I hope so. Good night and thanks."

"Good night."

Caitlin hung up the cell phone and pitched it toward her handbag on the bed. Before she lost her nerve, she left her room, went down the hall, and knocked on Cameron's door. There was no answer. She put her ear to the door. Nothing.

Going to Joshua's room, she quietly opened the door. He was sprawled on his stomach with the covers up to his neck. Cameron must have tucked him in again. Closing the door, she started back down the stairs, and heard a clinking sound coming from the direction of Cameron's room.

Retracing her steps, she stopped at the door next to his, listened, then knocked when she heard the sound again.

The door opened and she barely kept her jaw from

dropping. Perspiration dewed Cameron's face, beaded on his muscled chest. She recalled lapping the moisture from his body, his nipples. Fighting desire, she jerked her gaze upward. His flared nostrils weren't due to exertion from exercising.

He drank in the scent of her and her arousal. They might both deny it, but the attraction between them was still strong.

Chapter 6

"Yes?"

She tried to swallow to ease the dryness in her throat There was nothing she could do about the need pulsing through her. "I've decided to go along with your plan for the time being. Joshua should know he has a father."

"Thank you," Cameron said, both hands holding the towel wrapped around his neck. A bead of water ran down his chest. The urge to lap up the moisture with her tongue was so strong she had to grit her teeth. "It will be better for him if we're united on this."

She swallowed before she could speak. "I know, but it's still difficult for me to share him," she admitted. "It doesn't help that you keep threatening to take him from me. I couldn't stand that."

Releasing the towel, he reached out his callused finger to lift her chin. Too quickly the warm roughness of his finger was gone. She'd missed his touch. She just realized how much. "Then just think of how I feel. I just found him. I'm not ready to even think of him not being a daily part of my life."

Her cautious eyes met his. "I understand that, but I hope you realize that I won't leave him."

He nodded and stuck out his hand. "Truce."

She scrunched up her face, but stuck out her hand. "It probably won't last a day."

"Then we'll keep trying until it does." His hand closed over hers. A tingling sensation ran up her arm. Somehow her gaze lowered to his mouth, full, sensual. Heat pooled in her belly.

"Caitlin." Her name was a rough thread of sound, tinged with need.

She snatched her hand back, almost stumbling in her haste. She flushed. "I better go check on Joshua. Good night, Cameron."

"Night, Caitlin."

Caitlin quickly entered Joshua's room and closed the door behind her. What had almost happened? She shook her head at the idiocy of the question. She had almost kissed Cameron. And since one kiss had never been enough, it would probably have led to other things, especially since it had been five years since he'd held her, made love to her. Her body quickened with need and greed.

That couldn't happen.

Trying to put Cameron out of her mind, she went to Joshua's bed, pleased to see he remained under the covers and slept peacefully. She couldn't fall into the trap of loving Cameron again.

She wouldn't survive this time when they parted. No matter how much she might foolishly wish otherwise she had to accept that she was on borrowed time.

* * *

By eight the next morning Cameron had completed his five-mile run, checked that his race car and motor coach had arrived safely, spoken with his crew chief, and was finishing cooking breakfast. His mother might have insisted he be self-sufficient, but it was Brandon who had taught him to cook.

He heard Caitlin and Joshua before he saw them. His lower body stirred. He cursed softly under his breath. Good thing he'd decided to wear dress pants instead of jeans. She still made his blood run hot. Bad, bad. She couldn't be happy with his life, and he couldn't be happy without racing.

"Good morning, Cameron," Joshua greeted.

"Morning, Joshua. Caitlin. Grab a seat. Breakfast is almost ready."

"Good morning. Can I help?" Caitlin asked.

"Thanks. There's a pitcher of orange juice in the refrigerator." Expertly balancing two plates on one arm and carrying a third plate in his other hand, Cameron placed the yellow and black stoneware on the table. "Waffles with maple syrup, soft scrambled eggs, hash browns, and pan sausage."

She wondered if he remembered she loved breakfast. She seldom cooked it because Joshua was into his cold cereal phase. A month ago it had been cooked cereal, and before that peanut butter and jelly sandwiches. Of course, Cameron hadn't thought about her when he was cooking, she reasoned. He liked a filling breakfast and had often cooked for them when they were together. He must not have noticed the cereal in their shopping cart yesterday at the grocery store.

Caitlin poured the juice and set the pitcher on a metal trivet on the small round table. Maybe if she didn't make a big deal out of it, Joshua would eat the waffles and pan sausage on his plate. The eggs were out.

Cameron pulled out Caitlin's chair. Their eyes met briefly before she turned away, but not before he saw a new kind of fear in her eyes. She was fighting the attraction as much as he was. Good. He needed all the help he could get.

"Where's your coffee?" Caitlin asked as she took her seat.

"Got it." Taking his mug from the counter by the oven, he returned and pulled out his chair.

"I'll say grace." Finished, Caitlin watched Joshua as he poured syrup over his waffles. She took the pitcher before he drenched them.

"Are we going to see the car today?" Joshua asked, picking up his fork.

"After breakfast." Cameron forked in a bite of waffle.

Joshua cut into his waffles, tentatively put the food in his mouth, then he opened wider, his teeth closing over the food. "This isn't so bad," he said around his food.

Caitlin was so stunned that she didn't reprimand Joshua for talking with his mouth full. He'd never eaten the waffles or pancakes she'd prepared.

Cameron smiled. "My best friend taught me how to cook. He and I have been friends since we were five."

"I'll be five in August," Joshua proclaimed proudly.

Cameron paused as he picked up his coffee cup. "What day?"

"The fifteenth." Joshua looked at his mother. "I'm having a big party and inviting all my friends. Isn't that right, Mommy?"

"Yes," she said, her gaze flicking to Cameron.

"You can come, too," Joshua said, picking up his juice.

"Thank you. I'd like that."

Caitlin knew he was thinking of all the birthdays he'd missed. The look in his eyes said he wouldn't miss another one. She'd been reminded again of what her actions had cost him. No more. They were ending as of now.

Things were changing too fast. She couldn't control what was happening. Cameron was in charge, and they both knew it. Yet, the hardest part was ahead of them—telling Joshua he was Cameron's son.

Caitlin would have put off the moment if Cameron would have let her. He hadn't given her a chance. As soon as Joshua had forked in the last bite of his waffles, drained his glass of milk, Cameron had scooped him out of his chair and headed for the great room.

Caitlin was left with little choice except to follow. The bright room, done in sunny shades of yellow with cherry woods, couldn't diminish her apprehension.

Cameron placed Joshua in one of the side chairs in the living room sitting area, then sat on the round coffee table in front of him. "We have something important we want to tell you, Joshua."

Caitlin wanted to sit beside Joshua to hold him, but realized that wouldn't be fair to either of them. Joshua had to know, as Cameron indicated, that they were united on this. Slowly, she sank down next to Cameron on the coffee table.

Joshua, his eyes wide, watched her. Sitting on furniture was breaking the rule. "I've been good," Joshua said.

"Of course you have," Cameron and Caitlin said almost in unison. Cameron placed his hand on Joshua's knee, Caitlin palmed his cheek.

Caitlin kept swallowing, the reassuring smile on her face seemingly more difficult to maintain with each passing second. It was going to be up to Cameron to get them through this.

Cameron prayed for the right words. How did he explain to a four-and-a-half-year-old that his father had "found" him? At least Caitlin hadn't claimed he was dead. "Your mother and I want to talk to you about something very important."

Joshua looked from one to the other. "I won't play in the fountain or go down to the lake unless an adult is with me. I remember."

"I know you won't," Caitlin said. "This is about—" She paused, bit her lip.

"Your father," Cameron finished for her. Dragging it out certainly wasn't helping anyone.

"You know my daddy?" Joshua asked, his small voice filled with wonder.

"Yes," Cameron answered.

Joshua, his eyes round with excitement, jumped

up from his chair and went to stand in front of Cameron. "Where is he? Can you take me to him?"

Things were moving too fast for Caitlin. "You remember I said that your father loved you, but we decided we didn't love each other and we went to live separate lives, that we didn't know how to find each other."

"Did he find us?" he asked his mother. Her mouth trembled, but she didn't say a word.

"I'm your father, Joshua," Cameron answered quietly, his voice unsteady.

Joshua looked at him as if he couldn't quite comprehend what he'd just been told.

Caitlin knew it was time. "He's your father, Joshua. He's found you."

"You're my father?" Joshua asked, his voice as unsteady as his father's had been earlier.

Cameron swallowed, swallowed again. "Yes, son. I'm sorry it took me so long to find you, but I'm here now and I plan to stay."

"Daddy!" The boy launched himself at Cameron, his arms wrapped tightly around his neck. "I knew you'd come! I knew it! I told Mommy you'd find us one day, and you did."

Over Joshua's head, Cameron caught Caitlin's strained features. If he didn't miss his guess she was beginning to realize how much she'd deprived Joshua. He knew that with Caitlin's tender heart, it wouldn't be easy for her to accept.

Hefting Joshua up with one arm, Cameron stood and asked, "You about ready to see my race car?"

"Wow."

Cameron smiled. He was fast learning that "wow" was Joshua's favorite word when he was excited. "Caitlin, do you need to get anything before we leave?"

"Maybe he should go another day." She stood as well, her hands curled into tight fists.

Cameron thought he knew why she was apprehensive. "I've already alerted the crew that we're coming. No practice race is scheduled for today. We'll have lunch."

She was living her greatest fear. How could she save her baby? "He's probably tired from the trip. Maybe tomorrow."

Cameron set Joshua on his feet. "I left my cap on the dresser in my room. Could you please go get it for me?"

"I'll get it, Daddy." Joshua took off running.

Cameron had to swallow. *Daddy.* He'd never in his wildest imagination thought Caitlin might be carrying their child. They'd always used protection. As soon as Cameron heard his son's pounding footsteps on the stairs, he stepped closer to Caitlin. "Today, Caitlin. Putting it off won't change anything. I want to show Joshua the stock car, introduce him to my crew."

"I—"

"I'm leaving in ten minutes, and when I do Joshua is going to be with me."

"I don't want that life for him," she said, her voice trembling.

"That's not for you to decide."

Joshua came running back into the room with the cap. "Here it is, Daddy."

Daddy. Emotion clogged his throat again, then laughter escaped. Cameron scooped Joshua up in his arms, took the cap, and put it on his son's head. "This way I won't lose it again.

"You coming?" Cameron asked.

"I need to work on the strip." She tried to smile and failed miserably.

"Thank you." He knew what it cost her to let her son go without her. She'd walk through hell for Joshua. He didn't agree with her decision to keep Joshua's birth a secret, but he knew she had done it out of fear, not malice.

To let him go without her to a place she feared said a great deal about her love for Joshua. She was putting his needs above her own. She wanted them to have this time together.

"We'll be back in time for dinner. I'll bring take-out." Cameron promised. Walking over to Caitlin, he leaned Joshua toward her. "Kiss your mother good-bye, and tell her you love her so we can go."

Joshua dutifully leaned over, put his arms around his mother's neck, and kissed her on the cheek. "Good-bye, Mommy. I love you."

Her arms clung to Joshua for a moment before she stepped back. "You mind, Ca—your father."

"Yes, ma'am."

Cameron wished he could get his own hug. Heck, he wanted the kiss as well. "He's safe with me. He'll never be out of my sight."

"I know," she said. Her voice trembled, she blinked rapidly.

He started from the room, then pivoted and came

back to her. He didn't ask, didn't pause. He simply curved his hand around her neck and brought her lips to his. She gasped in shock, allowing his tongue to thrust inside her, swirl, taste the heady sweetness that was uniquely hers, and maple syrup.

Joshua's giggles brought him back to his senses. The kiss had been an impulse, but no less enjoyable. From the flare of desire in her dark eyes, she had enjoyed it as much as he had.

"You looked as if you needed that." His gaze narrowed on her moist lips again. "I'd forgotten how—"

He abruptly stopped. Caitlin's wide eyes were now fastened on Joshua, who was studying his parents with interest. "We'll be back by dinner." This time when he started from the room, he never paused.

Sean Hilliard had started Hilliard Motorsports Racing team because of his fascination with vintage and racing car restoration. He'd taken a hobby and turned it into a professional NASCAR racing business fifteen years ago. The four-man racing team and their crews were housed in a state-of-the-art forty-five-thousand-square-foot automotive shop.

The spotlessly clean area was a cornucopia of sounds—the clink of metal against metal, drills, the revving of motors, the good-natured conversation as the men worked on the cars.

Cameron had always been proud and pleased that he drove for one of the best teams in the business. The other three drivers were having a good year and all were in the top twenty.

Cameron couldn't keep the proud grin off his face

as he introduced Joshua to his crew as Caitlin's and his son. There wasn't a raised eyebrow in the bunch. It had helped that he had called Mike and asked him to share the news with them, but no one else.

Cameron trusted his crew. They worked hard. They were loyal and a cohesive unit. They had to be to work in sync during race day. A slow or disgruntled team member could cost the driver a race. A driver learned quickly that he couldn't win the race by himself; it took team effort.

Most of his crew had been with him when Caitlin left. He'd have a talk later with Hilliard, the three other drivers on his team, and Hope. She'd know how best to handle the media. He didn't want Joshua or Caitlin ambushed or embarrassed.

Although NASCAR people were loyal, they were still human. There was going to be talk. He had an idea of how to handle the talk that was bound to come, but he needed Caitlin's cooperation. For now, it was just him and his son, and he planned on lots of memories.

"This is my car, Joshua. Number twenty-three."

Joshua's eyes rounded to the size of saucers. His hand reached out to touch the bright purple hood. Frowning, he looked up at his father. "Where are the headlights?"

Cameron snapped a picture with his camera, then hunkered down. He planned his own memory book. "Besides not having a door, stock cars don't have head or tail lights, or a speedometer."

"Why?" he asked, inspecting the decal headlight.

"They're not needed," Cameron explained. "We race on the track, not the street. Would you like to get inside?"

"Really? I can?"

Smiling, Cameron put his newly purchased digital camera on the roof of the car. "I'm going to pick you up. I want you to keep your legs together as you pass through the window."

"I will, Daddy. I'll remember."

"I know, son." Picking Joshua up, he guided him through the window and settled him in the seat. Emotion caused his throat to ache. Swallowing, he grabbed his camera and took another photo to give him time to compose himself. "How do you like it?"

Joshua's face was a picture of awe. "Wow."

"That about sums up how I feel when I get inside." Cameron leaned in the window. "The passenger and back seats are taken up with equipment. It's just you and the car against all the other drivers."

"I bet you're the best."

Cameron chuckled. "I'm trying. Let's get you out of here and I'll show you the hauler where they keep a spare car."

"Wait until I tell Mommy."

"Yes," Cameron said. He could just imagine how that would go over.

Caitlin was waiting at the front door for Cameron and Joshua when they returned that evening. From her son's glowing face she could tell he had thoroughly enjoyed himself. Even before he reached her, he was telling her about the wonderful time he'd had with his father. Caitlin tried her best to look pleased instead of anxious as she helped him wash up, then set the table for them to eat the takeout Cameron had brought back.

Through everything, Joshua kept telling her over and over about his outing. Like an indulgent father, Cameron had looked on proudly.

"Daddy let me sit in the driver's seat.

"You can peel the windshield off if it gets bug splatter or dirty, Daddy said.

"There is an extra car in the hauler in case Daddy needs one.

"Daddy says a whole team of people and specialists help to make his car faster."

Barely touching her food, Caitlin listened to each excited word and knew that in just a short space of time, Cameron had already carved a permanent place in Joshua's heart. "Daddy" was peppered into almost every sentence. Cameron's expression was just as pleased.

She was relieved when they finished eating dinner and Cameron suggested watching one of the movies he and Joshua had picked up on the way back from the garage—until Joshua dropped a bombshell.

"Stephen's mother and father let us watch movies in their bed." Joshua glanced expectantly between his parents. "We have popcorn. They let me and Stephen climb into the bed with them."

"Sounds like fun," Cameron said. "I have a sixty-one-inch plasma screen in my bedroom."

"Yeah!" Joshua shouted.

"You better take your bath and chance into your pj's then," Cameron advised.

Enthused, Joshua hopped up and down, then caught his mother's hand. "Come on, Mommy. You have to turn on the water."

She cut a weary look at Cameron. "We could watch the TV in the media room and be more comfortable."

"It wouldn't be the same," Joshua told her, his face solemn.

It wouldn't, but it would be safer for her unruly mind and body. She was remembering too much about Cameron's tempting body, the warmth, the hardness, the pleasure. From his suddenly narrowed eyes, he was remembering the same thing.

"I might have to search for my pj's," Cameron said softly.

Caitlin recalled too vividly his nude body. Her own traitorous body tingled. "Then we'll put it off."

"No, Mommy," Joshua pleaded. "I want to do it tonight. Please. It will be another memory for my book." He looked at his father. "You can take a picture of us, can't you? Just like the ones you took of us today."

"You betcha."

Despite her uneasiness, she would enjoy seeing father and son together. It hit her again how much she had deprived Cameron of. She couldn't deny Joshua. He probably had so many things in his little head that families did, and he wanted to do them all. "All right."

"Yeah," Joshua said.

Caitlin hurried away, feeling Cameron's hot gaze on her until she disappeared up the stairs. In Joshua's room, Caitlin helped him with his bath and into his pajamas.

"Now it's your turn," he told her.

"What?" Taking her hand he started for her room across the hall. "You have to be in your pajamas, too. Just like Daddy."

Cameron happened to be coming down the hallway and heard Joshua. "I was just on my way to find a pair."

Caitlin felt her face heat. She didn't dare look at Cameron. He didn't wear pajamas, not even in the winter months. His feet were always icy, but once he touched her, started making love to her, she forgot all about his cold feet. The nightgowns she'd worn had ended up on the floor in less that a minute. After making love, they'd sleep naked in each other's arms. He'd often asked why she bothered with a gown.

"We can just wear regular clothes," she suggested. She didn't know if she could take looking at Cameron's naked chest again.

"There is no way I'm not going to do the first thing our son asks us to do as a family." He leaned down and placed his hand on his son's shoulder. "Once your mother is in her pajamas, I'll meet you in the kitchen to fix the popcorn and then we can all climb into my bed and enjoy a movie together as a family."

Caitlin was pulled to her room by Joshua, but not before she saw the gleam in Cameron's eyes. He was enjoying this, and if she wasn't careful, she'd begin to enjoy them being a family, too.

"Wait until I tell Stephen I have my own father."

Cameron's throat tightened. He was glad he didn't have any popcorn in his mouth. Between them on top of the covers, Joshua's neck had to be hurting because he kept looking from one to the other, grinning, saying things that tore at Cameron's heart.

He'd caught Caitlin's pained expression a couple of times as their son talked of having a father, being like his best friend, Stephen. She hurt for him. Her arm around his slim shoulder, her cheek pressed to his forehead at times, told Cameron as much.

"Isn't this fun, Mommy?" Joshua asked.

"Yes."

He dug his little hand into the bowl of popcorn in his lap. "I always knew it would be if my daddy were there instead of Stephen's." As soon as he swallowed the popcorn, he continued. "I like Mr. Howard, but it's not like having my own father, is it, Mommy?"

She swallowed. "No." The word had come out rough and raspy.

Cameron lifted his arm over Joshua's and swept it over her hair in a soothing gesture, just as he'd done countless times in the past. Her gaze lifted to his. His heart clenched. Her eyes were moist.

"Caitlin—"

She shook her head. She didn't want his sympathy, or maybe it would make the tenuous hold on her composure shatter. Joshua was her world. Unlike

Cameron she didn't have any other family. She wasn't ready to share him yet.

She hated that she had deprived Joshua of a father, but no one had to tell him that she hadn't changed her mind about her dread of Joshua driving one day. Boys liked cars. Cameron had started racing quarter-midgets when he was nine.

She wasn't pleased, either, about the attraction between them. He hadn't been at first until he stopped being angry long enough to realize he still cared about her, wanted her. If he could build on that, bind her to him with sensual pleasures, he could have her *and* his son.

If he was able to help her get over her fear. NASCAR was safe. He was more likely to be injured on the way *to* the race rather than actually racing. But for Caitlin, who had lost her father to racing, and who had seen a fatal accident, it was going to be an uphill battle to convince her.

"Movie's over." Caitlin practically leaped from the bed, tightening the sash of her silk robe. Beneath were matching blue silk pajamas. Cameron knew it had been wishful thinking on his part that she'd wear one of the nothing gowns she'd worn when they were engaged. "Bedtime."

Joshua looked up at Cameron instead of getting out of the bed. "Is it all right if I stay in here with you a little while longer, Daddy?"

There went that knot again. "Sure." He glanced up, saw the frightened look on Caitlin's face. "You can stay, too."

"I—I need to finish the strip." She cleared her throat. "I'll be back to put you to bed, Joshua."

Joshua kept his head angled up to Cameron's. "Daddy can do it."

Cameron looked at Caitlin. She blinked several times, then hurried from the room. He wanted to call her back, but what could he say?

"Tell me about when you were a little baby, Daddy."

He smiled down at his son. They had so much to learn about each other. "I was born and raised in Santa Fe. That's where I met your mother."

"Really?" He rose up to his knees. "Did she draw then?"

"No, she wrote for a newspaper." He leaned closer. "I'll tell you a secret, if you don't tell anyone."

Frantically Joshua shook his head. "I won't."

"The first time I saw your mother I thought she was the most beautiful woman I'd ever seen." He leaned in closer. "I still do. And you know something else?" Joshua shook his head.

"This you don't have to keep a secret. The day I learned I was your father was one of the proudest days of my life. I love you, Joshua. Always know that."

Joshua went into his arms, squeezing him tightly. "I love you, too, Daddy."

Cameron held on to the solid warmth of his son. With fatherhood came responsibilities. Joshua wouldn't be happy with just one parent or with them fighting over him. Somehow he had to unite his family.

In NASCAR racing he was used to coming from

behind and winning. Besides the other drivers in his path, there was the unknown he had to contend with. It took grit, nerve, and coordination to be a NASCAR driver. Fatherhood required just as much tenacity on his part.

He'd win this time as well. It was too important not to.

Chapter 7

"Be sensible, Caitlin. He's just intrigued with having a father. In a few days he'll be back to being all yours." Saying the words out loud didn't lighten Caitlin's somber mood or her fear of losing Joshua. Right now, Cameron was the big attraction. There was no way for her to compete and win.

Sitting on the bed with the drafting pad in her lap, her eyes shut tightly, Caitlin clenched the charcoal pencil. Who was she kidding? The second Joshua learned he had a father, he had ceased being just hers. She was having a difficult time accepting that. Even as a child, she'd never liked sharing her toys or her daddy.

Her eyes opened. She could still visualize him, strong, tall, and always laughing. Except when he and her mother were fighting over his racing. Her mother never went to a race and she forbade Caitlin to attend. He'd defied her once and taken her. He'd won that day, calling her his good-luck charm. Her mother had been waiting for him when he'd returned. Their fight had been the worst ever. And she had been caught in the middle, trying to be loyal to both of the parents she loved.

The next weekend he'd had his fatal accident. For a long time she blamed herself. If she had been there, perhaps "his luck" would have kept him safe and he would have come home.

She didn't want to put Joshua in the unwinnable position of choosing between his parents. Joshua was outgoing, affectionate, and lovable. He was too young to understand the reason for his parents' bickering, only suffer the consequences. There would be no winners—only losers.

He wanted a father.

And as Diana had pointed out, he was one of the lucky ones to have a father who loved him, wanted to spend time with him. No one had to tell her that the last two days had been unusual. As a NASCAR driver, Cameron had a great deal of responsibility to sponsors and owners, yet he'd hung around the house and taken time for his son. He was putting him first.

Just as she should have done.

And that nagging thought made her feel small. Cameron's capacity to be generous was larger than hers. She'd seen him watching her during the movie. Even after she'd kept Joshua a secret from him, he'd been able to feel sorry for her.

Just like she was feeling sorry for herself now.

A knock on the partially opened door brought her head up and around. Cameron peeked inside. "I didn't want to disturb you, but I thought you might want to help me put Joshua to bed."

Joshua lifted his head from Cameron's shoulder to yawn. "I'm not sleepy, Daddy."

Caitlin stood in an instant. She'd heard the same

words from Joshua too many times to count. "Well, you will be when your head hits the pillow."

"Your mother is right," Cameron said. "I used to tell my mother the same thing, and you know what? She was always right."

Joshua yawned. "But I'm not sleepy."

Cameron smiled down at her. Before she thought of a reason not to, she smiled back. "He's my son, all right."

It hit her at once that if Joshua hadn't looked like Cameron, he might have thought he wasn't his. Their meeting in the emergency room might have ended differently. Then, she saw the way, even in sleep, that Joshua clung to his father, the gentle way Cameron held his son. She wouldn't have wished it any other way.

In Joshua's room, Cameron handed their sleepy son to her. "You hold him while I pull back the covers."

She readily accepted Joshua, glad to have him in her arms. She suspected Cameron sensed as much. His willingness to forgive her and share Joshua made her feel even smaller. Why couldn't Cameron have an ordinary, safe career?

Cameron pulled back the covers and straightened. "He brushed his teeth in my bathroom, but he hasn't said his prayers yet. He said you always said them together. If you don't mind, I'd like to join you tonight."

"No, of course not." Caitlin eased Joshua down by the bed. Cameron knelt beside him.

Joshua yawned again, then noticed his parents on either side of him. For a long moment he stared at one then the other as if committing them to memory. Linking his small hands, he bowed his head.

"God, thank you for letting my daddy find us. Bless Mommy, bless my daddy, bless Stephen and his mommy and daddy, and bless all the children in the world who don't have a mommy or a daddy like we do."

Getting up, Joshua hugged Caitlin and Cameron and then climbed into bed. Caitlin tucked the covers around his neck, knowing he'd kick them off two seconds after he fell asleep, but she needed to fuss over him just a bit.

Brushing her hand over his forehead, she pressed her lips there. "Good night, sweetheart. Mommy loves you with all her heart."

"So does your daddy," Cameron said, his voice a thick, husky rumble.

Joshua smiled up at them, then closed his eyes. In seconds he was asleep.

"Come on."

Caitlin resisted Cameron's hand on her arm for a split second, then reached over to turn out the lamp on the bedside table. Joshua didn't stir. By the soft glow of the night lamp they slipped from the room, leaving the door partially open.

"Are you all right?" he asked.

Cameron read her better than anyone. He always had. Her mother had been so deep in her own grief and guilt she hadn't paid any attention to the lonely, needy child who was just as devastated by the sudden death of her father. "I will be."

His knuckles brushed down her cheek, then his

palm was gliding down her arm to her hand. Linking her hand with his, he started down the hall. Expecting him to release her when they reached her door, she didn't resist. Just for a moment, she took the comfort he offered.

However, when they passed her door she snatched her hand back. "What do you think you're doing?"

His eyebrow lifted. "What do *you* think I'm doing?"

His calm question threw her. The last thing she wanted to do was overreact and let him know she was still very much attracted to him and not doing a very good job of fighting her emotions. "Why are we going to your room?"

"To talk." He took her hand and started walking again. "In case you didn't notice, I have a sitting area that leads out to a terrace and a koi pond. I recall you mentioned you always liked seeing them at the Japanese restaurant we visited in Los Angeles." He didn't pause as he entered his room. "It also has a minifridge. You only nibbled at dinner. The same with the popcorn."

She tried not to let it matter that he had remembered such a small thing about her. They'd gone to the restaurant the first time he'd visited her. "I'm not hungry."

"We both know why." Stopping in front of a small built-in refrigerator, he released her hand. Bending, he took out the cup of minestrone soup she hadn't wanted with her dinner. Opening the microwave door, he set the timer.

"Why aren't we in the kitchen doing this?" she asked with suspicion.

"Because neither of us want to be far from Joshua in the kitchen," he answered, crossing his arms over his chest.

It made sense, but his bedroom, although as large as her living room, felt too intimate with his bed in it.

"If you're going to keep up with Joshua, you need to eat." Cameron smiled. "He has more energy than a bumblebee and moves about as fast."

"He's very inquisitive."

"So I'm finding out." The timer went off. Carefully removing the soup. Cameron took it to the small round table in the sitting area. "Come on, before your soup gets cold."

"I don't need anyone to take care of me," she told him. The idea appealed too much to her.

"That's debatable." He went to her, taking her arm and guiding her into a chair. "I'll get you a napkin and a spoon."

He prepared the food so effortlessly, charmed her so completely, she idly wondered how many other women had been there before her. "Why is your room so well stocked?"

Lifting her soup bowl, he spread the black place mat, then put her matching napkin and spoon beside it. "I get in late sometimes. I want to be able to shower, eat, and fall into bed without going all the way back to the kitchen."

She picked up her soup spoon and began to eat. She wasn't going to let her mind get hung up on Cameron being naked in the shower. "The house is big."

"Yeah." He crossed his long legs and linked his fingers over his flat abdomen. "Pierce and Faith's do-

ing. He said I needed a tax break and she picked out this one."

She returned the spoon she had lifted to the bowl and frowned. Selecting a house was personal. She had looked at over fifty before she found one she liked. "Why didn't you pick it out?"

He shrugged. "It didn't matter that much."

A strange feeling came over her. She straightened, watching him closely. "How long have you lived here?"

"Almost four years I guess."

What could she say? She'd said it all before. "I didn't mean to hurt you."

"But you did," he said, his eyes so intent they burned. "And you'd do the same thing again if given the opportunity, wouldn't you?"

There was only one honest answer. "Yes."

"Thought so." Uncoiling, he picked up her almost empty bowl, placemat, and spoon. "I'm flying to Chicago in the morning to meet with one of my sponsors and do a photo shoot and commercial. I want Joshua and you to come with me."

The thought of refusing was fleeting. She owed him, and her debt was getting larger by the hour. "What time do you plan to leave?"

"Eleven. It's cold there, so we'll stop at the store on the way to the airport," he said casually.

Obviously, he'd never shopped with a small child. "The stores don't open until ten."

He shrugged. "They're opening for me at nine. The shoot isn't until four. If we run late, I'll let the pilot know so he can file another flight plan."

The casualness of having a store open early and a jet wait for him was stunning. And it also reinforced how much his owner and sponsors valued him, and his income and power. The top NASCAR drivers made in the high seven figures, but Cameron hadn't cared about the money; his focus had been on racing and winning. And a win or placement in the top ten meant more recognition and sales for the driver's sponsors.

The make of the winning car often meant increased sales for that auto maker. Since all the cars adhered to NASCAR specifications inside and out, the cars looked similar. To help spectators tell them apart, the makes of some cars were written on the hood.

"We'll take their corporate jet to Midway and spend the night at the Palmer House."

The downtown Chicago hotel was noted for its excellent service, rich architecture, and fantastic food. "Oh."

"I have two connecting suites. Joshua can sleep with me."

She felt her face heat. She kept jumping to conclusions. He didn't want her. "We'll be ready. Thanks for the soup." She hurried to the door.

"You can't take care of Joshua if you're sick."

He cared about his son. Not her. She mustn't forget. "Well, good night."

"Not quite." He moved so quickly she didn't have time to evade him. Or perhaps she didn't want to. She wanted his mouth, his hands on her. She was lonely, feeling more adrift with each passing hour. If only for a little while, in Cameron's arms she wouldn't feel that way.

His mouth took hers. She opened for him, sighed into his mouth with remembered pleasure. Her arms went around his neck, deepening the kiss, enjoying the rush of passion zipping though her veins. It had been so long, and no one had ever kissed her the way Cameron did, all-consuming and all-powerful.

His hand closed over her breast and she whimpered. They'd always been sensitive and he knew it. He also knew just how to caress, to mold them in his hand to give her the most intense sensations. He hadn't forgotten.

And she remembered too much, craved too much.

His head lifted, he stared down at her, his breathing as off-kilter as hers. "Feel free to come back anytime."

She didn't know what to say, not with her body still humming, unmet need clamoring to be fulfilled. He wasn't immune to her. But making love with Cameron, although satisfying, would only lead to more problems.

"We can't stay here forever."

"You're here now." He stepped back. "Night."

"Night." Turning, she went down the hall, aware that Cameron's hungry gaze followed her all the way.

And that she was just as hungry for his body. It was going to be a long, long night.

Cameron watched Caitlin go into Joshua's room to check on him. He wondered whether she would remain there, hiding from him. He felt a spurt of admiration when she came out of Joshua's room, but she quickly went across the hall into her own room. Not once did she look in his direction.

He blew out a breath. He shouldn't have kissed her. Did he regret it? No. Would it complicate matters? His mind shouted a resounding yes. But she'd needed comfort and he hadn't been able to resist giving it to her.

He closed the door to his bedroom, striping off the T-shirt he'd used as a pajama top. Luckily he'd found bottoms. He had no idea where the top was to the set his mother had given him a couple of years ago after he'd dislocated his shoulder. Opening the hamper in the bathroom, he dumped the tee, reached for the pajama pants, then paused.

Sleeping naked wasn't a good idea with Joshua and Caitlin in the house. Cameron grinned. Although it might not be so bad if just Caitlin saw him. She'd certainly been checking out his body while she was eating. It had taken considerable willpower to remain seated and act nonchalant. But the kiss had singed him.

She still had the power to reduce him to a quivering mass of need, but he was keeping that to himself. She was a bit off balance, feeling guilty, and scared as hell of losing Joshua. She'd go along with him on the trip, but race day was a different story.

He just had to show her that her fears were unfounded. If he couldn't, they were heading for a confrontation that neither one of them would emerge from victorious.

* * *

The plane ride to Chicago Midway Airport was almost as tense as the one from California to Charlotte. Joshua's happy chatter kept her silence from being so noticeable. She'd become annoyed with Cameron when he'd insisted on purchasing her a full-length ranch-mink coat. He'd become just as annoyed because she kept insisting that, living in Fontana, she wouldn't need the coat.

"There will be a car to meet us," Cameron said, tired of the silence as they made their way down the concourse. "We'll go straight to the hotel to check in and have a late lunch. Then the driver will pick us back up at three."

"Can I have a hamburger with that k-b meat?" Joshua asked.

Cameron smiled at Joshua's attempt to pronounce "Kobe." The smile died as he saw people turning toward him, whispering. He increased his pace as much as Joshua's short legs would allow. He would have picked him up if he hadn't known it would put his son even more in the spotlight.

"Cameron," Caitlin said.

"I know." He heard the nervousness in her tense voice. "We're almost to the escalator. The escort is at the bottom, waiting for us. His name is Gus. The sign he's carrying will say 'North.' He'll take care of you if things get a bit crazy. The limo can't park, so the driver will circle until we come out."

Caitlin picked up Joshua and stepped on the escalator. Cameron stepped on behind her with Caitlin's suitcase and his satchel. This part, when he slowed, was always tricky. With the slow ride, he was more likely to be recognized, and fans had time to go down the stairs to head him off. He hadn't wanted Caitlin hurrying down the stairs in the long mink coat and possibly tripping.

He saw two, then three people gathering just beyond the escalator and accepted that he wasn't going to escape. NASCAR fans were loyal and intense. He loved them. It had taken a long time for them to accept an African-American driver, but they were equally verbal about their dislike of any driver, no matter the color of their skin.

He'd won them over by being himself and winning races. It had helped that the big racing stars had good things to say about him, and supported him whenever possible. Fans had helped him get where he was. There was no way he'd refuse to sign the pieces of paper some had out already, while others searched for anything for him to write on.

Caitlin saw the crowd growing, and looked back up at him. "Cameron, are you sure?"

"There's Gus just ahead. He'll muscle his way through if necessary to get the luggage. You can wait in the car."

Seconds before Caitlin would have reached the bottom of the escalator, a security officer arrived to push the crowd back so the passengers on the escalator could step off. They did as directed. However, the second Cameron came off the escalator the crowd surrounded him.

At any other time, he would have kept moving. He'd become adept at signing his name while walking, because once you stopped, like now, fans would surround you, making it impossible to move.

"Mr. McBride, can I have your autograph?"

"You're a heck of a driver."

"My husband just loves you. I wish he was here."

Cameron listened and thanked everyone shoving a pen and a scrap of paper toward him, his gaze on Caitlin as she stood off to one side with others who just watched. As expected, Gus managed to get through the crowd to pick up the luggage. Cameron never stopped signing. As long as no one bothered Caitlin, he didn't mind.

"Ms. Lawrence?"

Caitlin swung from staring at Cameron to see the driver Cameron had pointed out to her. With his wide shoulders, he had been easy to spot. "Yes."

"I have your luggage. Cameron's instructions were for you to wait in the car if he was detained. I've already alerted the driver," Gus told her.

Because of Cameron's height, she could see his head. He had on a plain black baseball cap. For some odd reason, she was loath to leave him.

"I tell you what. I'll take the luggage with me and see if the limo has made it."

"Why are all those people crowding around Daddy?" Joshua asked.

Caitlin refused to look at the driver. "Perhaps it's best if we go with you."

"Follow me, please."

Caitlin grasped Joshua closer to her and followed

the man out the door. Joshua had called Cameron his father at the store while they were shopping, but it hadn't been when anyone could hear. Neither of them had thought about that happening. They might have a problem.

The Palmer House was an elegant hotel with impeccable service. Cameron, holding Caitlin's arm and Joshua's hand, went straight to the private elevator. Swiping his room card, he punched in their floor. He caught Caitlin staring at him. "You all right?"

"Yes. We need to talk once we're in the room."

He frowned, glanced at Joshua, then nodded. The elevator doors opened and he stepped off after Caitlin, who was holding Joshua's hand.

"Welcome to the Palmer House." The receptionist at the concierge desk on the floor stood and greeted them. "I'm Marla. If we can do anything to make your visit more pleasurable, you only have to ask."

"Can I have a cookie?" Joshua's gaze was glued to the service area just beyond the desk that was stocked with cookies, fruit, coffee, and soft drinks.

Marla smiled. "With your mother's permission."

Caitlin didn't have a doubt that the woman knew who Cameron was. She was being diplomatic and cautious. "After you've eaten."

"But they might be gone," he said.

Cameron took him into his arms. "Then we'll have them bake some more."

Joshua grinned. "Then there will be more for me."

"Exactly." Setting Joshua on his feet, Cameron picked up the suitcases.

"Do you need assistance finding your room?" Marla asked

"No, thanks." Cameron passed the service desk and turned to the left.

"You've stayed in the suites before?" Caitlin asked.

"Yes." He stopped and opened a door at the end of the hall. "Only then, the connecting door was locked."

Caitlin didn't know what to say so she took Joshua's hand and entered the suite. A large bouquet of fresh flowers stood on the coffee table. There was also a fruit basket and a small tray of crackers.

"This must be your suite." She started for the connecting door.

"Nope. It's yours." He handed her the key.

She looked from the long-stemmed yellow roses to the artful basket of fruit and the cracker tray Joshua was examining. "I don't understand."

"They're late, but the flowers are for Joshua's birth. You were probably the only woman there with no one."

She was and had never felt lonelier . . . until the nurse had entered the room with Joshua. "Holding Joshua, healthy and in my arms, was enough."

Cameron nodded. "Just the same. Thank you." Dropping a casual kiss on her cheek, he went into the connecting suites with their son.

Caitlin stared after him, her heart melting. *What had she gotten herself into?*

Chapter 8

"We need to talk," Caitlin whispered, keeping an eye on Joshua as he watched a cartoon on the widescreen TV.

"We sure do," Cameron agreed. "You go first."

"I think it's best if we stay here." Caitlin didn't want to imagine what might have happened if they'd gone to a restaurant to eat. "Joshua called you 'Daddy' while we were waiting for you. I don't want this getting out."

Cameron's relaxed pose stiffened. "I want the whole world to know he's mine."

"Think, Cameron. What will happen when the circumstances surrounding his birth become public gossip? People can be cruel."

"Believe me, I know," he said tightly.

Caitlin didn't want to go there. "I realize you want him with you just as much as he wants to be with you, but how did you plan to introduce him or me?"

By the frown on his face she knew he hadn't thought that far. "You said it's a photo shoot with a mock-up of your car. I'm sure you won't be in and out. Joshua might be fascinated for a little while, but then he's going to get restless."

"He didn't get restless when I showed him around the shop," Cameron told her.

"Because you were with him."

His mouth tightened. "So you'll be with him this time. He'll be fine."

"Cam—"

"He's going."

Caitlin looked at Cameron's stubborn face and knew it was useless trying to reason with him. Cameron could be stubborn. One of the many reasons he did so well at racing was that he didn't give up, no matter how far behind he might be. "I hope you know what you're doing."

"I've had a lot of practice dodging questions."

She stiffened. "I guess the truce is over?"

"Nope, just pointing out fact." Spinning on his heels, he went to where Joshua sat on the floor and hunkered down. "You ready to go, now?"

Joshua scrambled up. "Yes, Daddy."

"Then let's go."

Cameron had an advantage over Caitlin in that he knew the photographer in charge of the photo shoot was a man in his late forties who apparently knew a great deal about filming, but who was a perfectionist, high strung and unfazed by the popularity of his subjects. He didn't like to be watched while working and allowed few people not connected with the shoot.

More concerned with lighting and angles, the photographer had dismissed Caitlin and Joshua the second after Joshua introduced them as "friends of mine." Since he was so exacting, those working with him had pleasing the thin, gray-haired photographer on their minds more than who might be with Cameron.

She was right about Joshua. Twenty minutes after they arrived, he was asleep in Caitlin's lap. During a break for light adjustment Cameron told her to go back to the hotel. She was up and out of there in a flash.

The filming for the commercial took another two hours before the director was satisfied. Cameron had left as fast as Caitlin had earlier. Downstairs, he'd instructed his waiting driver to take him back to the hotel. In the heavy Chicago traffic it had taken thirty minutes to reach his hotel several blocks away.

Now staring down at the two of them asleep, her arm thrown protectively around Joshua, Cameron wondered if there was a place in her heart for him. There were so many obstacles facing them.

Reaching into his pocket, he pulled out his cell phone and took several photos to add to his memory book. Toeing off his Italian loafers, he climbed into the bed, wrapping his arm around Caitlin.

"Cameron."

Cameron had heard the sleepy voice before on many occasions. Sometimes he'd have to work late at the garage and would come to bed with her already asleep. Always, always, the moment he slipped his arm around her, pulled her snugly against him, she'd murmur his name.

He absorbed the fact that she hadn't forgotten him,

wished he could nip her on the ear as he had done so many times before, wished he could kiss her everywhere his mouth and hands could touch, slip into her waiting heat. His body stirred, remembered, hungered.

Not now, but soon. Kissing her head, he closed his eyes and drifted off to sleep with his family in his arms, just where he planned on keeping them.

Caitlin came awake by degrees. She felt Cameron's strong arm around her, the hard outline of his body pressed against her backside, his arousal against her hips. She didn't open her eyes, she wanted to hold on to the dream fantasy as long as possible. It was the warmth of her son's body that finally pulled her completely from sleep.

In an instant she realized it wasn't a dream. She stiffened. Unable to scramble out of bed without waking Joshua, she looked over her shoulder and straight into Cameron's dark gaze. The look seared her. With his arousal pressing against her, there was no denying he wanted her.

She opened her mouth to tell him something, but his lips, warm and tender, touched hers and she forgot the words, only remembered the pleasure. In the shelter of his arms she always would.

"Mommy," Joshua said slowly, stirring. Caitlin stiffened, pulled her mouth away, and looked down at Joshua.

"We'll finish this later." Cameron rolled from the bed and headed for his connecting room.

Her body on fire, her mind in a turmoil, she watched him open the connecting door and close it softly after him.

Caitlin was nervous. After they'd awoken, they'd ordered room service and eaten in. Now it was past eight and time to get Joshua ready for bed. Perhaps she should have insisted on another room.

The kiss had made her more aware of Cameron, more aware of her body's wanting something it couldn't have. Make that shouldn't have. From the sizzling looks Cameron kept giving her, and his arousal pushing against her hips when they were in bed, he was more than ready to give it to her.

"Aren't you going to sleep in the same bed?" Joshua asked, staring up at them from the sofa where they were all seated. "Stephen's parents do."

Cameron looked at Caitlin, as if the problem lay with her. "You're sleeping with your father tonight," she said before he could say anything. "I'm going to do some work on the next strip. I don't want to disturb your father when I come to bed."

A half-smile curved Cameron's lips upward. "You wouldn't bother me."

Caitlin frowned at him. "Your father is just being courteous. I'll be in the other bedroom. He's going to sleep with you."

"It will be another memory," his father said, but he was looking at Caitlin, his gaze hot and intense as if he were remembering another time with just the two of them in bed creating their own memories, living out their fantasies.

Her throat dry, Caitlin swallowed. Would there ever be a time when Cameron didn't make her want and shiver with desire? She hoped so, but she wasn't taking any bets.

Joshua got up to look around the room. "Where is your sketchbook?"

Caitlin stood and did the same. She distinctly remembered putting it in the truck. "Oh, no. It's still in Cameron's truck." She shoved her fingers through her hair. She'd been so annoyed with Cameron about the fur coat that she'd forgotten it.

"There's an all-night drugstore a block away." Cameron picked up his black baseball cap, put it on his head and snagged his leather coat. "I'll go see if they have some type of sketch pad you can use until we can get what you need tomorrow."

She was so stunned by his suggestion that for a moment she didn't say anything.

"Can I go with you?"

Cameron placed his hand on Joshua's head and smiled down at him. "It's getting late. You stay here and take care of your mother."

"Cameron, it can wait until tomorrow," she told him. She didn't like the idea of him out at night in a strange city.

"You need to be able to work." He opened the door. "I should have checked to make sure we had everything."

"Cameron, it was my responsibility. Not yours." She walked over and closed the door. "You are not going out."

He lifted a dark brow. "Trying to protect me?"

"Call it what you like." She placed her hand on Joshua's shoulder. "Let's get you ready for bed."

As usual he resisted, but with a different ploy this time. "You know, Stephen said his mommy and daddy let him sleep with them one night."

Caitlin jerked her gaze to Cameron. He wore that slow sexy smile that made her stomach feel as if she had just taken a plunge on a roller coaster. "Well, er . . ."

"You'll have to settle for just me tonight." Cameron scooped his son up and set him on his shoulder, heading to the connecting door, then turned. "But your mother should feel free to join us if she'd like."

Needing to help Joshua get ready for bed, she followed them into the bedroom. As if he'd done so a thousand times before, Cameron helped Joshua with his bath, then into his pajamas and helped him brush his teeth. Back in the bedroom, Joshua knelt to say his prayers. Finished, he climbed up into the king-sized bed. He looked expectantly at his parents. "It's big enough for all of us."

Caitlin tucked the covers under his chin. "Go to sleep. Your father will join you soon."

"I wish you were coming to bed with us."

Caitlin fussed unnecessarily with the covers. Her stomach did a jitterbug. "Not tonight, sweetheart." Leaning over she kissed him on the forehead. "I love you."

"I love you too, Mommy."

"Now go to sleep," she told him.

"Good night, son."

"Good night, Daddy." Yawning, he blinked several times before his lids remained closed.

Sitting on the side of the bed, Caitlin watched Joshua fall asleep. She didn't want to face Cameron, but after Joshua kicked off the covers and turned over on his stomach, signaling he was halfway to settling in for the night, she had no choice. Rising, she tiptoed across the plush carpet out of the bedroom suite and into hers. Cameron followed, leaving the door partially open.

"He and Stephen must be a handful."

"They are," Caitlin agreed, feeling restless and afraid she knew the reason. Trying to be nonchalant, she went to the desk and pulled several sheets of hotel stationery from the drawer. "I was lucky to find good neighbors. Diana is my best friend."

Cameron followed, leaning against the side of the desk mere inches from her. If she got up, it would be too obvious that he disturbed her. "How long have you lived there?"

"Three years. I bought it the year my comic strip syndicated and I was sure I could pay the mortgage."

"You're doing something you love."

"Yes." She picked up one of the hotel's black ballpoint pens and made sure, quick strokes across the paper. "It allowed me to stay at home with Joshua."

"Guess you won't be happy doing anything else?"

Her head came up. The question wasn't an idle one. "My work isn't dangerous."

"I keep telling you NASCAR is one of the safest sports around, and will be even more so by next year with the Car of Tomorrow," he said, mild annoyance in his voice. "How would you feel if someone said you had to give up what you love?"

"That's not going to happen." She stood, recognizing her mistake immediately. He was closer to her than before. "Good night."

Cameron looked at her a long time, then straightened to his full height. "You want to tuck me in?"

He'd said the words teasingly, but there was nothing teasing about the heated gaze. Or the sudden tightening of her nipples, the undeniable quiver in her lower body. "Cameron, don't do this."

"I just asked a simple question." The back of his knuckles brushed down the side of her face.

Shivers raced over her body. She wanted to go into his arms, press her lips against his, taste the exposed column of his strong throat. She couldn't because it wouldn't stop there. "Good night, Cameron."

"Good night, Caitlin." Leaning over, he brushed his lips against hers, then he was gone.

Caitlin watched until the door closed. That made two nights he had kissed her. She couldn't let it happen again. Each touch made her crave more, made her remember how good he felt against her body, how happy she'd been with him.

Biting her lip, she plopped down in the chair and stared at the drawing of Joshua. Her trembling fingers traced his smiling face. Their love had created him. She wouldn't allow it to put him in danger. No matter how she felt, somehow, someway she'd see that Joshua didn't follow in his father's footsteps.

*   *   *

Caitlin woke up tangled in the top sheet. No wonder. She'd had a very erotic dream. Cameron had done delicious and wicked things to her body. She'd gladly returned the favor. She groaned. It had been difficult to get over Cameron years ago. She'd ached for him. She wouldn't fall into that trap again.

They had to be friends for Joshua's sake. Just friends, she repeated to herself. Now if her heart would just listen.

Blowing out a breath, she rolled over and glanced at the bedside clock radio. Seven forty-five A.M. So much for beating Cameron up and being dressed. Throwing back the covers, she went to the bathroom to wash her face and brush her teeth. She'd finished and just reached to turn on the faucet for her bath when she heard a knock on the connecting door. She started for the robe on the end of her bed. She didn't make it.

The door opened and in rushed Joshua, a smile on his face. "Good morning, Mommy. We have a surprise for you."

Stunned, Caitlin's gaze went to Cameron's. He had a breakfast tray in his hands. His gaze swept over her like silent caressing fingers. She had on a long, sleeveless cotton gown. She thanked what foresight she'd had to keep on her bra and panties. Joshua barreled into her, throwing his arms around her. "Me and Daddy ate."

"Good morning, Caitlin," Cameron greeted, setting the tray on the desk. "Joshua was getting anxious to see you."

"Daddy let me order for you all by myself,"

Joshua said proudly. Taking her hand, he led her back to bed. "It will be just like Stephen and his daddy did for Mrs. Howard on her birthday."

Her lips trembled. She had no idea he paid that much attention to the Howards. He wanted that loving relationship for him and his family. With Cameron in his life, he was finally getting it. But what would happen when Cameron was gone?

"Having you hug me is just as good as breakfast in bed." She hugged him and kissed the top of his head. "Thank you," she mouthed to Cameron. Whatever their problems, he was enabling their son to live out the things he thought a family did together.

Releasing Joshua, she returned to bed and scooted back against the headboard. "It smells good."

Joshua put both hands on one side of the tray to "help" his father place the tray on her lap, then he climbed onto the bed. "Do you like it, Mommy?"

She lifted the lid. "It's perfect." There was bacon, sausage, French toast, fruit, jams, breakfast breads. There was enough food for two people. And Joshua was bursting with pride that he had ordered by himself.

Cameron sat at the foot of the bed. "A car will pick us up at ten to take us to the airport."

Caitlin was glad. It must have showed.

"I'll be glad to get home, too." He stood. "Come on, Joshua, and let your mother eat her breakfast. You can help me pack."

Smiling, Joshua piled off the bed and hurried to his father. He was happy. He had a father. And she had to take that away.

* * *

Cameron couldn't contain his excitement. He'd been planning this since the night he found out he had a son. He couldn't be more pleased that it had happened sooner than he had expected. They'd no more arrived at his house in Charlotte than he caught Joshua's hand and headed for the great room. "Joshua, I've got a surprise for you." Grinning, Cameron opened the door.

His family was there, just as he'd known they would be. His mother stood with Faith and her husband and Cameron's best friend, Brandon, while his father was on the other side of Duncan. If Cameron needed a reminder that love hurt and that it could turn sour in the blink of an eye and bite you on the backside, he was getting it up close and personal.

His parents were standing as far apart as possible. Growing up, he thought they had a great marriage. Apparently so had his father. It had taken him a lot of years to finally get over his wife divorcing him, then marrying another man. She'd surprised them again a month ago by filing for divorce from her second husband.

"Joshua, I'd like you to meet the rest of your family." With Joshua's hand in his, Cameron took him first to his mother, who visibly fought tears. "This is my mother, your grandmother, Stella McBride."

Tenderly, she palmed Joshua's little face, then looked at Cameron. "No wonder you recognized him." Then to Joshua. "Would you like to call me 'Grandmother'?"

He nodded, then found his voice. "Yes, ma'am."

"And this is my father, your grandfather, Paul

McBride." His father hunkered down to eye level. "I'm proud to know you. Maybe we could go fishing together someday."

"I never been fishing before," Joshua said.

"We'll have to remedy that," Grandfather McBride said, and pushed up to his full height of six feet.

"And this is my sister, Faith, and her husband and my best friend, Brandon," Cameron said. "Your aunt Faith and uncle Brandon."

Faith enveloped him in a hug. "You're a handsome young man. I know we're going to be great friends."

"Yes, ma'am."

"Hello, Joshua. I can tell you that your aunt Faith makes a great friend," Brandon said, smiling down at Joshua.

"And this is my brother, your uncle Duncan."

"When you come to visit, I'll teach you how to ride and we'll go camping," Duncan said.

Six feet four of conditioned muscles, Duncan wore a white shirt, jeans, and a denim jacket. He seldom left his ranch. If he kept busy, he didn't have to think of the woman who had married and left him within a year.

The McBride curse had left its mark on both brothers. Thank goodness Faith had escaped the curse, but then she was the first female born to the McBride family in seven generations.

"You have a horse?" Joshua asked.

"Yes," Duncan answered, his handsome face wreathed in a smile. "I live on a ranch in Montana."

The little boy looked from one new relative to the other. "Now it just won't be me and Mommy."

Cameron's mouth tightened. It shouldn't have been that way in the first place. He'd missed—they'd all missed—so much because of Caitlin's fears.

Duncan scooped up the little boy. "I have a surprise for you. Let's see if they fit."

Sitting the little boy on the chair, Duncan produced a pair of cowboy boots. "Every cowboy needs boots." Slipping off Joshua's tennis shoes, Duncan lifted Joshua back down and helped him slide his feet into the boots. They fit.

Grandfather McBride placed a fishing rod in Joshua's hands. "I know just the spot for our first fishing trip. There's nothing like feeling the tug on your line, then reeling in your catch."

Joshua's eyes kept getting larger and larger. Caitlin knew he wanted a father, but she hadn't realized how much an extended family would mean to him. Her father's parents had died when she was an infant, and her mother's parents were cordial, but they weren't loving. They lived two hundred miles away and seldom visited.

Her hand flexed. Trying to protect him, she had also deprived him. It was difficult to weigh one against the other.

Joshua was the center of attention. He had a father, and now he had his family to love him. It was his birthday and Christmas all rolled into one. His eyes sparkled. He couldn't stop grinning.

"He's a bright, handsome young boy, just like

Cameron was at his age," his mother said from beside Caitlin.

"Thank you," Caitlin answered. She'd hung back from the celebration. She hadn't wanted any hard feelings Cameron's family had about her to interfere with Joshua's celebration. She needn't have worried. There wasn't one look of censure—which made her feel worse.

"No wonder he recognized him immediately," Mrs. McBride commented. "Cameron said Joshua even kicks the covers off and sleeps on his stomach."

"And he's just as fearless."

"I'm glad he found you and my grandson," she said, staring straight ahead at Joshua laughing with his grandfather. "Life has given you another chance." Her face pinched, she looked at Caitlin. "Don't throw it away."

She stared at Cameron's mother. Behind the strained smile, she saw the loneliness and the love shining in her eyes. She hungrily watched Cameron's father, the man she had divorced.

"The car should be outside, I have a few more surprises for my son." Scooping Joshua up in his arms, Cameron headed for the front door. "I don't want you to forget this day."

"I won't, Daddy."

Caitlin knew she wouldn't, either.

Chapter 9

Cameron came through on his promise. Even before they all piled into the stretch limo, the driver had taken a family picture. Cameron's long arm had drawn Caitlin to his side. Out of the corner of her eye she saw Cameron's dad place himself farthest from his ex-wife. Sadness touched Caitlin.

She'd come to admire both of them. She didn't want her and Cameron to end up polite strangers.

"Everyone in the car." Taking the camera from the driver, Cameron waited until they were all inside and then set Joshua on his feet. "The fun begins."

They went for a boat ride, to the petting zoo, played miniature golf, stopped at a pizza parlor with games. It was late in the afternoon when they arrived back home.

Faith crouched down to Joshua and blinked back tears. "I'm glad you're my nephew. You come visit me real soon."

"That goes for me too," Duncan said.

"I will," Joshua promised.

Brandon glanced at his watch. "We better head to the airport. We're supposed to take off in an hour."

Caitlin's eyes widened in alarm. "You should have left an hour ago. You'll never make it through security in time."

"Don't worry," Faith assured her. "Blade and Sierra happened to be in Santa Fe and he offered us his Gulfstream. We couldn't coordinate everyone's air flight. And we have to get back to work."

Blade Navarone, the once reclusive billionaire, was the man Cameron mentioned that would help take her son. Blade's wife was Brandon's sister.

Brandon, his arms around Faith's shoulders, smiled tenderly down at her. "I'm not sure if Sierra or Faith got us the airplane."

"The important thing is that we're here." Mrs. McBride hugged her children, then Brandon. "I'll see you two in a couple of weeks and you the following week, Duncan."

"Good-bye, Dad," Faith said, hugging him.

Her father frowned and looked at his ex-wife. "You aren't leaving?"

"No." She touched the heavy turquoise necklace at her throat. "I've decided to stay the night."

He didn't say anything, but his mouth flattened into a thin line.

Duncan stepped forward to stand beside his mother in the awkward silence. "If you want to come visit sooner, you know the door is always open and you're welcome."

Cameron shook his head. "Wait your turn. Joshua and I have her now."

"Well, I've reserved Mom a suite at the hotel and you know how I hate a cancelation, so next week she's mine and Brandon's," Faith said. "She'll get to see the changes I've made since she was there for our wedding."

"I'm sure it's beautiful," Mrs. McBride said. "You're a natural at running the hotel and taking care of the guests. The hotel is in good hands."

"It's not like we gave her a choice," Mr. Bride muttered. From the sharp intake of his ex-wife's breath, she heard him.

"Come on, Dad. You can see us off," Duncan said, taking his father by the arm and leading him out the door. Brandon and Faith walked behind them.

Cameron, with his mother, slowly followed everyone to the waiting car. "Thank you for coming."

"Good-bye Aunt Faith, Uncle Brandon, Uncle Duncan," Joshua called, waving as they climbed in a big black Lincoln.

"Why don't you and me go out back to the lake and practice casting with your new rod?" Mr. McBride suggested as soon as the limo pulled away.

Wide-eyed, Joshua looked excitedly from his mother to his father. "Can I?"

"Sure." Cameron put his hand on his son's shoulder. "Mind if I go with you?" Wildly, Joshua nodded his head. "Then let's go."

Caitlin trailed behind them to the back of the house. A wall of glass allowed an unimpeded view of the lake. A thirty-foot pier extended from the bank into the man-made lake. A few sailboats were on the lake, but most were speedboats.

Halfway there, Cameron stopped on the green lawn and hunkered down to eye level with Joshua.

From the shaking and nodding of his head, she suspected Cameron was reminding Joshua that he was forbidden to go near the water without one of them with him.

"My first grandchild," Mrs. McBride said softly. "Thank you."

Caitlin still felt it difficult to comprehend that none of them wished her ill. Especially Faith, who adored her brothers. "You don't hate me for not telling Cameron?"

"You didn't have to have Joshua," Cameron's mother said.

Caitlin gasped. "Not having him never occurred to me. Joshua has given me far more than I ever imagined."

Mrs. McBride nodded. "Loving the man makes the love for the child even stronger."

"Cameron and I—"

"Still have feelings for each other," she finished, finally turning to her. "You can tell by the way you look at each other." She turned back to see Joshua bring the rod over his right shoulder, then forward. Her mouth curved. "Joshua brought you two together, but you'll need more if you're to make it this time."

Caitlin wrapped her arms around herself. "It will never work. I don't want Cameron racing and he wouldn't be happy doing anything else."

"At first I was frightened as well. I thought his wanting to be a NASCAR driver would pass. There weren't many African Americans in the sport, but that only made him more determined," his mother recalled fondly.

"He began racing quarter-midgets. He won his second time out and never looked back. The first time I saw another driver intentionally bump Cameron when he refused to give up the lead, I was irate at the other boy and scared because Cameron had to fight for control."

"They're still bumping. Only now he's racing a thirty-four-hundred-pound car going in excess of one hundred eighty miles per hour," Caitlin said, her voice strained.

"And relishing every moment," Mrs. McBride said. "You'll have to face and fight your fears. Otherwise you'll be alone." Her arms wrapped around herself. "Take your second chance, Caitlin. You and Cameron were once as happy as Faith and Brandon."

"As you said, that was then. Joshua and I can't stay here."

Cameron's mother sighed sadly. "Then you'll lose, and regret it every day for the rest of your life." She lowered her head, then lifted it. "Believe me, I know."

"Mrs. McBride—"

She shook her head. "I think I'll join them." Opening the door, she started down the path. Mr. McBride looked up to see her. The smile on his face died. He turned his back to her. Mrs. McBride paused briefly, then continued.

If Caitlin didn't miss her guess, Cameron's mother regretted the divorce. The sad thing was, Mr. McBride didn't appear to care. She'd lost him.

Caitlin ached for Cameron's mother, and was afraid one day soon, whether or not she wanted to admit it, she might be in the same position—loving a man who no longer loved her back.

* * *

"Dad, what's going on?" Cameron and his father were sitting on the terrace off the great room after dinner. The built-in television over the unlit fireplace was on, but neither man was watching the movie.

"I take it you mean your mother," Mr. McBride said, his hands linked over his stomach.

"You know I do." Cameron blew out a breath in frustration. "A blind man can see she's trying to let you know she's interested in you."

"Too little. Too late," his father said flatly.

"Dad, if—"

"No." His father cut him off. "You know, when she left me, I wasn't sure I could go on. I wasn't worth warm spit. Faith was fresh out of college and had to run the hotel by herself. I'll always regret that I dumped it on her. I knew full well she had planned to travel after she graduated."

"I admit it was challenging for her at first, but she loves running Casa de la Serenidad. She's proven that she can handle it."

His father nodded. "She took the hotel from three stars to five. I couldn't be prouder of her." He faced Cameron and reached over to place his hand on his shoulder. "Of all of you."

"The same goes for the way we feel about you."

Mr. McBride's hand fell. "It wasn't always that way, and we both know it. Your mother leaving shattered me. It wasn't until I became interested in competition bass fishing that I finally began to come out of my downward spiral. Something about the water and testing my skill against the other fishermen helped take the hurt away. But I guess you know what I mean."

Unfortunately Cameron did. "You know I lost fifteen races straight before I pulled it together." Only Faith and Duncan knew he had been fired. He hadn't wanted his parents to know he was so close to the edge.

"And since then you've always finished the season in the top ten and last year you won the Chase Cup. This year you're going to win a second," his father said proudly.

"I want that win, and I have the car and crew that will help me get it," Cameron said with conviction. "We're going to do everything to make it happen."

"This might sound harsh, but having Caitlin around with nothing settled is going to mess with your concentration," his father said. "With the new point system for the Chase, wins are going to count more toward the total scoring than the years before. Number twenty-three needs to consistently win."

"I can't have Joshua without Caitlin," he said, well aware that there was more to it than that. "She won't affect my concentration. I'll win."

"Then you're a better man than your old man." Mr. McBride blew out a breath. "There is no way I'm letting your mother back in my life. I couldn't, *won't* go through the hell she put me through again."

"I know it's tough, but if she wants to get back with you, can't you at least talk with her?" Cameron suggested.

"Would you, if Caitlin wanted to start over?" his father asked.

Even before the question formed clearly in his mind he knew the answer. "Caitlin is afraid for me when I race. There is no future for us unless I can change her mind and, frankly, I'm not sure I can accomplish that."

"I'm sorry to hear that, especially with Joshua."

"Caitlin did a great job raising him and it couldn't have been easy for her," Cameron mused. "She used her savings to pay for the doctor bills. Coming up with the comic strip was a godsend, she says, because it allowed her to stay at home with Joshua. He's smart and loving."

"I agree. He's a wonderful little boy who needs both parents."

"For the time being, that is what he has," Cameron told him flatly. On that, he didn't intend to budge.

"At least your mother waited until you were all grown before she divorced me."

Cameron heard the anger and hurt in the clipped words. "And she obviously regrets her decision."

"I could care less. In fact, I'm seeing another woman."

The motion lights flooded the terrace. Cameron and his father turned to see what had activated them and saw his mother. From the strained, hurt expression on her face he knew she had heard everything.

"Caitlin sent me to get you two," she said in an unsteady voice. "Please come up. Joshua won't go to sleep until his father and grandfather come up and say good night." After delivering the message, she went back inside the house.

"Dad—"

"We better go see Joshua so he can get to sleep." His father walked to the terrace door. "Then I want to call my friend."

Cameron picked up the control and shut off the television. "Are you sure that is what you want to do?"

He paused. "I've never been surer of anything else in my life."

Cameron stared at his father's steadfast gaze, then headed for the stairs. He wished things could have been different for his mother, who apparently still cared about the man she'd divorced. Unfortunately, it showed that some decisions were irrevocable and carried far-reaching consequences.

If he didn't want the same unhappy consequences, he had to figure out a way to help Caitlin overcome her fears or there would be no future for them as a family.

Caitlin had never felt so heartbroken for anyone as she did for Mrs. McBride. The older woman had looked shattered when she'd returned from getting Cameron and his father. As soon as Joshua had climbed into bed, she'd gone to the guest bedroom on the ground floor. Unable to get her mind off Cameron's mother, Caitlin had gone to see her. She'd found her packed and ready to leave.

"Mrs. McBride, your flight isn't until the morning. Please stay. I can take Cameron's truck and drive you," Caitlin told her.

"No. I've already called a cab and secured a room at a hotel at the airport." She picked up her luggage from the bed. "Please tell Joshua good-bye for me."

"What do I tell Cameron?" she asked.

"Not to make the mistake I made and that goes for you as well." She gave Caitlin a brief hug, started from the room, and ran straight into Cameron.

"Mom, don't do this."

Her smile trembled. "I don't think I can face him after—Please."

Cameron took the suitcase from her hand. "There is no reason for him to come downstairs until breakfast. I can call my travel agent, get you an early flight, and take you to the airport."

"Cameron, I don't know."

"I do." Setting the suitcase down, he pulled her into his arms.

"How could I have been such a fool?" she sobbed. "I still love him and now it is too late and it's my own fault."

"Mom, I wish things were different."

"So do I." She lifted her head from his shoulder. Tears coated her lashes. "Don't make the same mistake I did. Either of you."

Caitlin couldn't help but look at Cameron. His expression was unreadable. The only reason he wanted her there was for Joshua. He might want the side benefit of her in his bed, but sex wouldn't solve the bigger issue. "If you'll give me the information, I'll cancel the cab and the hotel, and you and Cameron can talk."

Sniffing, Mrs. McBride opened her purse and took out a small piece of paper and handed it to Caitlin. "Thank you."

"I'm the one who should be thanking you. Joshua

couldn't have a better MeMa." Impulsively she kissed the other woman on the cheek, careful not to touch Cameron. "I hope we can keep in touch and visit often. Joshua's maternal grandparents are living, but they've chosen not to have much contact with us."

"I'd like that."

"Good night."

"Good night, Caitlin."

Quietly, Caitlin left. In her room she canceled the cab and hotel, then dressed for bed, all the time thinking how similar Mrs. McBride's situation was to hers. Both had left the man they loved, both had had a child involved, both regretted the decision, both were reaping the bitter consequences.

But there was one major difference. If Mrs. McBride had the chance to do it all over again she'd stay with her husband. Caitlin would still leave, and ask God, as she'd done every night, to watch over the man she would always love.

A knock sounded on her door. Cameron. She'd half expected him, dressing in the cotton pajamas she'd purchased at the specialty store. She pulled on the matching robe and opened the door.

He looked tired and miserable. She stepped aside for him to enter and closed the door after him. "I'm sorry."

"Yeah. I wish . . ."

"I know," she said, reaching out to touch his arm.

"I don't want us to end up like that. Hurting each other because we're afraid of being hurt." He shook his head. "Dad worshiped Mom, but he's erected this wall."

"You said it—he doesn't want to be hurt again," she said.

Cameron stared down at her, then trailed a finger along the side of her face. "I'm finding there are worse things."

Her breath hitched. "We said we'd keep this impersonal."

"We said a lot of things." He pulled her into his arms, his mouth finding hers. There was a sweet desperation in the kiss. So many things were against them. Lifting his head, he went to the door. "Sleep well, and thanks for caring about my mother."

"Good night. She made it easy." She closed the door. Caitlin, she thought, you're going to be in big trouble if you keep on letting him touch you, but you enjoy it too much to stop him. Tonight she wasn't going to worry about it.

Cameron woke up early to take his mother to the airport. He cursed inwardly when he saw her red, puffy eyes, but knew nothing he could say would change anything. Only his father could do that and apparently that wasn't happening. One thing he had been able to do was book her on the first flight to New York.

At the security checkpoint at the airport she'd clung to him as tightly as she had last night, and issued just as dire a warning. "Swallow your pride or whatever it takes, but don't end up like me with regret and thoughts of what might have been."

He'd stayed until she'd disappeared down the concourse, then he'd gone home to find Caitlin and his father at the breakfast table. Apparently she had cooked breakfast. Their family might have been in the hotel business, but his father was next to worthless in the kitchen.

Cameron's helplessness turned to anger. He hadn't even been able to get his mother to drink coffee, and his father had a full plate of food in front of him. Cameron opened his mouth to say something mouthy to his father, but then he looked up. Just for a moment his father's eyes held the same bleakness they had when his mother had walked out on him and filed for divorce.

"Good morning, Cameron," Caitlin said.

Cameron jerked his gaze to her and saw the almost imperceptible shake of her head. "Morning," Cameron amended, and took a seat next to his father. "You sleep all right?"

"Yes." His hands remained curled around the coffee mug.

It was a lie that Cameron had no intention of challenging. It would solve nothing. His father was hurting just as badly and determined not to show it or let himself be hurt again. Last night had all been an act to protect himself. Cameron wondered if there really was a woman.

"Would you like breakfast?" Caitlin asked.

"Please." Cameron pulled out a chair and took a seat. "It looks good."

"Caitlin found me in the kitchen and took pity on me," Mr. McBride said, finally raising his cup to his mouth.

"Since your flight isn't until this afternoon, why

don't you come to the race shop with me this morning? We can drop back by here to pick up your luggage and you can say good-bye to Joshua then," Cameron suggested, accepting his plate filled with bacon and eggs, noting they were fluffy instead of the hard pebbles that once were all she could cook.

"Yes, I can cook," Caitlin said, with no animosity in her voice.

"How is it, Dad?" he asked, hoping to jar his father into eating. "Caitlin used to be almost as bad as you are in the kitchen."

" 'Used to be' is the operative phrase. Help me out here, Mr. McBride," Caitlin said, apparently catching on and trying to help.

The older man looked at his plate as if he'd forgotten it was there, then picked up his fork and took a bite of fluffy soft scrambled eggs. "They're good."

"See," she said smugly, folding her arms.

Cameron took a bite, then lifted a brow. "He's right. They are good."

Caitlin smiled with undisguised pleasure. "Thank you."

Cameron turned to say something to his father and caught him watching him with a strange look on his face. Cameron didn't have to be a mind reader to know what his father was thinking; the same thing that was on his mother's mind. Only he wanted Cameron to get as far away from Caitlin as possible so he wouldn't have to go through the pain he was enduring, while Cameron's mother's advice was just the opposite.

Cameron had his own plan and he was putting it into action this afternoon.

"We have a surprise for you," Cameron said.

Joshua giggled. "I helped pick it out."

Caitlin looked up from her sketch pad. She wondered if she'd ever get used to seeing father and son together. Joshua was a miniature of his gorgeous father, who looked deceptively lean. She knew hard muscles were under the chambray shirt and tight jeans. Joshua was dressed just like his father, down to the cowboy boots.

"I guess your mother doesn't like surprises?" Cameron teased. "Maybe we should take it back."

Joshua shook his head and ran to grab his mother's hand. "Come on. It's something you need."

"Something I need," Caitlin repeated, trying to come up with what they had bought her now. The yellow roses he'd given her in Chicago were on the dresser in her room. They were the first thing she saw when she woke up. Cameron's thoughtfulness had touched her more she wanted to admit. What else could he want to give her? She balked. "It's not a car, is it?"

Cameron frowned. "No."

She could see the wheels turning in his head. "No car."

"Come on, Mommy."

"I've got a faster way, son." Grinning, Cameron picked up a startled Caitlin.

She gasped as Joshua laughed. "Put me down."

"Daddy picked up Mommy," Joshua singsonged.

"Lead the way, Joshua, while I bring your mother." Cameron hugged Caitlin close as she pushed against his chest.

He stopped and leaned his face closer to hers. "If you don't stop, I might have to kiss you."

She flushed, licked her lips.

His nostrils flared. The laughter left his face.

"Daddy, come on!" Joshua cried impatiently.

"Saved by an impatient four-and-half-year-old," he whispered. Out loud he said, "Coming, son."

Cameron walked into the glass-enclosed sitting area that looked out to the formal gardens, dancing fountain, and the pool pavilion. Caitlin was too busy trying to control the desire pulsing through her to be aware of anything except the man holding her so tightly.

"Surprise!" Joshua yelled.

Caitlin looked toward the sound and gasped. There was an easel and paintbrushes, almost identical to her work station at home. "How?"

"Joshua with a little help from Diana. We have one smart son."

"Daddy, put her down so she can see all her stuff," Joshua told his father.

"Spoilsport," Cameron whispered, but he set Caitlin on her feet and walked with her over to the easel. "I have the store's card. If you want to exchange anything or you need more supplies, all you have to do is call. They deliver."

"It's almost like my setup at home," she murmured softly.

Joshua patted the stool. "Sit down, Mommy. I tried it out and it works real good."

She smiled and took a seat. "Thanks for testing it for me."

"We wanted everything to be right." Cameron's face turned serious. "I realized that night at the Palmer House, when you didn't have your sketch pad, that sitting on the bed might not be the best thing."

"Thank you," she said, picking up one of the charcoal pencils. "I'll pay you back."

"Daddy used his credit card." Joshua picked up a package of small sketch pads. "Daddy and me are going to put them in the car and all over the house so if you think of something you can draw it."

"Cameron, I appreciate the offer, but your house is picture-perfect. I don't want to clutter it up with my work," she protested.

"I want you to be comfortable," he told her. "Is this all right? I thought you'd enjoy the light."

"Daddy bought me a portable PlayStation so I can watch movies and play games while you're working," Joshua said, proudly showing her the entertainment pack.

"I—"

"Before you object, there are learning programs on math and science, and he's promised me to put on an educational program between games," Cameron defended. "He even has headphones."

"Isn't this great, Mommy?" Joshua grinned up at her.

"It is. Thank you, Cameron," she said. "But I could just as well work in my bedroom."

"They're delivering another table in a couple of hours and will set it up in your room," Cameron said. "You'll still be able to work at night. I don't want your staying with me to change anything."

How could he say that? Living here changed everything, especially for her heart that wanted what it couldn't have.

His dark eyes narrowed for a moment as if he could read her thoughts. "I better get back to the garage."

"Daddy, can I go with you?" Joshua asked.

"Not this time, son. We're working on the engine and I'll be in and out of the car testing it, so it will be busy." Cameron took off his hat and placed it on his son's head. "Keep my hat for me, and take care of your mother while I'm gone."

"I will, Daddy."

Cameron squatted down. "Give your old man a hug." Joshua eagerly went into his father's arms. Cameron pushed to his feet and stared at Caitlin a full two seconds before pulling her into his arms. "If you want to worry about something, worry about what you're going to cook your men for dinner."

"This morning you were skeptical and now you want a full-course meal," she bantered back.

"We need our strength, don't we, son?"

"Yes, sir," Joshua answered dutifully.

Cameron stared down into her face. "I'll try to be home before seven." Kissing her on the cheek, he was gone.

"I wanna wait for Daddy."

"Honey, it's seven-fifteen. Daddy had someone

call. He's going to be late. He wanted you to eat and take your bath and go to bed."

Arms folded, Joshua had his head down with the cap Cameron had put on his head before leaving. "I wanna wait on Daddy."

They'd been having this "discussion" for thirty minutes, ever since one of Cameron's crewmen had called. There was a problem with the shocks and they wanted to fix it before they called it a night.

Picking up his plate, she placed it back in the warming oven. "Why don't we go get your bath."

"I wanna wait for Daddy."

Caitlin stared down at her son, and accepted that she had two options: get an attitude and remind him who was the boss here or accept that Joshua was as needy to be around his father as his father was to be around him. The back door opened and in rushed Cameron.

"Daddy!" Joshua was out of his seat in a flash.

"Hi, Joshua." Cameron picked Joshua up without breaking his stride. His eyes looked a bit anxious. "Sorry I'm late."

He should be. She folded her arms. Knowing the pose was combative didn't stop her. "Joshua refused to eat until you came home."

Cameron stared at his son. "Son, I'm thrilled you want to wait, but I want you to mind your mother."

"Yes, sir, but I missed you," he said, his lower lip trembling.

"The same goes here, but it would sure help me when I can't be here to know that you're minding your mother and you both are doing all right," he said. "Your mother worries about you when you don't eat."

Joshua looked at his mother. "I'm sorry."

She hadn't expected Cameron to come to her defense. But then she reflected that he backed her with Joshua . . . except when it came to matters involving racing. "Apology accepted. Your father can wash up and we can eat. You can get his glass and fill it with ice."

Joshua brightened and wiggled to get down. Cameron set him on his feet. "You're good at being a mother."

The compliment took her aback. "You let him know he was wrong, but that you loved him," Caitlin said. She turned and winced at the grinding sound as the ice maker attempted to spit out ice.

"Ease back a bit, Joshua," Cameron said, going to stand by his son. "Burn out the motor and you're in trouble."

Joshua pulled the glass back and glanced up at his father. "It can't run without a motor, just like number twenty-three can't."

"Right." Cameron accepted the glass. "Why don't you go get your mother's glass. It takes practice to develop just the right touch, just like in driving."

"All right." Joshua did a fast walk to the table for the glass.

Caitlin said nothing. Father and son were bonding more and more and, despite the danger involved, she couldn't regret that Joshua had his father.

* * *

"Caitlin, the hauler is leaving tomorrow for the Las Vegas Speedway. Frank, my driver, is taking my motor home that same day. The team owner has given us the use of his jet to fly down there on Thursday evening and we can all fly back late Sunday night or Monday."

Caitlin had known this was coming, but she still sat there on the sofa across from Cameron later that night and she still couldn't get the words out. His parents' unhappiness and their warnings were too fresh.

She might have been able to shake his mother's warning but his father's was tough. He had said she should leave now before she ruined Cameron's chance for a second Chase Cup. That bothered her the most. If she had thought he was being nosy or insensitive, she might have told him—respectfully—to mind his own business. But with the pain of his ruined marriage so vivid in his eyes and face, she couldn't do that. All she could say was that she never wanted to hurt Cameron.

"Caitlin?"

She lifted her head and stared across at Cameron. He wore the jeans he preferred, a T-shirt with HILLIARD MOTORSPORTS on the front, and on the back a picture of him in racing gear beside the number 23.

"You know how I feel, Cameron."

"I know, but Joshua is my son. I want him to know what I do for a living, and I want him there with me."

"No." She came to her feet. "I don't want him seeing the race."

His hands clenched, then he stood. "We'll talk about it once we get there, but he *will* be there."

She folded her arms. "I guess all that talk about us working together was just talk."

"If it was, I would take Joshua whether you wanted me to or not. I could hire a lawyer," he said, and kept talking as her eyes widened. "If you're unhappy he's going to be unhappy. I don't want us fighting over him. I'm willing to take this slow, but you have to be willing to meet me halfway, otherwise this isn't going to work."

She glanced away. "It's hard."

Crossing to her, he took her arms. "I know. The closer it gets to race day, the harder it will be for you."

She might have known he'd remember and understand, but he wasn't letting it sway him. "Why couldn't you have been a salesman like I thought when we first met?"

The sides of his mouth hitched up in a smile. "I saw you and that was that. I never wanted a woman to say yes to a date so badly."

"I couldn't believe you really wanted to go out with me," she admitted.

His arms slipped around her waist. "I'd tell you you were beautiful, but you probably wouldn't believe me now any more than you did then."

She shrugged. "I look in the mirror and just see me."

His hands cupped her face. "I see a beautiful, courageous woman. I see the mother of my child."

Her hands palmed his. "Not even close to being courageous."

"That's where you're wrong," he said. "There are

different kinds of courage. Falling in love takes courage. Being a good mother takes courage. It would be so easy to turn Joshua against me, but you haven't."

"I would never do that," she said, angry that he would even think she would.

"A selfish mother who cares more about what she wants or who hates the father might. One way to make sure Joshua never wanted to be near me or race would be to make him hate me." He smiled sadly. "You'll find a way to fight me, but not at Joshua's expense. That shows love and courage."

"And you want me here anyway?"

His thumb feathered over her lower lip. "Wanting you is all I used to think about."

Heat balled in her stomach. Her hands trembled and she realized she still held his. She lowered her hands and stepped back. She was more of a coward than he knew. "I probably should get to work."

"One more thing. I've been thinking about him being out of preschool. Do you think we need to hire him a tutor or maybe a nanny to take him places when we're busy?" he asked. "There are eleven more races before summer."

Eleven races meant twelve weeks. There was no race on Easter Sunday. Tutors and nannies meant permanence. "Cameron, surely you can see now that it's best for Joshua to have stability. I know and understand you want him here, but he needs friends his own age."

"If we work together he'll have that stability. You've had four and a half years. The least you can do is give me unrestricted time with him."

His being right didn't make it any easier for her to acquiesce to what he asked. She glanced away.

"I know I'm pushing hard and I know you can fight me on this if you want to take it that far."

Her head snapped back around. He meant lawyers and court. "No. We'll work this out for Joshua's sake."

"There are a couple of other things." Caitlin braced herself. "The housekeeper, Joyce, is usually here every day when I'm home, but I called and told her to wait until next week to give us time to get settled in. If you decide you want to interview a teacher or a nanny, I have a list with their contact information on my desk."

"I'll let you know. 'Night."

"Good night, Caitlin," Cameron said and left the room.

Not likely, she thought.

Chapter 10

She woke up in another tangle of sheets. Erotic dreams of Cameron—again. Throwing back the covers, she pulled on her robe and left to check on Joshua.

"Good mor—" The rumpled bed was empty. Panic hit her. She whirled, raced to Cameron's room and found the bed neatly made. She headed for the stairs. Surely Cameron wouldn't have changed his mind about working things out.

Two steps away from the stairs, she heard the shared laughter of father and son. Relief swept though her. She continued to the kitchen. They were sitting side by side at the table, their dark heads bent over a magazine.

She wasn't aware of making a sound, but Cameron looked up, frowning. "You all right?"

"Morning, Mommy," Joshua greeted. "Daddy was showing me his racing team in the magazine."

"I see." She barely glanced at the *Sports Illustrated*. "Have you two had breakfast?"

"Daddy fixed waffles, and I helped," Joshua said.

Caitlin placed her hand on his head. "I bet you were a big help too."

"That's what Daddy said." He grinned up at her.

"You didn't answer my question."

Cameron had that stubborn look she was all too familiar with. The one that had swept aside her opposition and landed her and Joshua in his home. She took a seat by Joshua. "He wasn't in his bed."

"And you thought the worst," he said, his voice devoid of warmth, the concern in his eyes a moment ago gone.

"I'm sorry." There was no sense in denying the truth. The upcoming trip had her nerves tied in knots.

Cameron grunted and stood. "Joshua and I are going to the garage."

Joshua came to his feet, picked up his cap to put on his head, turning it around backward just as his father did. "We have to make sure the car is ready for the race on Sunday."

It was happening, and there was nothing she could do to steer Joshua in a different direction—if she stayed at the house. "Do you mind if I come with you?"

Cameron's eyes narrowed. Before when they were together, she seldom visited the garage and only stayed for a few laps of the actual race. "The car is leaving in ten minutes."

"I'll be ready." Caitlin hurried to get dressed. This was for Joshua.

At the garage, Caitlin recognized many of the men working there. They nodded, then went back to work. They hadn't forgotten or forgiven her running out on Cameron. She could accept that. What she couldn't accept was Joshua following in his father's footsteps.

"Caitlin, how are you?" Mike asked.

"Fine, thank you, Mike." Caitlin stuck her hands into the pockets of her jeans after the brief hand-shake. "How have you been?"

"Great. Cameron is headed toward another Chase Cup and my daughter is on the circuit, too."

Caitlin remembered the beautiful, dark-haired young woman who had come to a couple of races. "She races, too?"

Mike chuckled. "I thought she might at one time join her brother in the Nationwide Series, but she likes promoting the drivers more. She's the PR rep for Cameron and some of the other drivers. She's good at it, too."

"Why, thank you."

Mike turned, a smile already forming on his round face. "It isn't nice sneaking up on people."

"With all this noise, who can sneak," Hope said, smiling back at her father, then her gaze centered on Caitlin. The smile remained, but it became restrained. "You must be Caitlin Lawrence."

"Yes," Caitlin answered. Mike might have forgiven Caitlin, but obviously his daughter hadn't, which was strange since she hadn't represented Cameron when they were together.

"Caitlin and Joshua came to look over the shop," Mike said by way of explanation.

Hope's dark brow arched. "I thought you didn't like racing."

Lines darted across his father's forehead. "Hope, she's entitled to her opinion."

"Not when it interferes with my client," Hope said, her voice as devoid of warmth as her face. "We're three races into the season with a big win at Daytona. He doesn't need any distractions."

"Hope—"

"I'm more aware than you will ever be of what Cameron needs," Caitlin said, cutting off Mike. "To me and Joshua, he's more than a paycheck."

Hope's dark eyes flashed, narrowed. "Why—"

"Caitlin," Mike said, catching her arm and leading her away from the other woman, who looked ready to pounce. "You'll have to forgive Hope. Her mother and I tried to teach her manners, and we did a good job until she followed her brother onto the race cir- cuit, getting to know the business and making con- tacts."

He led Caitlin inside the hauler. "She's learned to be tough in a man's world where she's in the minority. It was that or get stepped on or pushed aside or, worse, being harassed. My baby doesn't take any guff."

"Neither do I and I've had to be tough as well," Caitlin said tightly.

Mike opened a refrigerator. "Water, Pepsi, Gatorade?"

"Water." She didn't need the kick of the caffeine, she was wound up enough.

Unscrewing the top, Mike gave her the bottle. "Cameron didn't offer explanations beyond the fact that you two were back together, and if anyone made you or Joshua feel uncomfortable they'd have to deal with him."

Caitlin took a swig of her drink. "Guess Hope didn't get the memo."

"Tell Cameron she tried to chew on you, and you'll find out." He popped the top of a Pepsi. "You and Joshua mean a lot to him."

"Not enough for him to stop racing." Her hand clenched the bottle. There, she'd said it.

To his credit, Mike didn't throw up the sign of the cross. NASCAR was sacred to the men who were on a driver's team.

"Could you stop breathing?" he asked.

Caitlin didn't dignify the question with an answer.

"That's what racing is like to us. It's what we live and breathe, and to be on a winning team is as close to heaven as some of us will ever get." He stared down at his soda. "Cameron beat the odds to be here, just as Mario, my son, and Hope and I are doing. We had to be better because our skin was darker. We proved we belong here with wins and the Chase Cup last year. Look at the stats. Some drivers never get to Victory Lane. Heck, they don't even make the cut to the forty-three cars. Cameron has never missed qualifying."

"Are you saying that he may because I'm here?" she questioned.

"Qualifying is a lot different than winning the race. Las Vegas is a good track, wide with enough maneuvering room for a driver to pass, but it's still four grueling hours with nothing but you and the car, pitting your skills against the track and the other drivers. A man has to have his head on straight. If not . . ."

She knew Mike was thinking about the fifteen straight races Cameron had lost after she left him at the altar. "It might sound strange, but I want him to win."

"You just don't want to see it."

She glanced away from his piercing eyes. "There are reasons."

"I figured," he said as she faced him again. "Cameron is a grown man, but I'm crew chief. It's my job to get number twenty-three across the finish line first. You two will figure this out or you won't. We have to take race day as it comes. You can't run the race again, and the race will always come first."

Her chin lifted. "That is a lesson I already learned." She set her bottle of water on the counter. "Good-bye."

Cameron didn't like Caitlin being afraid. He knew that look as she came out of the hauler. He hadn't been able to get her to overcome that fear in the past. He didn't hold out much hope now.

Joshua was as outgoing as she was reserved. At the moment he was with his pit crew, and they were telling tall tales about his father. Thankfully, she hadn't let her shyness and fears keep their son from being inquisitive.

"Safety measures have changed in the past five years," he said as she approached him. "The crew is one of the best in the business. We work as a team. Number twenty-three car doesn't move unless we're sure she's in top shape."

"What about last Saturday?" she asked.

"We knew there were a few bugs in number thirty-six. The race was to find the problems."

"Instead you ended up in the hospital."

"Without any major injuries, and if I hadn't I wouldn't have found my son." There was censure in his voice, his direct gaze.

"I think I'll take Joshua home."

Cameron's brow lifted. She'd said "home" and not back to his "house." He pulled the keys to his truck from his pocket. "Joshua." He pitched his voice to be heard over the machinery.

Joshua looked around from watching two men work on number 23's engine. He started toward them.

"I'll see you tonight," Cameron said

"All right." She met Joshua halfway. Taking his hand, she left the garage without looking back.

Caitlin couldn't sleep that night and didn't waste her time trying. Instead she changed into lightweight sweats and went to the drafting table in a corner of the room. Every time she saw the table or recalled Cameron's thoughtfulness regarding her welfare, her heart turned over.

She told herself she was silly to put more meaning to it than his making it easier for her to stay, but she couldn't quite make herself believe that. She didn't want them to be enemies, and as her body awakened more and more to him, she couldn't deny that she missed the closeness they had once shared. Not just the intimacy, although that had been earth-shattering. No, she'd enjoyed talking to him, reveled in his love.

Hunching over the table, she studied the partially

finished comic strip. She had to stop thinking about Cameron. This paid the bills. She was lucky that she was a month ahead of the Sunday comic strip that ran in over 350 newspapers. That number could shrunk as newspapers merged or simply devoted the space to something else.

Her hand paused over the outline of Joshua's face. With Cameron, she no longer had to worry about having enough money for Joshua's college education. Instead she worried that Joshua might not stay with her or not want to go to college at all. Despite his mother's concern, Cameron had begun racing after obtaining an associate degree in business. He'd shown everyone that he was mature and disciplined enough to race and win.

Until she'd come along.

A knock sounded on the door. Cameron. She straightened, her hand automatically running over her hair before she caught herself and groaned. Giving in to the attraction between them was asking for trouble, and they had enough to deal with.

"Caitlin," Cameron called. "You awake?"

"Yes. Come in."

He came inside, closing the door after him. "I see you're working."

Trying, she thought, but she wasn't about to admit that. Any more than she would admit that it was becoming more and more difficult not to give in to the temptation of the signals Cameron kept tossing out. He smelled and looked good enough to bite, and she knew just the place.

She twisted on the stool. "Yes. I wanted to finish

this by the weekend." There was no way she'd be able to concentrate once they left for Las Vegas.

"It's after one."

She shrugged. "I often work while he's asleep." *And on those long lonely nights when memories of me and Cameron locked in passion and need haunted me . . . like tonight.*

Cameron peeked over her shoulder at the drawing and chuckled. "Something tells me that Joshua really did try to fry an egg on the sidewalk."

Caitlin's mouth curved upward. The little boy in the comic strip, spatula in hand, squatted in front of a raw egg on the sidewalk. The caption read: "Mommy's breakfast." "He's so inquisitive and bright. Watching him laughing and trying to catch a butterfly when he could barely walk gave me the idea for the strip."

"I wish I could have seen him then." The yearning in Cameron's voice made her heart ache.

"Perhaps you can." Putting the pad aside, she went to the dresser and picked up a five-inch-thick photo album. "I asked Diana to send this overnight. I thought you might like to see it."

She opened the album. The first picture was of Joshua and Caitlin shortly after he'd been born. She frowned over the picture as she usually did because her hair was a mess. She had on no makeup, of course, but she hadn't been able to stop grinning.

Quietly Cameron took the album and sat down on her bed and began flipping pages. After a moment's hesitation, she sat down beside him and smiled at a picture of Joshua, smiling back at her with one baby tooth, arms raised. "This was taken at eight months when he started walking. He hasn't slowed down since."

There were pictures of Joshua playing soccer, at church programs, at his first day of prekindergarten. Cameron's blunt-tipped fingers traced over the last photograph: Joshua and Caitlin standing beside their family science project and him holding a first-place ribbon.

"I missed a lot."

The regret in his voice tore at her. "Please try to understand. I only wanted to keep him safe." She swallowed the lump in her throat. "You can't imagine how difficult it was for me to always be afraid for you."

Trying to understand her fears, Cameron pulled her into his arms. Tears filled her eyes and streamed down her cheeks. "I don't want Joshua to find you just to lose you."

"Please don't cry." He kissed her forehead, the curve of her cheek, before settling on her mouth. Desire rushed through him. He gathered her closer, feeding off the sweetness of her mouth, reveling in the elegant length of her body pressed against his.

She was everything that he had ever desired. To have her in his arms, to be able to sweep his hand down her bare back, over her hips, feel her body awaken beneath his hand, was heaven on earth.

The hard buds of her nipples pushed against his chest. He had to touch them. His hand swept under her top, felt the smooth, satiny skin. His heart thumped like a jackhammer. Her breast was fuller, yet firm. It filled his hand. Moaning softly, she arched against him. She'd always had sensitive breasts. His thumb stroked the hard peak. Her hands flexed on his shoulders.

He wanted her naked beneath him. Grabbing the bottom of the sweat top, he lifted it, flinging it aside.

"We—" Whatever she had been about to say turned into a moan as his mouth replaced his hand, his breath warm, his tongue gliding around the underside of her breast again and again before finally closing on the turgid point. Her hand clutched his head to her as her lower body moved restlessly beneath him.

His hand slid over her quivering stomach into her heat, stroked the tight bud. She came off the bed, undulating against his hands. What little control he had snapped. He quickly finished undressing her, then himself before coming back down on top of her.

His sigh mixed with hers at the rightness, the pleasure of bare skin against bare skin, hard to soft. She was all the woman he would ever need.

"This won't change anything," she murmured, even as her nails dug into his shoulders, her eyes burned with need. His body was lean and hard in all the right places and she wanted him. This shouldn't be happening, but if he pulled away she might die.

His answer was to surge into her moist heat, filling her. She clenched around him. Both moaned at the rightness, the intense pleasure. Then he began to move. Heaven.

Lifting her hips, she eagerly met each thrust as he glided in and out, taking her higher and higher to the point of no return. She locked her legs around him, buried her face against his shoulder, and let arousing sensations sweep over and through her.

Each stroke pleasured her, thrilled her. He began to move faster, the delicious friction of their bodies taking her closer to the edge. Conscious thought became impossible.

His blood hot, he clamped his hand beneath her hips, deepening the contact. He felt his body tightening and fused his mouth on hers, his tongue imitating the driving motion of his hips. He jerked, spasmed, felt her go over with him.

His breathing harsh, he lifted his head and stared down at her. Slowly her eyes opened. Pleasure, not regret, stared back at him.

Rolling over, he picked her up and started from the room. "Cameron! Stop!" she shrieked as he shifted her in his arms to open her door. "Joshua."

"Is asleep—unless you wake him up." Nudging the door wider, he continued to his bedroom, swinging the door closed behind him

"Cameron, I can't sleep in here."

He placed her on the bed, coming down on top of her. "You won't be doing any sleeping for a long time."

She gasped. His hot mouth covered her, his tongue thrusting inside her. The faint embers of sated passion flared white-hot. Cameron made her body hot, made it crave what only he could give her—mindless passion.

She locked her arms around him. Time enough for regrets tomorrow.

* * *

"We're leaving this afternoon for the next race."

In bed that morning, sated from a night of love-making, she stared at Cameron, wished she were dressed. "Is that why last night happened?"

Cameron's face harshened "Last night had nothing to do with this and you know it."

"I'm sorry." She pulled the sheet tighter to her naked breasts. "It's just that he is so taken with you. He wants to be like you."

"And you think that's bad?" Cameron asked, his hands on his hips.

The softly spoken question didn't fool Caitlin. He was angry. "In some ways. You're honest, intelligent, caring, but you're also driven and single-minded when it comes to racing despite the dangers and the time it consumes."

"It's what I was born to do. There's only one thing that has ever come close to the feeling I get when I'm pitting my skills against other drivers. When I'm buried deep inside you, and you're clinging to me."

Caitlin's heart thumped. Her nipples tightened.

"We'll be gone through the weekend," he told her. "A driver is taking us to the airfield."

"If I refuse to go?"

"You won't. Despite your fears, you won't deprive Joshua of spending time with his father."

He knew her too well. "I would to keep him from following in your footsteps."

"Like I said, you might not have a choice." He glanced at his watch. "In the meantime, we have a plane to catch."

Chapter 11

Race day was filled with excitement for the more than two hundred thousand plus fans, the owners of the cars and their drivers and crew, the sponsors—large and small—and all the other people at the track who made NASCAR racing possible. The haulers with the race cars and motor coaches of the NASCAR drivers came in on Thursday, and the drivers usually arrived Thursday evening for qualifying races on Friday.

Saturday was spent fine-tuning the car, pushing it to get the maximum speed, learning the track, taking practice runs in anticipation for the big race day on Sunday.

No matter how many times Cameron raced, he never tired of it. The excitement was just as high, the anticipation just as thrilling.

Mid-morning Sunday he zipped up his suit, picked up his sunshades, put on his team cap. It was time for him to leave for the garage. Number 23 had already passed the NASCAR officials' inspection, a necessary and nerve-racking hurdle whose outcome you were never sure of. An infraction could cost a fine or disqualification. After the race the cars in the top five were inspected again.

NASCAR was concerned about all the cars being on an even playing field, but also that the cars were as safe as possible. If only he could get Caitlin to see that. He'd tried to get her to go to the inspections, but she wouldn't even take the track pass for the infield.

He stared at the bed they had shared. Last night she'd been almost desperate for him. The race was the reason. Once he left, she wasn't sure he'd walk back though the door again.

He found Caitlin and Joshua in the kitchen. Caitlin sat hunched over a sketch pad. Joshua had his arms folded across his chest, his small face mutinous.

His son wasn't any more pleased than his father that he wasn't going to watch the race. In the distance, Cameron heard the revving of motors, which meant some of the crews were still working on their cars prior to inspection. Once that happened all would be quiet. Car motors would be silenced and wouldn't come on again until the grand marshal said the famous "Gentlemen, start your engines."

Until that happened, the crew happily pushed the car to inspection, to get fueled up, and then onto the grass infield of the track, the adrenaline pumping in their veins.

"Why can't we go to the race to watch Daddy?" Joshua asked.

"Because I have to finish this and, since Cameron is racing, there would be no one to watch you."

"I bet we could find someone." Joshua was nothing if not persistent when he wanted something. Just like his father.

"I don't know anyone here."

He came out of his seat. "Yes we do. We know Hope and Mike, and the other men in Daddy's crew."

"They're all busy."

He plopped back into his chair. "I want to see Daddy race."

"No, Joshua, and that is final," she said in a voice that had Joshua tightening his arms.

"Can a fellow get a good-luck hug?" Cameron asked.

Joshua's face lit up. Jumping out of his chair, he ran to his father. Cameron scooped him up to hold him tight. No matter how many times he held his son, it still humbled him that he was his. And the woman staring at them with fear she tried to hide, was the reason. He held out his other arm.

Biting her lips, she came, burrowing into his chest. He kissed the top of her head. Words hadn't helped in the past; they wouldn't help now. "Joshua, how about tomorrow before we head home we go have some fun." His son's head lifted. "We can go see pirates and their ship, play games." He leaned closer. "And when Mommy's not looking, stuff ourselves with hot dogs and ice cream."

His son's eyes glittered for a few seconds. He leaned closer and whispered, "She always knows."

Cameron laughed, then sobered. "I love you, son. Take care of your mother." After another hug, he released them and went to the door.

"Take care of yourself," Caitlin said, trying to smile and failing miserably.

"I will," Cameron told her.

"Get the checkered flag," Joshua told him. Caitlin pulled him close.

"I'll do my best." Opening the door, Cameron went down the steps and headed for the garage.

"I wish I could have gone with Daddy," Joshua bemoaned over and over.

Caitlin felt like putting her head in her lap and weeping. She'd kept Joshua with her on numerous occasions when she was on deadline and had to finish a strip. He was too inquisitive to leave alone. The sofa incident indicated that. He'd never minded before, but then he didn't have a father he adored.

"Mommy, why can't I go with Daddy? I bet we could find someone to look after me."

A four-year-old could nag with the best of them and would never tire of asking why. An hour after Cameron left, Caitlin had a pounding headache. "All right. You can watch it on television."

He jumped up and ran to grab the remote from the counter. Since Cameron had had it on earlier while watching preracing, the stands of the Las Vegas Motor Speedway instantly filled the screen. "Gentlemen, start your engines."

"There goes Daddy's car!" Joshua cried, inching closer to the screen.

Her heart thumping in her chest, her palms sweaty, Caitlin glanced away. The start of the race, when the cars were so close and trying to position themselves better, was always scary to her. It only took a moment to cause an accident. To her, it didn't matter how much maneuvering room the cars had. A picture flashed in her mind of Cameron's crumpled car at the California Speedway. Crossing the room, she picked up the control and hit the off button.

"Mommyyy!"

"I've got a great idea. Why don't you help me finish the strip, and then you can help me make dinner for your father. He'll be hungry when he returns."

"I guess." But his head was cocked as he listened to the muted roar of the engines. They were in the infield, the racetrack surrounded them. In the stands the sounds were earsplitting.

She put her hand on his shoulder to turn him to her and distract him. "We'll make brownies for dessert."

Joshua's face didn't brighten the way she expected at the mention of his favorite dessert. Determined not to be deterred, she led him to the kitchen and turned on the radio to an easy-listening station. "This will be fun," she promised, turning up the radio.

He'd come around once they began making the brownies. He liked helping, and later licking the spoon.

They were halfway into the recipe when there was a knock on the door. Her heart lurched. She almost dropped the bowl she held in the crook of her arm.

"Daddy!" Joshua cried and raced to the door.

Caitlin couldn't move until Joshua reached the door. The race would last for hours. "No!" Her sharp command had him stopping and turning to her. The knock came again. Setting the bowl down with unsteady hands, she went to the door. Saying a prayer, she opened it.

Hope, in a short-sleeved pink blouse and skinny jeans, stood there wearing a headset. She didn't look happy. "Cameron asked me to check on you once the race started."

"He's all right, isn't he?" Caitlin drew Joshua closer.

The irritation in Hope's dark eyes vanished. "You really are—" She stopped abruptly and looked down at Joshua, who was intently staring at her.

"Can you watch me?" Joshua asked. "I want to see my daddy race."

Caitlin pulled him back to her. "No."

Hope hunkered down, a smile on her beautiful olive-skinned face. "It's pretty busy out there now, Joshua. The garage is red light, which means no one without a special pass can get into that area. The pit area is worse with the pit crews waiting for their drivers to come in, owners, the news media, and all the other people."

Joshua's head lowered. "Yes, ma'am."

Hope glanced at a silent Caitlin, who couldn't hide the misery in her face, then back at Joshua. "But I tell you what. I'll have my dad tell your daddy that you're pulling for him."

His head came up. Happiness glittered in eyes so like his father's. "You will?"

"I promise." Hope pushed to her feet and spoke to Caitlin. "At the next race I'm getting you a hot pass. You can use it or not, but if you need to get to the garage or infield area at any time, you'll have access. I need to get back. Bye." She opened the door and stepped outside.

There was a load roar from the crowd. Hope shot her fist into the air. "Wahooo." Grinning, she whirled around and leaned down to Joshua. "Your daddy just moved into fifth place."

Joshua grinned back and looked up at his mother. "You hear that, Mommy? Daddy said he never wants to be back farther than ten and five is closer than ten."

She'd heard, but that meant there were four cars ahead of him who would do their best not to let him pass, and a number of cars behind him who wanted his spot. "Yes, Joshua, I heard."

"Cameron is one of the best," Hope said, the words obviously meant to reassure.

"I know. He's just not invincible. Thank you for coming."

Hope nodded and went down the steps. Caitlin reached for the door.

"I can hear the cars!" Joshua said with excitement. "I wanna see Daddy race!"

The headache that had abated came back with a vengeance. Caitlin swung the door closed. "Cameron, at the moment I could strangle you."

"Cameron." Mike's voice came on the headset. "Your newest fan is pulling for you."

Cameron didn't say anything to the signal they'd worked out. There was a camera inches away from his face. He came out of the back stretch and straightened. He went low and passed car number 47. With his headphones on, he couldn't hear the crowd's re-action to his passing last year's winner of the race. He didn't have time to think about it.

"How am I doing?" The drivers couldn't tell how many laps or their speed.

"Great. Sixty laps. I think you need to come in for a four-tire change. I've got a feeling this one is going to come down to traction."

His crew could make the change in less than nine seconds on the three-bolt tire, but a quarter of a sec-ond had won a race.

"You've lost rubber, Cameron. Bring her on in. We'll be waiting."

He could argue, wanted to, but took the exit to the infield, slowing down only marginally and looking for the flag with number 23. The pit was hectic with the pit stops of forty-three cars separated by mere feet.

He spotted the number 23 sign and pulled into the assigned spot. Even before he stopped his seven-man team scrambled over the wall. A NASCAR official eyed their every movement.

The right side of the car lifted as two tires came off and new ones went on. He heard the whirring sound of the nuts being tightened. A bottle of water on a pole came through the window. Since he was wearing a fire-resistant suit, it was hotter than Hades in the unair-conditioned car. You sweated so much you didn't have to worry about a potty break. That's why drivers were always seen chugging drinks dur-ing interviews after the race.

The right side went down and the left came up. A crew member peeled off the dirty layer of the windshield. Three seconds ticked by. The car hit the ground with a bounce.

"Go!"

Tires grabbing for traction, Cameron sped off toward the entrance to the racetrack straight ahead.

"Number forty-seven coming fast on your right!" Mike and the spotter shouted in unison.

Cameron barely kept from cursing as he jerked hard to the left to keep from tangling with number 47 running all out to get back on the track. Haskell wanted his second win at the track and his first of the season.

There was no sense getting angry. He needed all of his concentration to win the race. Anger was a waste of time and energy and made concentration next to impossible. Cameron pressed on the accelerator and hit the track. "How am I?"

"You're one-half lap back and still in fourth place. Drive smart and you can get the flag. Your new fan is counting on it."

Cameron took the next curve with barely a decrease in speed. He felt the slight slide of the car in turns three and four but then the new treadless tires gripped the track and he was headed down the front stretch. He'd tell Mike he was right later. Now, car number 59 was in sight and Cameron intended for it to be eating his dust when they came around the track again.

He was winning the race.

* * *

Caitlin burned the brownies, which her son was only too happy to tell her about. If he wasn't usually a sweet-tempered child, she wasn't sure how she would have handled the long hours they stayed in the motor coach.

"Mommy, what are we going to have for dessert? You said the brownies were for Daddy."

Caitlin stared down at her son. No matter what they did—coloring, playing on his entertainment center— he always came back to the burned food.

Was he being sassy or merely making a point? With her head throbbing she couldn't decide. She massaged her temples. Perhaps she should have taken Joshua and left in the car provided for Cameron. What stopped her was the fear that if something did happen, she wouldn't be there.

"You said Daddy would be hungry."

The fingers of her right hand joined the left. Perhaps she shouldn't have taught him that he could always ask questions and say—as long as it was respectful—what was on his mind. He was obviously annoyed with her for not letting him see the race. There was nothing a parent liked worse than hearing "you said."

"You said—"

"Joshua." Her hands dropped to her sides. "I know what I said and I know you're upset with me, but you still can't go see the race." She put her hand on his shoulder. "Daddy will understand about the brownies."

"I wanted to see him race."

"It's hard to accept sometimes, but we can't always

get what we want," she told him. She knew that better than anyone.

"But I wanna see Daddy race. I bet the other drivers' children get to see their fathers race."

He was certainly pushing all the buttons. Next to "you said," being compared to other parents was guaranteed to make a parent bend or go left. "I'm not like other parents."

Down went his head again. "I know."

Caitlin couldn't determine if his reaction was a compliment or a put-down. She stared at the top of his head. "I love you, Joshua."

After a long moment his head came up. "I love you, too."

She picked him up just as the cell phone in her pocket rang. She pulled it out, saw it was Diana and answered. She needed the calming voice of a friend. "Hi, Diana. I'm glad you—"

"Quick. Turn on the TV. Cameron is going neck and neck with one lap to go." The line went dead.

Joshua heard what Diana had said. In a flash, he wiggled down and grabbed the control, clicking on the TV before she could stop him. The screen filled with two race cars—Cameron's in black and purple, the other in green and white—flying around the track. "Go, Daddy! Go, Daddy!"

"This is when the race comes down to skill. Two of NASCAR'S best drivers refusing to give an inch as they head down the stretch with one lap to go. Cameron McBride is looking for his second win of the season, but Burt Haskell has won two races on this track and isn't about to give up without a fight.

He almost tangled with McBride's car coming out of the pit stop earlier in the race," the race commentator said. "Wanna bet McBride hasn't forgotten and it's probably given him an extra incentive to win this one."

"I wouldn't doubt it," said another commentator. "Haskell is having a bit of problem with traction. He took on two tires when McBride took on four. That could cost him. McBride's crew chief, Mike Alvarado, made the right call, it seems. Both cars are refusing to give way as they go into turn three. This might get interesting."

Caitlin wanted her legs to move, her mouth to tell Joshua to turn off the television, but she was frozen. She watched as the cars entered the curve. Seconds into it, Haskell's car began to slide.

She gasped.

"Trouble for Haskell and for McBride if he doesn't get past Haskell, and lucky for number thirty-five, rookie Russ Simpson, who's behind them."

Her heart in her throat, she watched the back bumper of number 47 make contact with Cameron's front right bumper. She heard the collective gasp of the crowd, wasn't aware of her holding her breath, of crossing to Joshua and picking him up.

Cameron's car slid sideways for a car length, then straightened, but it was enough for car number 35 to pull even with Cameron's car.

"Number twenty-three has obvious damage to the front bumper. It doesn't look as if it is enough to bring out the yellow caution flag, but it might be enough to slow down McBride if that bumper touches his tire. Both cars are racing flat out toward the finish line, inches apart, their front bumpers almost even."

"Go, Daddy! Go, Daddy!"

"This is racing at its finest," the announcer said. "You never know what's going to happen in NASCAR. Rookie Simpson just might pull off an upset in only his third race of the season. Haskell has dropped back to fifth place."

"He can't beat my daddy!"

"Uh-oh. I see smoke coming from McBride's right fender. Can he sustain his speed with seconds to go and be the season leader with two wins?" asked the commentator.

"Go, Daddy!"

"This is it! This is it! Wow, what a photo finish!!"

Joshua looked at his mother. "Why are you crying?"

She couldn't do anything but shake her head and hold him tight.

Chapter 12

"Next time the race is mine."

"Not if I can help it," Cameron said, shaking the callused hand of Russ Simpson, the sandy-haired driver who'd recently come from the Nationwide Series to NASCAR. They were finally through with the interviews, the presentation in Victory Lane. He was anxious to get back to Caitlin and Joshua, but people seemed to keep getting in the way. "Great race."

"The same goes." Russ grinned. "At Atlanta, you might not be so lucky."

Cameron took the good-natured teasing as it was intended. Russ was a good driver. "Luck has nothing to do with it. I've got the best pit crew, chief, and car in the circuit."

"You also have the best PR rep in the business," Russ commented, watching Hope running toward them, designer sunglasses perched atop her head. "She won't give me the time of day."

Cameron had a pretty good idea why, but he was keeping it to himself. "Hi, Hope."

"Hi, Hope."

"Simpson," she said firmly, before lowering her

glasses to her eyes and turning to Cameron. "Let's walk."

"Catch you later, Russ." Taking Hope's elbow, Cameron started toward the infield. "What's the matter?"

"Not sure, but if I were you I'd get to your motor coach." She caught his arm as he took off. "VIP party at the Bellagio at nine P.M. Hilliard's suite. Be there."

He glanced toward the motor coach. "I'll see."

"No. Sponsors are crucial. This is not up for debate," she said firmly.

"Hope, you work for me."

She folded her arms, lifted her shades. Her gaze was direct. "Yes, I do, and since you hired me to get your name and face out there, to help keep the sponsors happy, I plan to do just that. Be at the Bellagio no later than nine P.M. The hotel has babysitting services." Turning, she walked away.

Cameron didn't have time to argue. He'd deal with the fallout later. Now he needed to get to the motor coach. Hurrying through the infield while being stopped by well-wishers took him seven long minutes.

Opening the door, he lifted his shades, not knowing what to expect. His chest felt tight as he saw all the signs on the walls, the cabinets. In the middle of them stood Joshua, a wide grin on his face, holding up one of the signs. *MY DADDY WON.*

His gaze lifted to Caitlin. Her eyes were red, her lips trembling. He couldn't get to her fast enough. He pulled her to him with one arm, with the other he hugged Joshua to him. "Honey, it's all right. I'm here and safe."

"You won, Daddy!" Joshua yelled happily. "Mommy helped me make the signs."

Kissing Caitlin on the temple, he squatted down to Joshua, putting his cap on his head. He took the sign with hands that weren't quite steady. Joshua had drawn Cameron's car and put his signature on the bottom. "Thank you, son. I'm going to frame this."

Joshua curved his arm around his father's neck and happily leaned against him. "I knew that other car couldn't beat you."

Cameron's head snapped up to meet Caitlin's gaze. He pushed to his feet. "You watched the race?"

"Mrs. Howard called. We saw the man hit your car," Joshua answered for his mother. "Mommy cried when you won. I knew you would."

Cameron felt as if a tight band were around his chest. He stood and pulled her into his arms again. "There was never any real danger," he whispered.

A small fist hit his chest, once, twice. He felt her shoulders tremble and held her tighter. "Joshua, please collect all the signs you can reach and lay them face down. I'll take the tape off later."

Joshua pulled down the nearest sign, which was attached to the back of the bar stool. "Daddy, you can put these in your memory book."

Every memory for him meant fear for Caitlin. His hand swept up and down her back. "That's an idea. When you finish, wash up and we'll go get something to eat."

"Mommy cooked, but she burned the brownies."

Joshua scrunched up his face. "They were supposed to be for dessert. They're my favorite."

Cameron lifted her face to his. "You burned the brownies?"

Caitlin swiped her hand across her wet cheek. "He hasn't let me forget it."

"Or that he couldn't watch the race, I bet," Cameron teased, hoping to help erase the fear in her eyes, the tension in her body.

Her lips slowly curved upward, then she placed her head on his chest. "An hour after you left I could have gladly strangled you."

"If you had, we couldn't do this." His mouth, warm and gentle, settled on her, reassuring her with the unmistakable heat and desire of his kiss.

Giggling, Joshua pushed his way between them. "I got all the signs I could reach."

Reluctantly, Cameron lifted his head and saw the same regret in Caitlin's face. "Good job. I'll get the rest, then shower so we can eat." His hand cupped her cheek. "Then we're going out."

"No, Cameron, and that's final."

"Come on, Caitlin. I need to go and I want you with me."

Caitlin folded her arms. Men. He stood before her looking impossibly gorgeous in a tailored wheat-colored sports coat, white shirt, and jeans. People, especially women, would be flocking to him. "We agreed we didn't want the media finding out about us."

"There'll be some media there, but not the crazy,

in-your-face kind," he said. "The hotel has a babysitting service."

Her hands dropped to her sides. She cut a glance at Joshua, who was watching his favorite animated movie. "It's already past his bedtime. I am not dragging him out to be watched by some woman I don't know."

He sighed, took her arms in his. "For once, trust me."

Her eyes widened. "If I didn't trust you, we wouldn't be here. You can't control every situation."

His dark brows lifted. "You mean like you're trying to do."

She stiffened and stepped back. "Think what you will. I'm not going." Stepping around him, she went to sit beside Joshua. "Five more minutes and it's bedtime."

"Ah, Mommy," he said, glancing at her briefly as Mumbles pretended to sing to win the attention of Gloria, a female penguin. Mumbles' deception almost backfired in his face. It was always best to be yourself and that's what Caitlin was doing. There was no way she could change. It was time for Cameron to accept that.

"Hope, I'm not coming."

Caitlin jerked her head around. Cameron, speaking into his cell phone, stared back at her.

"Yes, taken under advisement. 'Night." Disconnecting the call, he pulled off his coat, placed it on the back of a chair, and sat beside her.

"You said your major sponsors would be there,"

Caitlin said. "After you won the race, they expect you to be there. It's a big PR event."

He ran his hand through her hair. "There'll be other events."

"I don't want to disrupt your life," she told him, meaning it.

Unrepentantly, he smiled. "Perhaps it's payback. I certainly disrupted yours, but I hope in a good way."

"For the most part," she said.

He eased closer and whispered in her ear. "I bet I know the parts."

Heat and desire rushed through her. Unable to hold his sensual gaze, she looked away. With their son sitting right there she shouldn't feel the rush of desire, the need to have his lips, his hands on her. The more they made love, the more she desperately wanted his loving.

His fingers caressed her neck. She shivered. His cell phone rang again.

"Hope?" she said.

"Or Hilliard." Getting up, he pulled the phone from the pocket of his jacket and answered. "Hope, I—" His gaze went to Caitlin.

"What is it?"

"She wants to speak to you." He held out the phone toward her.

After their conversation in the garage, Caitlin could well imagine what his PR rep wanted. "I need to get Joshua bathed and to bed." Picking up the control, she turned off the TV.

"Mommy," Joshua protested, but the word was slurred with sleep.

"Bathtime," she told her son.

"You want me to ask her what?" Cameron said, his frown increasing.

Caitlin paused while picking up Joshua. "What does she want?"

"Me to ask you if you had a cocktail dress," he answered.

Leave it to another woman to bust her. "That is none of her concern."

"No, she doesn't," Cameron answered, ignoring the glare Caitlin sent him. "Eight. All right. We'll look for you when we arrive." He spoke directly to Caitlin. "Hope booked us a suite so we could sleep late and enjoy the day with Joshua tomorrow. The babysitter is her cousin who came to Vegas to watch Hope's brother race in the Busch Series. Hope will get you a dress."

"I'm not wearing one of her dresses." Indignant, Caitlin said the words loud enough for the other woman to hear.

Cameron got a strange look on his face and disconnected the call. "Ah, the limo should be here in thirty minutes. Hilliard isn't happy that I'm not there to hobnob with the sponsors. He almost cut me when things weren't going well. Another owner might have. I owe him."

Caitlin hefted Joshua in her arms. She was the cause of "things not going well." She didn't want or need any more guilt when she left, and no matter what either of them wanted. "I'm not wearing her dress."

Cameron took Joshua from her. "Pack a few things. We're flying back on Hilliard's jet tomorrow afternoon."

* * *

The Bellagio Hotel towered into the sky and glittered with lights. Directly in front were the dancing fountains, a spectacular water show in the man-made lake. The streets teemed with people going in and out of the casinos. The limo pulled to the end of the circular driveway and stopped beside several other limos. Almost instantly, the back door opened.

"About time," Hope said. "Cameron, give Joshua to me. Dad is waiting for you by the elevator. I'll take Caitlin and Joshua up and introduce them to Abigail."

"I'll take him," Caitlin said, placing her hand protectively on his back.

"You won't be able to get out of the car holding him and, since you're late, more media have arrived."

Cameron ignored Hope and turned to Caitlin. "She's bossy, but she's usually dead-on."

"All right," Caitlin said softly.

Cameron leaned over to kiss Caitlin on the cheek, handed Joshua to Hope and got out of the car. "If you don't come to the party, I'm coming to get you."

Caitlin emerged and immediately reached for Joshua. Hope stepped back.

"He looks too much like Cameron and, as you just heard, Cameron wants you two to be together at the party," she said.

"Cameron might take orders from you, but I don't have to. I want my child."

Hope hissed several rapid-fire words in Spanish, before switching to English. "And if he wakes up and calls you 'Mommy,' and one of the reporters hears and happens to see you later with Cameron, then what? Or if Cameron is still in the lobby and Joshua calls him 'Daddy,' how do you propose to handle the situation?"

"That's a long stretch," Caitlin said, but it wasn't impossible to imagine.

"I pride myself on avoiding those long stretches." To the patient driver who stood by his door obviously giving them privacy, Hope said, "Thanks, Curtis. I'll call you when Daddy and I are ready to leave."

"Yes, Ms. Alvarado." Tipping his hat, he returned to the car and drove off.

"Now," Hope said to Caitlin. "Let's get Joshua to bed, and we can have the conversation you're aching to have."

Caitlin fell into step beside the other woman, keeping a watchful eye on Joshua. For once, Hope was right. She had a few things she was itching to say to the other woman.

Inside the opulence of the hotel, the lobby was cavernous. She was about to point out to Hope that no one would notice them as they headed for the elevator, but was glad she'd remained quiet when she saw the crowd just off the lobby. Cameron was surrounded by people. The long shot had paid off.

Cameras flashed. She thought the crowd was a mixture of fans and the media. She wasn't sure, but from his downward-angled head, she'd bet he was signing autographs. Mike stood beside him.

"The private elevator is this way," Hope said, quickly moving past them.

Through the glass windows Caitlin saw the immense swimming pool and cabanas, and what looked like a white stone villa directly behind.

Swiping the card in her hand, Hope stepped on and punched in the penthouse floor. "I'll take him." Caitlin reached for Joshua as soon as the door closed.

"You need to work on trusting others," Hope said, but she released Joshua.

"So I've been told," Caitlin commented, stroking up and down on Joshua's back.

"I don't doubt it." Hope folded her arms and turned away.

Caitlin immediately liked the sweet teenager waiting for them in the palatial suite. Thank goodness she was nothing like her bossy cousin. She had come prepared with several books to read. Caitlin liked that as well. An iPod or a radio with headphones would have prevented her from hearing Joshua if he woke up.

After giving the sitter her cell phone number, Caitlin went over Joshua's routine of settling in for the night before stepping outside the smallest room of the two-bedroom suite with Hope.

"What did you say to Cameron when I said I wouldn't wear one of your dresses?" Caitlin asked the moment the door to the bedroom closed.

Hope lifted a perfectly arched brow and smiled, showing beautiful white teeth. "That you should be so lucky."

The other woman's answer was so far from what Caitlin had thought she was going to say she was momentarily taken aback. For the first time, she really looked at Hope. The other woman was stunning, with an hourglass figure and small waist that men would love. The silver sleeveless dress stopped at mid-thigh and had side lacing. The gown was expensive and provocative and a size too small and five inches too short for Caitlin.

"I guess I deserve that."

Hope's dark head tilted as if she were just as surprised. "I might have misjudged you."

"You think?"

Up went that dark brow again, then Hope laughed, and shook her head. "I've been known to speak before I think at times."

"Your father said it wasn't easy for you gaining credibility in NASCAR, that you had to be tough," Caitlin commented.

"He doesn't know how rough, and none of my family ever will," she said. "Since I was a woman and a minority, people didn't know how to take me, or they just wanted me gone. NASCAR was a good-old-boys sport when it started. Now women and the rest of the country are finally getting in on things. NASCAR is pushing diversity, and that helped. But you must have the skills, and not hesitate to speak your mind and stand up for yourself."

Caitlin admired any woman who could gain entry into a man's world. "I guess you have to be a little pushy and thick-skinned."

"More than a little," Hope agreed. "You're seeing more women in positions of power and authority in NASCAR in part thanks to NASCAR's policy of inclusion, but you have to be able to take the heat and show your mettle when you get the chance. Just as Cameron, my father, and my brother have done."

"You get the chance, but it's what you make of it," Caitlin said, knowing it was true in life as well.

"Exactly, and we all plan to prove we have what it takes." She hooked her arm through Caitlin's and headed for the main bedroom in the suite. "Let me show you the dress I selected. Perhaps after seeing it, you'll forgive my bad manners."

It would have to be some dress, Caitlin thought but she remained quiet. They both had just extended the olive branch. Obviously Hope wanted what was best for Cameron, and for that Caitlin would give her a pass.

Inside the bedroom, Hope released Caitlin's arm and picked up the dress on the bed. "Well?"

Caitlin didn't know what to say. Slowly, she took the dress from Hope and turned to the floor-length mirror in the corner. The dress, iridescent bronze, sleeveless, and straight, was fabulous. She couldn't wait to try it on. Since Joshua's birth she'd had few chances to dress up, and she had to admit she wanted Cameron to be proud of her when she went to the party.

"You're forgiven."

Hope smiled, then sobered. "Sponsors are needed for drivers. A race team is extremely expensive to run. A sponsor might come on for the season, but there is no guarantee they'll come back the next. A winning driver, if he's inaccessible, won't get people buying the sponsor's products."

"I want Cameron to be successful even though every time he races it ties my stomach in knots."

"Then you know for Cameron it's not about the

money, but the race. For that, he needs sponsors willing to shell out the big bucks. He can't have one without the other. I'll do what's necessary to make sure he has what he needs."

Caitlin saw the determination in the woman's gaze. It couldn't have been easy for her. She placed the dress over her arm. "Thank you."

She nodded. "Cameron is a great guy. He deserves to win. And I don't plan to let anything stand in his way."

Caitlin understood that while Hope might be willing to help Caitlin and Joshua, her main focus was Cameron, because what happened to Caitlin and Joshua ultimately affected Cameron. "This might sound strange, but I'm glad he has you in his corner."

"Thanks. The other day I wouldn't have cared what you thought." She picked up the shoes and handed them to Caitlin, then went to the door. "Luckily, Cameron knew your shoe size. You better hurry and get dressed."

Caitlin accepted the items, but didn't move. "Why does it make a difference now?"

"It should be obvious." Hope opened the door. "You love him."

For the second time that night Hope had shocked Caitlin. "Y-you're mistaken."

"I think not, but don't worry. Cameron won't hear it from me," Hope assured her. "I don't interfere in my clients' personal lives unless it affects their performance or presents problems like it did tonight. Besides, if Cameron knew how you felt, I don't think he'd let you go."

Caitlin clutched the clothes to her chest. "He won't have a choice."

"I wouldn't be so sure about that." Hope closed the door before Caitlin could ask what she meant.

Chapter 13

Cameron tried to keep an eye on the door to the room where the party was going on, but someone always got in the way: Hilliard, a sponsor, a member of the media, a fan or, as now, a woman who wanted more than his autograph or his photograph.

"Seeing you race always gives me goose bumps," the dark-haired woman said, sliding closer to Cameron with each word.

"Me, too," said her companion, managing to press her breast against his arm.

Mindful that they were fans and related to one of his biggest sponsors, Cameron smiled. "Thank you, ladies. If you'll excuse me, I need to speak to Mike."

Both women pouted and protested, but Cameron made good his escape. He spotted Russ Simpson and Mario by the bar and headed in their direction, surprised they weren't being pursued. He said as much when he neared.

Mario, darkly handsome, looked at Russ and grinned. "Should we tell him?"

"It will spoil the fun," Russ said, taking a sip of his beer.

"Tell me what?" Cameron asked, a frown marring his brow.

Just in the nick of time, it seemed, because the door across the room opened. Hope and Caitlin walked in. For a moment, they stood there. If it had been any other women, Cameron would have said they were doing it for effect and not just to get their bearings. He knew better, but the result was the same.

Like a ripple effect, one man after another turned to stare. It was impossible not to. Caitlin and Hope were dazzling. Both had a gleam in their eyes that said they were up for any challenge. Men would fight to get in line to take that challenge.

Cameron had no intention of letting any man near Caitlin. He started for her. This time, he didn't let a reporter or the two women who tried to waylay him again stop him. With a smile, he sidestepped each one and kept moving until he stood in front of Caitlin.

"You're stunning."

"You're not so bad yourself," she said, a smile tugging the corners of the mouth that he planned to kiss later on that night. Heck, he planned on doing a lot more than kissing. He introduced Mario and Russ.

"Hello," Caitlin greeted.

Mario folded his arms. "I can see why Cameron was watching the door so much. You're worth waiting for."

"Ease off, Mario," Cameron warned. "She's taken."

Mario held up his hand in mock surrender, then winked at Caitlin. She laughed.

"Evening, Caitlin, Hope," Russ greeted, then turned firmly to Hope. "You look beautiful."

"Don't tell her that," Mario said with a laugh. "She's difficult enough to live with."

"Mario," Hope cooed. "You know I'll pay you back when you least expect it."

He frowned, then smiled. "I'll tell Mama."

"No you won't," she said cryptically. This time the frown on Mario's face remained.

Cameron chuckled. "You know she will, too. Glad I'm not in your shoes."

"It looks as if all the fun is over here."

Cameron looked around to see Sean Hilliard, tall, broad-shouldered, and elegant. Like everything he did, Hilliard wore his tux with panache and ease. He'd come from old money and made bucketloads of it on his own. Rumor was that his ex-wife had tried to get her hands on a lion's share when they divorced four years ago. A prenup, the best lawyers in the country, and Hilliard had stood in the way. Hilliard wasn't a man you'd want to cross, not if you didn't want to keep looking over your shoulder.

"Hello, Caitlin," he said, extending his hand. "It's nice to see you again."

"Thank you, Mr. Hilliard," Caitlin said.

"I thought we agreed on Sean," he said smoothly.

Cameron frowned. Of course Caitlin had met Hilliard when they had been together and engaged, but she hadn't been around him much. Hilliard hadn't been as hands-on with the racing teams as he was the last two seasons.

Cameron watched the man he supposed some women would call handsome watch Caitlin. Was his owner trying to come on to Caitlin or just being nice?

Hilliard was always more magnanimous after a win. But just to establish his claim, Cameron curved his arm around her waist.

Caitlin glanced up at him and smiled as if she'd read his mind. "It looks as if everyone is having a great time," she finally answered Hilliard.

"If the amount of liquor is any indication, they are," he said with a smile. "I believe there is going to be dancing later on. Isn't that right, Hope?"

"Yes," Hope said, her voice flat, then she faced Russ with a flirtatious smile. "Why don't we go check it out and get the dancing started."

Russ's eyes sparked like a boy with his first quarter-midget. "Lead the way."

"If you'll excuse us." Hope curved her arm through his and walked away.

Hilliard and Mario watched them. Cameron studied Hilliard. He held his body stiffly, as if the sight of Russ and Hope together bothered him.

"Excuse me, too," Mario said. "I better make this night count while I can."

"Surely you aren't afraid of your sister?"

He looked at Hilliard and Cameron before answering. "No offense, but women are more devious than men, and some have it down to a fine art. Nice meeting you, Caitlin."

Cameron felt Caitlin shiver and knew she was thinking about her keeping Joshua's birth a secret. He pulled her closer. "What do you say we hit the dance floor as soon as Hope gets things moving?"

"I'd like that," she said. The words were barely out

of her mouth before the sounds of "Break Every Rule" filled the room.

"Ladies and gentlemen," Hope said, mic in hand. "Hilliard Motorsports thanks you for coming to celebrate the second win of the NASCAR season by Cameron McBride."

People in the room searched until they found Cameron and Hilliard. Applause erupted. The way they were standing, it was difficult to tell who Caitlin was with, especially when Hilliard stepped closer.

"We'd also like to thank the sponsors of number twenty-three, and the other cars that make up Hilliard Motorsports," Hope said, calling out the names of the sponsors. More applause. "Tonight we celebrate the phenomenal driving skills of Cameron McBride under the awesome leadership of Sean Hilliard that you, the sponsors, make possible. It's fitting that the song leading off the dancing tonight is 'Break Every Rule,' because Hilliard Motorsports's racing team is going to break records in NASCAR. Let the party begin!"

Two men pushed back a screen to show the seven-piece band. Giving the mic to one of them, Hope crooked her finger and Russ joined her, taking her into his arms and swinging her out. Hope did a smart turn, shimmied, laughing all the way.

"She can really dance," Caitlin said.

"There isn't much Hope Alvarado can't do," Hilliard said, his voice tight. "If you'll excuse me. I need to circulate."

Cameron glanced from Hope on the dance floor

enthralling Russ to Hilliard talking to an elderly man, his back to the dance floor.

"Are we going to dance or what?" Caitlin asked.

Cameron grinned down at her, then swung her into his arms. "Dance. The 'what' comes later."

Caitlin grinned back.

Chapter 14

Life was good. Legs crossed at the ankles, his arms folded, Cameron leaned near the side door of the hauler on the infield of the Bristol Motor Speedway preparing to watch the replay again of the crash at the California Speedway. While Mike readied things, Cameron let his mind wander.

Since the night in Vegas, he and Caitlin had continued to grow closer. They were becoming a family. She hadn't protested when they left Charlotte last week for the Atlanta Speedway, nor this week when they headed to Tennessee. He didn't fool himself into thinking they didn't still have some bumps, but he believed this time their love for each other and Joshua would see them through.

Their love. Neither one of them had admitted it to the other yet. It was as if both were afraid of unsettling the delicate balance.

"Ready, Cameron?" Mike asked.

"Ready." The film began to roll.

Cameron admitted it was a jolt the first time he saw the car ram head first into the wall, then slowly slide back down the track. It was a blessing that no other cars had hit him, and although number 28 had clipped him, the car hadn't sustained any major damage and was able to finish the race.

Crashing was bad enough. Taking out another car with you twisted your gut. Although it was an accident, it was as if another driver were paying for your stupidity or bad luck. The results were the same.

Out of the race through no fault of your own.

"Cameron, we think the problem was the shocks," Mike said. "The gearshift is a bit tight as well. That's what we believe you were experiencing before the blowout. Which, I think, was just a bad coincidence."

"Probably. Let's see it again. I felt a slight vibration just before the tire blew." Cameron straightened as the film zeroed in on him. He'd had a camera on him at the time. The helmet prevented a clear picture of his face, which he thought was a good thing.

The impact jolted through him as if he were going through the accident again. The camera was knocked out. There was static until the other TV cameras zoomed in on him again.

His head peeked out of the escape hatch on the roof. The TV camera caught every disjointed movement as he hoisted his body out of the car. He jumped to the ground, staggered, then righted himself and removed his helmet.

"Daddy!"

Cameron jerked around to see Joshua, his face pale, his little body trembling, his frightened gaze glued on the TV monitor. "Stop the tape!" Cameron yelled, scooping up Joshua and quickly leaving the hauler, heading for the motor coach.

"I'm all right, Joshua," Cameron soothed. "It was just a film. I'm all right." His hand stroked his son's trembling back.

The desperate grip around Cameron's neck didn't lessen. He increased his pace on feeling moisture dampen his T-shirt. Tears.

Bounding up the steps, he opened the door, calling Caitlin's name, heading down the hall to the second bedroom where she worked. "Caitlin. Caitlin."

"Cameron!" she cried, running into the hall.

"He saw the accident footage," Cameron explained. "I didn't know he was there."

Caitlin's gaze lanced up to his, then she stepped to his side so she could see Joshua's face, stroke his trembling back. "Your daddy is all right," she soothed. "I know it was scary, but it happened the day you had your accident. Just like you're all right, he's all right."

Joshua finally lifted his eyes. The misery in his son's little face tore at Cameron's heart.

"Your daddy is fine," Caitlin repeated.

Cameron's gaze met Caitlin's. He knew she was thinking of her father, and of his teammate who was killed, of his son seeing his father die.

He wanted to promise that it wouldn't happen to him, that he'd always come back. But accidents happened; there were fatalities. He couldn't promise what he couldn't control.

"Why don't we go for a drive and get some ice cream?" Caitlin suggested.

Joshua placed his head back on his father's shoulder, his arms curled around his neck. "You're going, too, aren't you, Daddy?"

"Sure." He had planned on going to the garage after watching the footage. That would have to wait until Joshua had settled down. Cameron grabbed his car keys off the ring in the kitchen. "We can make an afternoon of it."

Caitlin's worried gaze caught his. He just hoped it was enough, but somehow he knew it wouldn't be that easy.

"Daddy!"

Cameron was out of the bed before Joshua's cry faded. His heart pounding, he raced down the hall, Caitlin on his heels. Going into the room, he picked Joshua up. His eyes were closed, but tears coated his lashes.

Caitlin clicked on the light, rushing to her son in Cameron's arms. "Baby, it's all right."

"Wake up, son. It's all right. Wake up."

Joshua's lashes fluttered open. He stared at his father, his lips trembling. "I'm scared."

"Oh, Lord," Cameron cried, clutching Joshua tighter to him.

"Joshua, your daddy is here and safe, and so are you," Caitlin soothed, swallowing and blinking. "Would you like to sleep with us?"

He nodded.

"Come on." Taking Cameron's arm, she guided him back to their bedroom. "You can sleep in the middle."

Cameron leaned over to put Joshua on the bed, but his grip tightened. "No."

"It's all right," Cameron soothed. Lying down, he tucked Joshua against him with his face toward him. "Go to sleep. We'll leave the light on so if you wake up you'll know that your father and mother are here."

Joshua didn't say anything or close his eyes.

Helplessly, Cameron looked at Caitlin. "I'm sor—"

Shaking her head, she began to hum a lullaby, stroking Joshua's head.

Cameron rested his head against Joshua's. Caitlin might not blame him, but he blamed himself. He should have been more careful.

Cameron didn't go to sleep, neither did Caitlin. Saturday morning, he eased away from Joshua, then stood and simply stared at the sleeping child. There were tearstains on his cheeks. The first time he'd seen his son cry had been his fault—and he had promised to protect and love him.

"This isn't your fault," Caitlin said softly.

He looked across at her, leaning on one elbow. "You were afraid I'd hurt him."

Getting out of bed, she went to him. "You're a good father. Joshua loves you."

"I'd give anything if this hadn't happened," Cameron said, his voice hoarse.

"I know." She looked back at the sleeping Joshua. "Why don't you shower and get dressed in the other bedroom? I want to be here when he wakes up."

"Maybe I should can—"

"No," she interrupted. "You might be back before he wakes up."

"I'll be back as soon as I can," he promised.

"I know." Standing on tiptoe, she kissed him on the jaw. "Now get dressed and get out of here."

Caitlin watched Cameron grab his racing suit and underclothes. The two people she loved most were hurting, and there was nothing she could do about it. She'd wanted Joshua to dislike racing, but not this way.

Sitting on the side of the bed, she watched Joshua sleep. He'd fought going to sleep and had held on to his father tightly. Of all the problems that could have occurred, she'd never imagined this one. If there was blame, she'd have to share it. She'd been daydreaming about Cameron instead of watching Joshua. He'd slipped out of the motor coach, and she hadn't even noticed.

Cameron appeared in the doorway in his racing suit and baseball cap with the team's logo. "Hope called. There are about a hundred people already in line for the autograph session."

"Most of them are probably women," she quipped, wanting to ease the self-recrimination in his face.

He crossed the room and pulled her into his arms. "It doesn't matter. I'll be thinking about you and Joshua."

Her arms slid around his neck, loving him, wanting him to know she understood, wished things were different. "Just like ours thoughts will be with you."

A whimper came from the bed. She wheeled around to see Joshua sitting up and crying. "Don't go, Daddy."

Caitlin's heart ached for him. She scooped him up

in her arms and set him on her hip so he could see his father and be reassured. She'd lost her father, knew the mindless fear. "It's all right, sweetheart. Daddy isn't going to race."

"I'm just going to sign the pictures," Cameron said. "Just like when you helped me."

"I don't want you to go," Joshua cried, tears streaming down his cheeks.

"Son, don't cry," Cameron urged. "I won't go near the car. You can come with me."

"No!" he cried. "I don't wanna go! I don't want you to go, either."

Cameron looked at Caitlin for help. "Why don't we all go?" she suggested.

Cameron had never had a more difficult time keeping a smile on his face. He tried not to keep looking at Caitlin and Joshua, side by side and holding hands, but he couldn't quite manage it. It helped that Mike and Hope stood beside him to give the crowd and media more to talk about. Yet he was thankful when he'd signed the last picture, answered the last question, so he could leave.

"That's all. Thank you for coming," Hope announced.

They'd learned the hard way that fans got upset with the drivers when they ended the autograph session. He didn't need that now.

Cameron waved. "Thank you." Clutching or admiring their photographs, the crowd moved slowly away.

Caitlin started toward the trailer with Joshua, and

Cameron followed. The crew and drivers knew they were living together, but thus far they had been able to keep it from the media.

Cameron entered the motor coach after them. "Joshua, you want to play with your Legos or the entertainment center?"

Joshua shook his head and went to his room. Cameron stared after him. If he was around, Joshua was usually like his shadow. He wanted to be with him, imitate him. During the autograph session, he'd barely looked at him. "He won't even look at me," Cameron said, his voice filled with remorse.

Caitlin placed a comforting hand on his rigid arm. "He's scared and confused. I better go talk to him."

"Tell him I love him."

"I will," she said, and went into Joshua's room.

Cameron hadn't felt this helpless since Caitlin walked out on him. He'd felt lost then just as he did now.

He did know he had to get his mind on something else. He glanced at his watch. It was almost time for his practice run. Skipping practice would let Hilliard, the team, and the sponsors down. He reached for the doorknob. He just hoped that in the garage, he'd be able to fill his mind with an image other than his son crying.

Cameron came back to the motor coach a little after seven that night. His practice time had been slower than his qualifying time. Plus a couple of times the car had gotten loose, the back tires losing traction on the pavement. The crew chief had wanted to know what adjustments needed to be made.

It had been difficult to tell him. The fault lay with him, not the car. Mike, being an outspoken man, had two words he'd used numerous times before. "Fix it."

Cameron blew out a breath. He'd like nothing better. Bristol was nicknamed "the World's Fastest Half-Mile Track." Cars lapped the oval-shaped track in fifteen seconds. With the concrete racing surface and steep banks, a driver had to have his mind on the race. His wasn't.

Going to his room, he put away his driver's suit and changed into jeans and a black T-shirt. Dressed, he started down the hall and saw the suitcase. His heart squeezed, his mind rebelled.

He stepped in the doorway to see Joshua sitting by his mother on the bed. Caitlin looked up. Joshua, wearing headphones, kept playing the handheld video game.

"Hi, Joshua."

There was total silence. Cameron reasoned he hadn't answered because he hadn't heard him. His worried gaze went to Caitlin's. "Why the suitcase?"

She kissed Joshua on the forehead, then stood. "I'll be back, sweetheart."

His head came up, his eyes wide. "Where're you going?"

She brushed her hand across his head before answering. "Just into the hall to talk with your father."

"You're coming back?"

"Yes."

Joshua stared at her a long time, then went back to playing his game. Caitlin stepped into the hall.

Taking Cameron's arm, she urged him into the kitchen.

"Why the suitcase?" he repeated.

"I think it's best that we leave before the race tomorrow, for both of your sakes."

"No," Cameron said. "He needs to stay. He'll be all right once the race is over."

"I don't think so." Caitlin blew out a breath. "The reason for the headphones is that he became upset when he heard the sounds of the cars practicing."

Cameron glanced skyward for a brief moment. "I'll get you a room in a hotel in Bristol. As soon as the race is over, we'll fly home."

"Unless I keep him in the hotel room, he'll be reminded of the race almost everywhere we go."

"Let me talk to him." Cameron went down the hall and into Joshua's room. He fought to keep the smile on his face when Joshua never looked at him. "Looks like you're having fun."

Silence.

"I bet we can find a video arcade where we could play together."

Silence.

Cameron placed his hands over Joshua's, effectively stopping him from playing. "Son, look at me. I love you."

Joshua lifted his head, but he looked at his mother. "Can I have some water?"

Caitlin had to swallow before she could get her response past the lump in her throat. "Your daddy says he loves you."

"Can I have some water?" Joshua repeated.

Cameron pushed to his feet. "Let him go."

"Yes," Caitlin said.

Placing the video game on the bed, Joshua left the room, never once acknowledging his father's presence.

"I'm sorry," Caitlin said, her heart aching for Cameron.

"Have you made reservations yet?" Cameron asked.

"Ten forty-five tonight," she told him. "I got the last flight just in case . . ."

"That's not about to happen. I'll get my keys."

All the way to the airport, Cameron kept glancing in the rearview mirror, hoping to catch Joshua's eye. It never happened. It was as if he were invisible. Once at the airport, Cameron parked the truck and stood by and let Caitlin unbuckle Joshua.

Cameron didn't know how he would have taken it if Joshua had pulled away from him. It was difficult enough being ignored. His chest was tight, his throat ached, and he felt completely helpless. Guilt rode him hard.

Instead of carrying Joshua into the terminal as he'd done all the other times, he was relegated to carrying the luggage and, once inside, helping Caitlin print out the boarding passes.

Silently he went with them to the security checkpoint. Perhaps he didn't look approachable or perhaps there were no NASCAR fans around. Cameron wasn't sure how he would have reacted to a request for an autograph or a picture.

"Thank you, Cameron. I'll call." Clutching

Joshua's small hand, Caitlin stopped at the entrance for first class passengers.

Time had run out for him. Cameron looked at Caitlin, who looked as miserable as he felt. His hand slid around her neck. He pulled her gently to him and brushed his lips across her trembling ones. She hurt for him and Joshua. Despite her fears, she would never want Joshua to be afraid.

Reluctantly releasing her, Cameron squatted down in front of Joshua. His son looked up at his mother.

"I love you, Joshua," Cameron said, hugging his son's warm, limp body tightly. He closed his eyes against the stinging he felt. Just that morning, Joshua had squeezed him tight and told him good-bye.

Swallowing the lump in his throat, he pushed to his feet. "Take care."

"You take care," she said, blinking back tears. "He'll be all right. He loves his daddy."

Cameron swallowed again. "Good-bye."

"Good-bye," she said, then curved one hand around his neck, kissing him deeply.

Needing her reassurance, the connection, he pulled her tightly to him, kissing her back. Slowly he lifted his head.

Her fingers trailed from his cheek to his chest, as if reluctant to stop touching him. "When it's over, call."

She meant the race. He glanced down at Joshua, who was looking across the aisle at a gift shop. His hand flexed on her arm. "I will."

Her smile brittle, Caitlin caught Joshua's hand

again. Together they went through the first class security checkpoint. Cameron watched them go, his heart aching.

He might have lost his son and the only woman he would ever love. And it was his fault.

Chapter 15

Cameron was up at dawn, and in the garage with his pit crew at eight. He'd tossed and turned most of the night. Caitlin had called when the plane landed. They'd taken a cab home. Once she had gotten Joshua to bed, she'd called again.

He'd promised himself he wouldn't ask, but had been unable to help himself. "Did he mention my name or ask about me?"

The silence was his answer even before she said, "No, but he went to sleep once the plane took off."

Both knew it was a flimsy excuse. Joshua spouted his father's name all the time. "Get some rest. I'll call as soon as the race is over."

"We might be out." She gave him her cell number. "Cameron, he'll be all right. Just be careful. The track—"

"Caitlin, don't worry," he said, cutting her off. Thinking he'd frightened his son was hard enough to handle.

"You just call," she repeated.

He could imagine her gripping the phone. He

should be there to reassure her, reassure his son. His fault. "I will. Get some sleep."

" 'Night."

" 'Night." Cameron had hung up the phone and lain in bed staring at the ceiling. She and Joshua were safe and back in their world without him. His loneliness was a deep endless ache inside him that he wasn't sure he was going to be able to overcome this time.

And this morning it had only gotten worse. He needed to keep his mind occupied. Dressed, he left the motor coach and went to the hauler and later to the garage. He moved from the hauler to the garage bay—talking to reporters and fans, discussing race strategy.

Mike kept looking at him. Cameron knew the question when he asked him to follow him back to the hauler. The moment the door closed he gave him the answer.

"Joshua and Caitlin went back to California last night."

Mike caught the expletive before it formed completely. "You're in good standing to make it back to the NASCAR Sprint Cup Series. You came in second last week at Atlanta. Wins count more for a shot to be in the Chase for the Cup this year, but Hilliard and your major sponsor don't want you finishing out of the top ten when the dust settles."

"I know." He'd told Joshua he always wanted to be in the top ten.

"Why am I not reassured?"

There was a brief knock on the door before it opened. Hope stuck her dark head inside. "The reporter is here for the interview, then we have to hot-foot it to the stage for the check presentation for winning the pole."

Cameron grimaced. Joshua had been so happy when he had the fastest qualifying time, which enabled him to start the race in front. "I'd forgotten about that."

Hope's perfect brow arched. "The check is for your own charity. You just played golf Thursday."

Joshua had been his junior caddy. "Doesn't matter." Cameron moved past her. "Let's get this show on the road."

Hope looked at her father. The look he gave her wasn't reassuring as he followed Cameron out of the hauler.

"Gentlemen, start your engines."

Cameron flipped the switch to start his car and pulled off. He was the lead car on the outside of the track. Next to him was the second-place qualifying car, number 35 driven by Russ Simpson.

Cameron wouldn't maintain that position for all of the laps, but he needed to be there when the white flag came out, signaling the last lap for the lead car. To achieve that goal, he needed to focus on the race and not on the tears on his son's face. Impossible, yet somehow he had to do it.

His mind elsewhere could get himself and another driver into trouble. The Bristol Motor Speedway had spit out better drivers than him.

"Cameron, how are things?"

"Fine," Cameron answered. They'd been around the track twice. He had to get it together.

The next time the pace car came to the road leading to the infield he took it. The flagman waved the green flag.

Cameron stomped the accelerator. Showtime.

Sunday afternoon Caitlin tried to keep busy and not watch the clock, but it proved impossible. Neither her local TV channels nor the radio stations were carrying the race. The TV stations and radio stations that did were on cable or radio-satellite stations. She didn't have either. She didn't want to chance upsetting Joshua, so she found herself doing something she never would have done before today.

While Joshua happily played in the park with Samuel, and another classmate named James, she listened to her newly purchased portable radio with earplugs. The news wasn't good. With thirty laps to go Cameron was in fifteenth place. The commentators kept speculating on the cause of his worst showing in years.

"The last time car twenty-three ran this bad was the beginning of the season five years ago. His crew had been in top form under his crew chief's directions. Whatever the cause of Cameron McBride's poor showing today, it isn't because of his crew."

"I agree," came the voice of the other announcer. "This looks like a completely different driver than the one who leads the series."

Caitlin clenched her hands and watch Joshua agilely swing from one bar to the next on the monkey bars. She'd been scared to death when she'd first seen him attempt the maneuver. Diana had calmed her, held her back, saying being overprotective wasn't good for him.

Caitlin wished she knew what to do now for her son. He hadn't mentioned his father since that last day they were with Cameron. But what hurt the most was his leaving Cameron's name out of his prayers. He had distanced himself from his father, and she didn't know how to help him get over his fears when she was still dealing with them herself.

"Look out! Look out!"

Caitlin surged to her feet at the excited voice of the announcer. "Cameron. Please, God, let him be all right."

"Cars number sixty-seven and eighty-two tangled on the front stretch. The red flag is out and all cars have stopped on the track. Both drivers are all right, but they're out of the race."

Caitlin sank back to the wooden bench, her body still trembling.

"Too bad," the announcer continued. "They were eighth and tenth in the race. Rookie Russ Simpson moves up to seventh place. Burt Haskell, in car forty-seven, remains in the lead. Only twenty-three cars remain. In last place is a car I'd never imagined to see there, number twenty-three, Cameron McBride."

"Oh, Cam," Caitlin whispered, her eyes closed as tears streamed down her cheeks. "I'm so sorry, for both of you."

"Mommy, Mommy," Joshua yelled.

Her eyelids flew upward as Caitlin surged to her

feet again already moving forward at the frightened sound of Joshua's voice. Her heart rate didn't steady as she saw him racing toward her. She ran to meet him. He didn't stop until his arms were wrapped tightly around her. She felt his body tremble.

Her heart ached as she gently tried to remove his arms so she could kneel and look him in the face. She wasn't sure if the panic in his voice was for her or if something had reminded him of his father. He'd awakened last night calling her name. He'd transferred his fear for his father onto her. He'd gone to sleep in her arms.

"It's all right, Joshua. It's all right." Holding his arms, she knelt. The ache intensified as she saw the fear in his eyes.

"You were standing and then you sat down with your head down. You aren't sick, are you?"

She smiled through her tears. "No, sweetheart. I feel fine."

"You're crying," he said, watching her closely. "You haven't cried since before."

With an effort, Caitlin kept the smile on her face. "Since before" referred to the time with Cameron. Joshua had to be extremely upset if he brought up the incident, but it also showed that by not mentioning his father, he wanted nothing to do with the man he once adored.

"Crying doesn't always mean a person is sad." She ran her hand over his head in reassurance. "I cried when you were born. It was one of the happiest days of my life."

He stared at her a long time. She'd always been

honest with him except when it came to his father. She was shading the truth again. Remorse hit her. Perhaps if she had handled this differently, the father and the son she loved wouldn't be in so much pain.

"I want you to come and watch me," he finally said.

"All right." She pushed to her feet. Joshua, who had always been independent, now wanted her close. Cameron would blame himself even more if he knew. "Let me get my things."

"I'll go with you."

She took his hand and silently they went over to the bench. Picking up the radio she had dropped, she clicked it off and dropped it into her oversized handbag. Perhaps it was just as well. Listening to Cameron's defeat and looking at her son's troubled face was more than she could bear.

Slinging the wide strap of her handbag over her shoulder, she smiled down at Joshua. "Race you."

He smiled, quick and easy. "I'll win." He took off running, laughing as if he didn't have a care in the world. Wishing it were the truth, Caitlin took off after him, careful to stay a couple of feet behind.

"I won. I won," Joshua shouted as he reached the monkey bars where his friends continued to play.

Caitlin picked him up, swinging him around so he wouldn't see her tears. Today, his father wouldn't be able to shout those same words and, more than the loss of the race, he'd mourn the loss of his son—perhaps forever.

* * *

Cameron felt like crap. He'd come in dead last. He'd let his fans, his team, Hilliard, and all of his sponsors down. He hadn't been able to concentrate on the race. Five years ago at his worst, he hadn't done this poorly.

He came off the track as Burt Haskell celebrated his win. Cameron wanted to keep driving so he wouldn't see the disappointment in his crew's face in the garage. They worked hard to give him the best car with the best speed to win. Wins not only meant money, they also meant prestige and a deep sense of accomplishment. No one worth anything worked on the teams strictly for the money.

He cursed to see cameras and newspeople already waiting for him at the entrance to his bay. This was one time he wished there was no such thing as hot passes, which permitted certain individuals to be in the garage area at all times. He would have preferred the media had cold passes, which prevented the wearer from being in the garage area one hour before and one hour after the race.

Mics were thrust in his face even before he flicked the switch to climb out of his car. He kept his helmet on so they wouldn't see his anger, the disappointment on his face.

"Cameron, what went wrong out there?"

"What are your thoughts now?"

He worked hard to keep the expletive from escaping. In no other sport was the professional put on the spot so quickly. Others had time to go to the locker room, cool off, and regroup, but in NASCAR you were thrust into the spotlight immediately. Words spoken in the heat of the moment had come back to haunt a lot of drivers. He had never felt less like talking.

"How do you plan to make up for this loss?"

"What do you say to your crew, your crew chief, or Hilliard?"

Cameron wanted to ram the mic down the throat of the reporter who had just asked the last question. Then he remembered his family, in particular his older brother Duncan, who no matter how hard life had slapped him down always held his head up. Cameron remembered Faith, who still didn't know he'd learned she called in a favor with Blade Navarone to use his far-reaching influence to keep Cameron on Hilliard's race team.

Probably none of his family had watched the race, but all would hear one way or another about his piti-ful showing. When they did, their TV would come on and his cell phone would ring. When that happened, he wanted them to see him with his head up despite the knot in his gut, the pain in his heart.

And there was always the possibility, albeit a long shot, that Joshua and Caitlin were watching the race. If they were, he wanted his son to know that no matter what, a man always took responsibility for his actions.

He removed the helmet. The glare of the TV cam-eras, and the flash of the film cameras caught every nuance of his face. "I have the best crew and crew chief in the business. No driver could ask for better. The loss today stops at my door and I take full re-sponsibility. I congratulate Haskell on his win."

"No driver that I can think of has ever won the pole and finished last. Any comments?"

Yeah, Cameron thought. *I'd like to rearrange your face.* "If you were hoping to make me feel even worse for my owner and team, you've succeeded."

"Thank you, ladies and gentlemen, but Cameron is wanted elsewhere." Hope stepped up beside him, her smile as beautiful and playful as always. "I'm sure you understand." Curving her arm through Cameron's, she led him away.

"What you wanna bet Hilliard is waiting to let McBride have it with both barrels?" Cameron heard a male voice ask.

"Yeah. I wouldn't want to be in his shoes," a female voice answered. "It won't matter if his teammate came in eleventh. Cameron is supposed to be the man to beat this year."

"Not the way he's driving."

Cameron tensed, paused in mid-stride. Hope tugged at his arm. "They meant for you to hear them and you know it. Keep moving. Don't fall into their trap."

Cameron resisted looking over his shoulder to try and determine who had spoken. Words spoken in haste were repented not at leisure, but over and over and in print and on TV. He started walking.

"Father told me about the tape," Hope said, still holding his arm. "I'm sorry Joshua had to see that."

Cameron tried to blot out the image of terror on his son's face and failed. "He won't even look at me."

"Give him time." Hope steered him through the

rows of motor coaches owned by the drivers. "I'm betting it will be different tonight."

This time he did stop and frown down at her. "What?"

She took his helmet out from the crook of his arm. "Hilliard wants his winning driver back so he's made his jet available."

Cameron had a hard time accepting what he was hearing. Hilliard, while a fair man, could be hard and unbending. He wasn't a man to be cajoled. He understood his cars wouldn't always be in Victory Lane, yet it wasn't in his nature to cut the driver slack, especially one who had come in last. Cameron was positive Blade hadn't intervened. That left Hope.

She nodded toward a waiting black Lincoln. "The car will take you to Greensboro Airport. Hilliard's private jet is there to take you to LAX. Another car is there to drive you to Fontana."

"Hope—" He didn't know what to say. She could be as hard-nosed as Hilliard. "Thank you."

"Thank me by getting your mind back on the race." She handed him a white envelope. "Tickets for a late Monday-afternoon flight to Charlotte. When I see you again I want to see the old Cameron, the one who is going to kick butt at the Martinsville Speedway."

He almost smiled. "Now, that's the Hope I know."

She pushed him toward the steps of his motor coach. "Go shower, and remember what I said."

Cameron didn't need any more urging. He opened the door, stripping off clothes as he went. Hoping, praying that Joshua would welcome him.

Chapter 16

Caitlin opened her front door before Cameron rang her doorbell and stepped out on the porch. Although the night was warm, she wrapped her arms around herself. She'd peeked through the window for the last fifteen minutes looking for Cameron's car to pull up, praying she'd somehow find the words to tell him.

He stopped a few feet away, studied her face, then continued until he held her in his arms. "I thought—"

'I'm so sorry, Cameron," she said, holding him tight, trying to ease the misery he must be feeling. "Perhaps he just needs more time."

Lifting his head, he stared down at her. "I wish I could believe that." Bending to pick up his overnight bag, he curved his free arm around her waist and entered the house, closing the door after them. "I know he's asleep, but can I see him?"

"Of course," she answered, hating that he thought he had to ask. She wasn't used to an unsure Cameron. Turning, she led the way down the hallway to Joshua's room. The door was open, the night-light giving enough illumination for his small body to be seen. He was sleeping on his stomach.

Placing his bag on the floor, Cameron slowly approached the bed. For countless moments he simply watched Joshua sleep, then he knelt by the bed, tucking the already secure covers around the sleeping child's neck.

Joshua twisted restlessly away. Cameron immediately lifted his hands.

Caitlin, standing behind him, saw what had happened. "He's just restless," she explained. "He did the same thing tonight with me."

Seconds stretched into minutes before Cameron looked over his shoulder at her. His misery and disbelief were written clearly on his face.

"I wouldn't lie to you." Stepping around him, she adjusted the covers. Joshua didn't move. She didn't want to look at Cameron's face, but she did anyway, then turned her head away at the raw emotions she saw. For whatever reason, Joshua twisted beneath her hands. "It's all right, sweetheart. Everything is all right."

After a few seconds, Joshua stilled.

"I'm the cause of that," Cameron said, his voice uneven.

Caitlin wanted to deny the obvious. She repeated what she hoped and prayed was the truth. "He'll be all right. He just needs more time."

"Yeah," Cameron said, but he didn't sound any more convinced than she was. He pushed to his feet and walked into the hall.

Caitlin followed, her heart aching for him. She didn't think, she just pulled his head down, her mouth covering his, trying to soothe away the hurt she saw in his eyes, felt in his trembling arms.

He jerked her to him, his hot mouth devouring hers. His hand slid beneath her T-shirt to touch bare skim. She shivered as his hand swept up and down her spine.

Picking her up, he crossed the hall and entered her bedroom. He placed her on the turned-down bed and came down on top of her, his mouth taking the lead this time, to ravish her mouth, trail kisses down the curve of her cheek, the side of her neck. When his lips touched cloth, he lifted his head long enough to drag the T-shirt over her head.

Almost immediately his hot mouth covered her nipple. She felt the pull in her lower body as he suckled, then his hand was there, cupping her through her sweatpants. Restlessly she whimpered, wanting the barrier gone.

His hand slid beneath the waistband, his fingers finding her heat and need. Wanting more, her hips came off the bed. "Cameron." His name was a ragged breath of sound.

"Lift your hips," he said, his voice hoarse.

She did as he asked, allowing him to slide the sweatpants and panties off her legs. Immediately she grabbed his T-shirt, sweeping it over his head and reaching for the belt buckle, the snaps of his jeans.

Her hand imitated his earlier actions. She cupped him, found him hard and rigid. He moaned her name then, pushing her hands away, he shoved off his jeans and came down on top of her.

Holding her hands, he feasted on her lips, the turgid points of her nipples until she was a quivering mass of need. "Cameron, please."

Lifting her hips with both hands, he surged into her. She took all of him, wrapping her legs around his hips, then she was spinning out of control, reaching for completion. She went over, tightening her arms around his neck. Shouting her name, he followed seconds later.

Breathing hard, he buried his head in the crook of her neck and held her securely to him. Loving him, she stroked her hand up and down his broad back, felt the muscled strength, the dampness of perspiration. This would be heaven . . . if only.

Cameron didn't want to move. In Caitlin's arms he'd found the first moments of peace since he'd seen the tears in Joshua's eyes. Trying to make the images disappear, he held Caitlin tighter.

"It's all right," Caitlin soothed.

Cameron lifted his head and stared down into the face of the only woman he would ever love. "Why aren't you crucifying me?"

Her hand lifted to cup his cheek. "Because I know you love Joshua. You would never do anything to hurt him. This has to be killing you."

Closing his eyes, he gathered her into his arms, rolling to one side so they faced each other. For a long time, they stayed that way. Finally, he opened his eyes. "I don't know what I would have done if you had blamed me or forbidden me to see him."

Surprise widened her expressive eyes. "I would

never do that. Besides, what I said didn't matter much before."

"And look at the way that ended up."

"Cameron, stop it." She palmed his cheeks. "No matter the obstacles, you've never let anything or anyone keep you from what you wanted. Don't start now. Together we'll find a way to get past Joshua's fears."

His eyes locked with hers. "As much as I've wanted to, I've never been able to assuage your fears."

Her forehead touched his. "I've tried, Cameron. I just can't. I lived it with my mother after my father was killed, then when Bobby—"

"It's all right," Cameron said, attempting to calm her. "Don't think about it."

Her head lifted. Tears glistened in her eyes. "Today, when there was an accident, I was so afraid it was you."

He frowned down at her. "You watched the race on television?"

"I listened on a portable radio," she confessed, chewing on her bottom lip. "I knew you wouldn't be able to keep your mind on the race and I couldn't stop worrying. The Bristol track has the steepest banks on the circuit. Cars lap the track in fifteen seconds. Accidents can happen."

He felt a muscle tic in his jaw. "Coming in dead last, I didn't have to worry."

She rose up on her elbow to glare down at him. "Because you were worried about Joshua. You finished ahead of twenty-four other cars and I'd say that was an accomplishment."

Cameron supposed so, but with Caitlin's tempting

breast hovering so close to his face, he forgot about the race. Opening his mouth, he gently closed his teeth over the turgid point, then swirled his tongue over the tight bud. Caitlin moaned and clamped her hand to his head, bringing him closer.

That was all the enticement he needed. His hand palmed the other breast, plucked at the distended nipple. Talking wouldn't change things and, for a little while, he could forget.

He kissed her, loved her with his hands and mouth until both were nearing the breaking point. Positioning her with her back to him he made them one. The pleasure was so intense he trembled.

Slowly he withdrew, then surged forward, stroking her hot sheath that held him so securely. Her cries of pleasure drove him on. One hand slipped between her slick folds to find the tiny bud, the other stroked her breast the same way he stroked her below.

The rhythm became faster and faster until he felt her body stiffen beneath his. He increased the pace, determined that this time they would find release together. Two strokes later, he found completion, taking her with him. He'd never felt anything so intense and realized he never would . . . unless it was with this woman.

Using his last reserves of strength, he wrapped his arms around her and lay down, fitting her body to his, so she faced away from him. He kissed the nape of her neck, felt her tremble, felt the little quakes that continued to ripple though her.

"Cam," she moaned sleepily.

"I'm here. Go to sleep." He kissed the nape of her

neck again, lightly closed his hand over her breast. She'd called him "Cam." Before she'd left him at the altar she'd always called him Cam. He wanted to believe that it meant something more than being caught up in a passionate moment.

And then what? His gaze went to the partially closed door. Worry gnawed at him. If he couldn't get Joshua to overcome his fear, it would mean nothing.

By Caitlin's even breathing he knew she was asleep. Gently easing away from her, he pulled on his pants and went to check on Joshua. If he happened to wake up, he wanted some clothes on.

Joshua remained on his stomach, the covers around his neck. Cameron pulled up a chair and watched him sleep just as he had when they'd first met. He had so many plans for them, first just the two of then, then as a family.

And now it looked as if none of them would work out.

Elbows propped on his knees, he put his forehead on top of his clasped hands. Caitlin was right about one thing; he'd always gone after what he wanted. This time he didn't know how.

Slender hands slid over his shoulders then stopped in the middle of his chest. Caitlin placed her chin on top of his head. "I was jealous at the time, but he was never happier than when he was with you."

"Until I ruined it," he said, self-recrimination in each word.

Caitlin knelt in front of him. "Don't let the last couple of days outweigh all the days of happiness you two had together. He loves you."

Cameron found that hard to believe, but he desperately wanted to hold on to the possibility if only for a little while. Rising, he pulled Caitlin to her feet, then picked her up in his arms, touching his head against hers. Together they watched Joshua sleep.

"Let's get you to bed." Cameron firmly turned and walked out of the room, wishing he could have kissed his son good-night, but afraid if he did Joshua would flinch. He might have gained Caitlin for a little while, but he very well mi ght have lost his son forever.

Caitlin slept in fits and spurts, and each time she woke up, Cameron was awake. She could tell by the way his arms held her so close to him. In turn, she'd held him just as tightly. It was almost seven. She wished she could hold back time. She'd wanted to stay in his arms as long as possible.

Angling her head upward, she kissed his chin. "Good morning."

" 'Morning," he said, his eyes troubled.

She brought a smile to her face. "I bet you're ready for your caffeine fix. I'll put the coffee on."

His arms slowly released her and he rolled out of bed. "You go ahead and get Joshua ready for school. I can take of myself."

She pulled her discarded T-shirt over her head before she spoke. "He's not going today. I have to reenroll him."

He paused with one leg inside his jeans. "Is that the only reason?"

She thought of lying, but quickly discarded the

idea. He deserved the truth no matter how difficult it might be for him to hear. "He likes knowing I'm nearby."

His sensual lips flattened into a thin line. "I not only made him afraid for me, but for you. What kind of father does that make me?"

She quickly went to him. "You're a good father. This was out of your control. He'll be fine."

"In the meantime, he won't look at me and doesn't want you out of his sight." He jerked on his jeans. "He was happy before I barged my way into his life."

"But he wanted a father," she reminded him.

"He didn't bargain on me scaring him half to death," he rasped.

"Cameron, you didn't mean to do that," she said, trying to get through to him.

"Yeah." He picked up the overnight bag he'd brought into the room. "Is Joshua a late sleeper?"

He wasn't going to listen, and answering his question wasn't going to make it any better. "He woke up around this time yesterday morning."

A muscle leaped in his jaw. "Is there another bathroom I can use?"

"The bedroom next to Joshua's has a full bath."

"Thanks." Without a word, he went out the door.

Caitlin wanted to hang her head and cry, but she didn't have the luxury. Cameron was hurting, and Joshua would soon awaken. Quickly checking on him to determine he was still asleep, she gathered her clothes and rushed to shower and dress. She needed to be there when Cameron and Joshua met again, for both their sakes.

* * *

Cameron came out of the guest bedroom and face-to-face with Joshua who was about to enter his mother's bedroom. The child simply stared at him. There was no bright smile, no hug. Despite the knot threatening to choke him, Cameron said, "Good morning, son."

Nothing moved on Joshua, not even an eyelash.

"I came by to say hi to you and your mother." Cameron wanted to take his son in his arms, but he didn't want to upset him. "Are you hungry? I can fix you pancakes."

Dismissing him, Joshua continued into Caitlin's bedroom. Cameron clenched his fists in impotent fury. He only had himself to blame for this.

"Good morning, sweetheart," he heard Caitlin say.

"Good morning, Mommy," Joshua said. "I'm hungry. Can I have cereal for breakfast?"

"I don't see why not." Together they came out of the bedroom holding hands. Caitlin paused on seeing Cameron. "Joshua, look who has come to visit."

"Can I have my cereal?" Joshua asked. "I washed my hands and brushed my teeth all by myself."

Caitlin's eyes widened in surprise at Joshua's announcement. "You are certainly growing up to be a big boy, but you haven't spoken to your father and he came a long way to see you."

Joshua folded his arms. "I'm hungry."

"Joshu—"

"No," Cameron said, cutting her off. Correcting Joshua would only make matters worse. "It's all right. I have some calls to make. I'll wait in the living room." Spinning on his heels, Cameron went to the spacious room, taking out his cell phone and activating it.

He wasn't surprised to see that he had fifteen messages. Most of them were from Faith and Duncan. He'd left brief messages for both that he was all right and would call Monday. He hadn't been in the mood to answer questions.

He still wasn't, but they had waited long enough. He glanced at his watch. It was a little after eight in Montana and Santa Fe. Duncan would be out already, working on his ranch. That meant his cell was off. Cameron left a brief message saying he'd call, then he dialed Faith's cell number.

She and Brandon moved between his apartment over his restaurant that Faith had renovated and her room at their hotel. Unlike Duncan, as executive manager of the hotel, she turned her cell phone on the moment she woke up and didn't turn it off until she was ready for bed. Since Brandon owned the Red Cactus restaurant, he understood her need to be available.

He was also crazy about his wife. They were both lucky. Cameron and Duncan had missed the mark.

The phone was answered on the second ring. "Tell me you're all right," Faith asked, her voice a bit breathless.

Cameron could think of a couple of reasons for her being out of breath this early in the morning. She and Brandon could have just come in from a morning run—which they did—or . . .

"Cameron," she said.

"He's all right, honey. Aren't you, Cameron?"

Cameron rubbed the back of his neck. "Yes, if I caught—I mean I can call later."

"You do, and you're dead meat after Faith worried about you all night," Brandon said. "Especially after she spoke with Ms. Alvarado."

Cameron frowned. "Faith talked with Hope?"

"Be glad I did," Faith said as she came on the line. "Or my next phone call would have been to Blade so he could call Shane to track you down. Luke is out of town with Catherine or I would have called him," she told Cameron, a mixture of pique and anxiety in her voice. "You should have called."

Cameron plopped into a side chair. Shane, a retired army ranger, once headed Blade's security. Married, he now ran his own prosperous security firm in Atlanta. Luke was Brandon's oldest brother and owned Manhunters, a private investigation firm in Santa Fe.

"I had a lot on my mind, Faith."

"I know," Faith said softly. "Hope explained about Joshua seeing the tape. I feel so bad for all of you."

He still couldn't take it in. "Hope doesn't give out information."

"It was either tell me over the phone or I was coming to see her in person," Faith said fiercely.

Hope didn't scare easily . . . if at all. There was more to it than that. Perhaps Hope had a soft side after all.

"Is Joshua up yet?" she asked.

Cameron swiped his hand across his face. "Yes, and he still acts as if I'm not there."

"He's hurting and confused, Cameron."

"I know that, but I can't help him," he said, angry at his own helplessness.

"That's why I've called so many times," Faith said. "Apparently you've forgotten that Brandon's sister-in-law, Catherine, is a noted child psychologist."

He was almost afraid to hope. "Did she say she could help? Did you tell her about what had happened to Joshua?"

"No, I thought you and Caitlin would want to do that yourselves, but I did call her and let her know someone I loved might call her this morning and ask her to help them. She doesn't have another workshop until this afternoon. She's waiting for you to call her."

"Do you think she can help?" he asked.

"If I had a child with a problem, she'd be the first person I'd call."

Laughter floated to him from the kitchen. If he walked into the room it would stop. None of them could go on this way. "Please give me the number."

Chapter 17

Caitlin was almost afraid for Cameron to make the call. From the den they looked out to the fenced backyard where Joshua swung on his swing set. After breakfast he'd ignored his father and asked to go play. She'd let him because making him stay or sending him to his room wasn't the answer. She wasn't sure what was.

"We both have to agree on this decision," Cameron told her.

Joshua stopped swinging and stared toward the wall of glass in the den. She waved. He set the swing in motion again. Her adventurous son was scared to let her out of his sight for long periods of time. She couldn't be with him twenty-four/seven.

"Caitlin?" Cameron asked.

"Make the call." They didn't know how to help their son; perhaps Dr. Grayson did.

Standing where they had a clear view of Joshua, Cameron activated the speaker and punched in the cell number on the phone on the end table in the den.

"Good morning. Dr. Grayson."

Cameron caught Caitlin's hand. He'd met Luke's

wife a couple of times in social situations. The last time was Sierra Grayson's wedding, but this was completely different. "Dr. Grayson, this is Cameron McBride. Faith told you I might call."

"Cameron, it's nice to hear your voice," she said, then, "Luke said hello. He's going into the other room to give us some privacy."

He glanced uneasily at Caitlin. "You knew I'd call."

"A guess. Faith showed us all the family pictures of Joshua," she said. "I don't blame her for being so proud. He's a good-looking boy. You were doing well in this year's NASCAR races until the race yesterday. There is a great deal of speculation as to the reason."

"Luke married a woman as smart as he is," Cameron said.

Dr. Grayson laughed. Her voice was soft, cultured. "Thank you for the compliment. How may I help you, help Joshua?"

She sounded calm, capable. He couldn't imagine Luke marrying a woman who wasn't. "I'm here with Joshua's mother, Caitlin Lawrence. We have you on the speaker phone."

"Hello, Ms. Lawrence," Dr. Grayson said. "Where is Joshua?"

"Hello, Dr. Grayson. He's in the backyard playing. We can watch him while we talk," Caitlin explained.

"Good, because this conversation is going to be intensely personal. I need you to answer honestly," she said. "We'll try this first, and if it doesn't work, you can bring Joshua to me or I can come to him, whichever I think would be less traumatic."

Caitlin edged closer to Cameron. His arm pulled her tighter to him.

"What do you want to know?" Cameron asked.

"Everything that led up to whatever difficulties Joshua is going through."

"That will take time," Cameron said.

"Then perhaps we should get started. Four-year-olds aren't known for their patience. Who will go first?"

They'd had to stop twice because Joshua came into the house for water, but Caitlin and Cameron knew the real reason was that he wanted to assure himself that she was all right. Cameron had spoken first, faltering when he told about being left at the altar. With tears in her eyes and stinging her throat, Caitlin had explained her fear, silently asking for forgiveness. The hardest part was explaining her decision to keep Joshua's birth a secret. To Caitlin's amazement and Dr. Grayson's credit, she didn't appear shocked or judgmental.

"How did Joshua react to learning Cameron was his father?"

"He was ecstatic," Cameron answered, his gaze glued to his son, who was playing with a ball. "My family came up, and we had a party. That's when Faith took the pictures. He went with me to the garage. At the autograph session he handed me my photographs to sign. We even went to Chicago to do a photo shoot and film a commercial."

"He adores his father," Caitlin said.

"Until he saw the film of my car crashing into the retaining wall." His fists clenched. "I didn't know he was there."

"It was my fault," Caitlin quickly said. "I was busy with a sketch, and he slipped out of the motor coach without my knowing it."

"Four-year-olds are extremely inquisitive and inventive when they want to do something they know they shouldn't," Dr. Grayson said. "He probably knows how engrossed you become and used your distraction to his advantage."

Cameron curved his arm around Caitlin's shoulder. "You're a good mother. This is not your fault. It's mine."

"I think it's time to take fault out of the equation and look for a solution. It's going to require both of you to work hard."

Cameron and Caitlin glanced at each other and both stepped closer to the phone. "Anything," they said in unison.

"I think you should hear what I have to say before you agree," Dr. Grayson said. "Is Joshua still occupied?"

"Yes," Caitlin told her. He'd abandoned the ball and gone back to his swing.

"Good. Cameron, you're first."

"Yes, Dr. Grayson."

"What is your goal when you race? Your best expectation?" Dr. Grayson asked.

Cameron frowned, looked at Caitlin, who seemed puzzled. "To win, and if I can't, to come in among the top ten."

"Have you shared this with Joshua?"

The questions were becoming weirder, but Faith trusted Dr. Grayson, and Luke had married her, so Cameron trusted her as well. "I told him, but I don't know if he remembers."

"He does." Caitlin faced him. "He told me when I let him watch a little bit of the race before I switched the TV off."

"Then, Cameron, you're going to have to do whatever it takes to come in among the top ten," Dr. Grayson told him. "When this is over Joshua will look back on this time and blame himself if you've lost because of him."

"It's not his fau—"

"She's right," Caitlin said, cutting him off. "Each time I read that you hadn't raced well, it tore me to pieces. I knew you wanted the cup, knew how much you loved racing, but, because of me, you were having the worst season of your life."

"Then why didn't you come back to me?" he asked, his voice low.

"Because, as much as I hated to see you lose, I was more afraid of seeing you hurt or killed the way my father and your teammate were," Caitlin said, her voice unsteady.

Cameron folded her into his arms. "Don't cry, honey. I'm safer on the track than on the freeway."

"Cars on the freeway aren't going in excess of a hundred eighty miles per hour," she countered.

"I see this is an old argument and, unfortunately, it's the key to helping Joshua," Dr, Grayson said. "Ms. Lawrence, children are perceptive. Joshua is obviously afraid. He's separating himself from his father because of that fear. Separated, he won't feel the pain as deeply if something were to happen to his father.

"He needs reassurance from the one person who has always been there, the one person he trusts implicitly, his mother. The only way to help Joshua is for you, Ms. Lawrence, to overcome your own fears," Dr. Grayson told them.

Shaking her head, Caitlin backed away from the phone, staring at it as if it were a poisonous snake. "I've tried. There must be another way."

"I'm afraid there isn't," came Dr. Grayson's calm reply. "Joshua is taking his cue from you. I bet if you think back over the course of time that you've been with Cameron you've shown Joshua your fear of his father's racing."

Caitlin's gaze sought Cameron's. "I wouldn't let him watch the race, and when I did, you and the other car were so close, I was so frightened that I picked up Joshua. When you won, I couldn't stop crying." Her balled fist pressed against her lips. "Cameron, what have I done to our baby? I never wanted him to be afraid."

"Shhh." Cameron pulled her fiercely into his arms. "Hush. Dr. Grayson just said we're not going to point fingers or blame anyone, just come together to help Joshua."

"I'll do anything to help him, but I can't do that. I can't."

"Yes you can," Dr. Grayson said firmly. "Your son is your motivation. Take yourself out of the equation and simply think of what is best for him. Face your fears. From what I've been able to bring up on the computer, NASCAR is one of the safest professional sports around and will become even more so with the car of tomorrow and all NASCAR safety measures for the track and the cars."

"I'm not sure I can."

"You'll have to if you want to help Joshua," came the somber reply of Dr. Grayson.

"Joshua's on his way back inside," Cameron said.

"Feel free to call me if you want to talk more. Good-bye."

Cameron hung up the phone just as Joshua opened the glass door to the terrace. He wasn't sure if he should let Joshua ignore him or push the issue. He'd forgotten to ask.

"Mama, I want you to come outside and play with me," Joshua told her, stopping a few feet from his mother.

Although Cameron was standing next to her, not by one glance did his son acknowledge him. "I could push you on the swing or we could play catch," Cameron said.

Joshua took his mother's hand. "Come on."

Helplessly, Caitlin glanced back at Cameron, then down at their son. "Nothing is going to happen to your father. What you saw on the video happened that day you hurt your arm. Joshua, you don't have to be afraid for your father."

"Can you come outside and play with me?" he repeated.

Caitlin blew out a frustrated breath. "I'll be out in a minute. You go ahead."

He didn't move. "I want you to come now."

"Joshua, please do as you're told, or you can come inside to stay," she said firmly. She might not be sure of what to do next, but she was sure that letting Joshua manipulate her wasn't a good idea.

Head tucked down, he went back outside, took a seat on one of the patio chairs, and propped his chin on his folded arms on the table.

Cameron swept his hand up and down Caitlin's arm. "If I'm hurting him, it's best that I leave."

"He can be stubborn," she said.

His lips curved upward. "Guess he gets that from his mother."

She turned to him, misery in her eyes. "Maybe Dr. Grayson is wrong. He'll get over his fear."

"Have you?"

Her eyes shut tightly. Warm lips brushed across her forehead. She opened her eyes to see Cameron walking away.

The glass door slid open. Joshua didn't stop until his arms were wrapped around her. "You aren't going, are you, Mommy?"

Her heart aching, she bent and hugged his trembling body to hers. "No, Mommy is not going anyplace." She had her son completely to herself just as she wanted, but the price was too high. Both Joshua and Cameron were hurting.

Cameron called Caitlin every night after Joshua was in bed. Each night he'd hope for some indication that Joshua missed his father. There never was.

The most promising event was Joshua's going

back to school on Wednesday. Caitlin had returned
for lunch and again at mid-afternoon to find him
busy in the play centers. He'd waved at her and gone
back to building a tower with blocks.

"I'm leaving for Martinsville tomorrow morning
to get ready for the qualifying races," Cameron said,
his feet propped up on his table in the sitting room at
his home.

There was a telling pause. "The track at Martinsville Speedway is the smallest track in the series.
There's no passing room. If you don't qualify well . . ."

Cameron dragged his feet off the table. "I plan to
be in the top ten and stay there. No way am I going to
let Joshua feel bad about my poor showing once this
is over."

"And, according to Dr. Grayson, it all hinges on
me," she said quietly. "The weakest link."

"Strongest," he corrected. "You can do this. You
have an extra incentive. You can begin by watching
the race on Sunday."

"No." The answer was quick, emphatic.

He could imagine her standing, pacing. He stood
as well. "Call Diana over to watch it with you . . . if
Joshua will let you. Otherwise, tape it and, once he's
asleep, we'll watch it together."

"I'm not sure I can do that."

"You won't know until you try," he said. "I asked
Hope to send you a few tapes of races. You were with
me for two months during race season. I had a couple
of fender benders and a lot of bumps, but I always
finished and always came back to you safely."

"And I stayed in the motor coach with headphones

on, waiting for Mike or someone to knock on the door the way my father's crew chief had come to tell my mother my father wouldn't be coming home," she whispered.

"Caitlin, I can't promise it won't happen to me or that I'll always come home. Accidents happen. Fatalities are rare now, but they have happened in the past. I can't promise what I can't control."

"Neither can I," she told him.

"Caitlin—" He stopped abruptly. He'd almost told her he loved her, but wondered if that would help her or put more pressure on her. There was one thing he could say. "I want you and Joshua in my life. I miss seeing his eyes light up when he sees me, miss him trying to imitate me. I miss having you in my bed, miss our talks."

"Cameron, I just don't know."

"I do. Watch the tapes. The race, if you can." He moved to sit on the arm of the easy chair. "And look for me early the morning after the race."

"But the track is in Virginia. You'll be across the country."

"That's what they have jets for. I want to see you and Joshua." He frowned. "Unless you don't want to see me."

"Stay safe, and I'll be waiting."

"I'll be there. 'Night, Caitlin."

"'Night, Cameron."

Cameron shut off the cordless and dropped it into the base. Picking up the control to the DVD player, he activated the tape of his last year's race at the Martinsville Speedway. He'd come in third after a fifth-place start. The bumpy track of concrete and asphalt had taken out a lot of drivers since it was built in 1947. Come Sunday, to save his family, Cameron didn't plan on being one of them.

Saturday morning, Caitlin carried the special delivery package into the house as if it contained explosives. In a way it did, she thought, as she placed the padded envelope on top of the television in her bedroom. Viewing the tapes might easily make matters worse instead of better.

If she let it. Cameron said she was strong. He knew she wasn't, and was patient with her anyway. She'd thought it was for Joshua's sake, but lately she had begun to think differently. Cameron had been her only lover, but her instincts told her that the loving way he cherished her body conveyed his deep feelings for her.

He cared, just as she did. They had both been cautiously feeling their way to becoming a family when Joshua had seen the film. If she wanted them to be a family—and she did—it was up to her to see that it happened.

"Mommy!" Joshua cried as he ran into the room with Stephen behind him. "Stephen's mother just dropped him off. We can all go to the movie now."

"And then get pizza afterward," Stephen added.

Caitlin smiled down at the two anxious boys. Each day Joshua was more like his old self, which was bittersweet because he never responded when Caitlin mentioned his father. It was as if Cameron had been wiped from his mind, his heart. Her smile slid away.

"You all right, Mommy?"

"Yes, sweetheart." She turned away to get her handbag from the top of the dresser. Dr. Grayson was right about Joshua's taking his moods from her. She slung the wide strap over her shoulder. "Who's ready to go to the movies?"

"Me!"

"Me!"

"Well, let's go." The boys took off running. Caitlin didn't even try to stop them. With one last look at the sealed envelope, she left the room.

Cameron had picked the wrong race for Caitlin to watch to overcome her fear. Six yellow flags and two red came out. When the race was over there were twenty-seven bumped and banged cars on the track.

Thankfully number 23 was sixth. He hadn't pulled off the win, but it was enough to get him the jet, dangled in front of him by Hope if he finished in the top ten. The lady knew how to bargain.

He just wished he knew how she kept pulling it off. Hilliard didn't coddle his drivers. At forty-nine, divorced, and tough as an old boot, he wasn't ruled by emotions. He'd caved for Blade Navarone as one successful businessman for another; Cameron was sure Hilliard didn't want to cross a man who wielded that much power and influence.

As soon as the car that met him at the airport stopped in front of Caitlin's house, Cameron opened his door. Caitlin met him halfway, throwing her arms around his neck, holding him tightly. The temperature was in the low eighties and she was shivering.

Since it was two in the morning, he didn't think any neighbors would be up and watching. Picking her up, he carried her inside, then set her on her feet.

She caught his hand. "I know you want to see Joshua."

He did, but it had felt good holding her, breathing in her sweet fragrance after hours of smelling gas fumes and rubber.

Opening the door to their son's room, she stepped aside. "He spent the day away from me and did fine."

Cameron went to Joshua's bedside and stared down at the sleeping child. Bending, he kissed the air just above his soft cheek. "I love you," he whispered. Turning away, he caught Caitlin's hand and went into her bedroom. Once inside, he pulled her flush against him.

"I'm here, and I'm safe."

"Then take me to bed and prove it."

"My pleasure." His mouth took hers, and he lost himself in their kiss. He loved this woman more than he thought possible. The thought of losing her again, losing Joshua, tied his gut in knots. They tumbled into bed and, for a little while, he could lose himself and forget.

"You ready?"

"No, but turn it on anyway," Caitlin said. The TV screen filled with cars racing around the famous Daytona International Speedway. Caitlin pressed back against Cameron, who was behind her on the bed. There was no sound for fear of waking Joshua.

"Racing takes skill, timing, and a bit of Lady

Luck now and then," Cameron whispered, his warm breath sending shivers racing though her. "For up to four hours the car becomes your entire world. Wearing the headphones inside your helmet, you're not even aware of the noise of the crowd, but you can see them in the Indy race because of the almost ninety-degree turn. You pit your skills against the track and the other drivers."

"I know that." She had read extensively about the tracks in the NASCAR circuit. She had wanted to know what he was up against. The Daytona Speedway was probably the most famous and where NASCAR racing had begun.

He leaned over to peer into her face. "Are your eyes open?"

"One of them."

"Try two."

She looked back over her shoulder to glare at him. He kissed her pouting lips.

"Now, back to the race. It's an adrenaline high." His cheek rested against hers, his bare chest against her back. "The only thing I can compare it to is when we're making love. I feel powerful, invincible."

She shivered. "It's incredible."

He instinctively understood she meant their love-making. "Do you remember the first time?" He pulled her earlobe into his mouth, bit gently.

"Y-yes." It was difficult to concentrate with his playful teasing. This was the carefree Cameron she remembered so well. "We met in San Francisco and stayed at the St. Regis Hotel. You filled the room with flowers."

"You wore a pink sundress with little white flowers. My hands were trembling so badly I could hardly get the buttons through the loops."

She looked back at him, knowing she was asking to be kissed again. "You remember that?"

His thumb grazed her lower lip. "I've never forgotten anything about you."

Her eyes closed tightly. "I've caused you so much pain."

"And countless moments of pleasure." His lips pressed against hers, his tongue lazily swirled inside her mouth. Slowly he lifted his head, waiting until she opened her eyes.

"Drafting."

"What?" Gently he turned her head toward the cars on the track.

"Single file. The cars can go faster, but it has to be an unspoken effort. If one car pulls out, it can slow the other car down."

Caitlin watched the cars circle the track. She knew she was concentrating more on the warm muscle hardness behind her than the race. The heat and temptation of his body negated the long white gown she wore. Cameron had a sheet across his lap, but nothing underneath. Her mind kept wandering to what was beneath that sheet.

Perhaps because Cameron was there and safe, the race didn't disturb her as much. Perhaps because she knew he had emerged safe and victorious that day.

"Are you paying attention?"

"Drafting," she repeated as Cameron's face came

on the screen. Looking gorgeous, he held his helmet casually in the crook of his right arm.

"Hi, Caitlin, we're going for a little ride," the TV Cameron said.

"What?" She tried to look back over his shoulder, but he turned her head toward the TV screen.

"First, we're going to look at twenty-three and how I get ready for the race." His hand swept down the front of his racing jumpsuit. "You already know that it's NASCAR regulation that my suit, the gloves, and shoes are fire-resistant. The year after you left, NASCAR mandated more stringent head and neck restraints. My helmet is specially made for me. After the little incident at the California Speedway, the helmet was sent to the manufacturer to be X-rayed to make sure it wasn't damaged."

"Was it?" she asked.

He kissed her. "Nope. Now turn around."

Caitlin turned around, wrapping her hands around his arms that circled her waist. He might take the accident calmly, but she didn't.

"When I'm inside the car, I'm essentially in a secure steel frame that is reinforced to further protect me during an impact. Officials inspect the car to make sure the roll bars are steel and not a lighter material that would make the car faster, but the driver less safe." He grinned. "And before you ask, Hilliard wants to win, but he doesn't cut corners. He's hard at times, but fair."

There was a snorting sound in the background. Cameron's grin widened.

"Who was that?" she asked, this time knowing not to look back.

"Hope," he answered from behind her. "I can't figure out what is going on between her and Hilliard. Russ might not even get in the race."

"The rookie? What race?"

"Doesn't matter. Listen, you missed me telling you about the roof flaps that keep the car from becoming airborne."

Caitlin went back to watching Cameron on the TV.

Tossing the helmet inside, Cameron holstered himself into the car, fastened his seat belt, and gave it a pull. "Seat belts are five adjoining belts that come over my shoulders and between my legs, and meet at a point around my waist. I'm putting the window net in place. That's what kept my head and arms inside after the accident."

She pushed back against him, holding him. Thinking about it still made her stomach feel jittery. She understood too well how it must have frightened Joshua. She had looked away when it was shown on TV. At the time Joshua hadn't been paying attention to the news, he was in too much discomfort with his arm.

Cameron spoke to her from the TV screen. "There's a camera mounted on the dash so you'll be able to see what I see, and one on the right door, so you'll be able to see me on a split screen." He put on his helmet.

"I want you to feel the excitement of the race. I want you to see why I love racing so much." The engine roared to life. "All right, Caitlin, let's go for a drive."

Caitlin saw the intensity, the pleasure in Cameron's face, recalled how he had told her the only thing that compared to it was when they made love. She'd watched him race a few times for brief periods, but there had been no camera to show his face, his emotions.

Racing was as much a part of him as his smile. Without it, he'd be only half alive. Racing was his world, but it was a world that Joshua wanted no part of. Until he did, there was no place in it for Caitlin, either.

Chapter 18

"Well?" Cameron asked as the film ended. When Caitlin didn't answer, he turned her face toward his. Misery stared back at him. His chest felt as if there were a tight band around it. "Caitlin?"

"I appreciate all the trouble you went though, but it just shows all the horrible things that can and have happened to drivers," she said.

For the first time, his anger flared. "That's all you wanted to see."

"Cameron, you're in a dangerous profession," she said.

"Can't you get past that?" he asked. Then without waiting for an answer he continued. "So are a lot of other jobs. I've tried to understand you, but I'm beginning to wonder if you're even trying to see my side."

She gasped, stood. "How can you say that? My father—"

"Died racing." He came to his feet as well. "I know that and can't begin to imagine how painful that must have been for you, but you refuse to move on. To consider the low ratio of drivers hurt to the number of cars racing, the safety measures that have been taken, the ones that will go into effect next year."

"If you're the one injured, statistics don't matter," she shot back.

Cameron stared at Caitlin; she stared back. "You won't even try. How can you expect Joshua to be any different?"

She sucked in a breath. "That's not fair. This isn't the way I've chosen to be."

"I'm not so sure."

Her head snapped back as if he'd hit her. "What do you mean?"

"It's easier for you to be frightened than face your fears. Until you do, you're condemning all of us to live apart." Afraid of what more he might say, he looked around for his pants. "I should be going."

"I thought you were staying the night."

After snapping his jeans closed, he shoved his arm through his shirt. "I have an interview at twelve."

Caitlin wrapped her arms around her waist. "Would you have stayed longer if we hadn't gotten into an argument?"

Picking up his shoes, he sat on the bed. "I planned to be gone before Joshua woke up. I'm not sure I can take him acting as if I don't exist again."

"Cameron." Kneeling, she hugged him to her. "He loves you."

"You said you loved me once, and you still left me at the altar."

She flinched, then slowly stood. "I can understand your anger, but not your cruelty."

He came to his feet, taking her chin in his hand. His eyes ignited. "How cruel was it to leave me at the church full of friends and family waiting like a fool for the woman I loved and was going to pledge my love to for the rest of my life? I kept the guests waiting for over an hour until Faith asked the on-duty manager at Casa de la Serenidad to check your room." He dropped his hand. "The unlucky man personally delivered your note to me."

"It would have killed me to see you get hurt."

"It almost killed me when you left." Stepping around her, he ignored her strangled cry of pain. He stopped at the door. "If you want to change, to give us a chance to be a family, you know where to find me." He walked though the bedroom door. This time he didn't stop.

Eyes closed, Caitlin sagged onto the bed as she heard the front door close. Cameron was gone, and this time he wasn't coming back. Misery welled inside her. She couldn't even cry. Joshua would see her red eyes and know. Instead, she crawled to the head of the bed to get under the covers, pulling the sheets and light blanket up to her chin.

She was cold. With Cameron gone, she wasn't sure if she'd ever feel completely warm again. Through the ordeal with Joshua, she'd thought they'd grown closer. He'd just proven her wrong. Worse, he blamed her. That hurt the most.

She huddled beneath the covers, her knees drawn upward toward her chin. Her fear wasn't something she could turn off and on like a switch. She'd lived with it since she was a little gi—

She stilled, tilting her head to one side, straining to hear. She thought she heard a sound. Lifting up on one elbow, she stared at the baby monitor speaker. Joshua hadn't had any problems sleeping for the past few nights.

Throwing back the covers, she went across the hall to check. Joshua slept peacefully, the covers up to his neck. She turned to go, then stopped, and went back to his bed. Outwardly he might appear not to have a care, but that wasn't so. Even though he acted as if his father didn't exist and tried to push him from his mind, there had to be times when he wasn't successful.

She knew because she had done the same thing for five years. On some days she was more successful than others. The difference was that she had willingly turned her back on Cameron and his love.

"It almost killed me when you left."

She went to her room and back to bed. Cameron's words kept returning to her. Perhaps it was fitting, because this time his leaving was the most difficult thing she had ever had to endure.

"It didn't work."

"Good morning to you, too," Hope said as she greeted Cameron at her front door.

Although it was barely eight in the morning and he hadn't called to tell her he was coming over, he wasn't ready for her sarcasm. He was in a foul mood.

"Come on in." She stepped aside. "I'll make coffee."

He shook his head as he stepped onto the tiled floor in the small entryway of her house down the street from her father's. "No, thanks. I already had a cup."

"Breakfast?"

"Not hungry." He stuck his hands in the pockets of his jeans, feeling restless and on edge.

"I am. Let's go into the kitchen." Taking his arm, she went through the family room and into the small but ultramodern kitchen in yellow and white. Releasing him, she waved him to a seat at the island with bar stools. "You want anything to drink?"

"I want my family back."

Leaning against the counter near him, she folded her arms. "You want to talk about it?"

Cameron propped his arms on the granite counter. He needed to talk to someone. Faith and Duncan were out. They were worried enough about him. The same with Brandon since he and Faith didn't keep secrets from each other. His parents wouldn't be of any help. They couldn't help themselves. He didn't want to end up like them.

"I thought the tape would work," he finally said.

"I wasn't so sure, but I'd hoped it would."

His head lifted, annoyance flared in his eyes. "Then why didn't you say something earlier?"

Hope merely lifted a brow. "Because, as I said, I hoped it would, and because you needed to do something besides mope. When I went to check on her and Joshua in your motor coach at the race in Vegas, she was terrified for you. I was prepared not to like her until then."

Cameron's shoulders snapped back. Hope used her sharp tongue indiscriminately. "Did you say anything to hurt her?"

"Caitlin might look shy, but she can take care of herself." Hope retrieved her glass of orange juice from the counter by the oven and returned. "I like her. She did a good job raising Joshua. I've seen too many bitter single mothers trying to punish the father through the child."

Cameron's gaze narrowed at the sharpness in her tone. Her comment sounded personal. "You dating a single father?"

"What?" She straightened. "Why would you ask a thing like that?"

He shrugged carelessly. "You just sounded as if you had firsthand knowledge."

"I don't have time for a man," she said, taking a sip of her juice. "We were talking about you and Caitlin."

Cameron had seen an evasive Hope before, but he'd never seen her flustered or nervous. There was the tiniest tremor in the hand holding the glass.

"So what happened after the film?" she asked.

Her question thrust everything else from his mind. "She said it just showed how dangerous my job was."

"Ever think you're giving Caitlin too much leeway?" Hope asked, placing the glass on the counter.

"Last night after she saw the film." He looked her in the eye. "I won't need the jet after the race Sunday."

Hope didn't even blink. "Good, because I'm not sure I could talk Hilliard into letting you have it again."

"How did you do it the other times?" he asked, watching Hope closely.

She busied herself with her juice. "Trade secret. Now get out of here. I have lots to do before I meet you at the television station for your interview."

He'd never felt less like being "on." "Can't you postpone it?"

"No. Clarice might be a friend, but she'd have a hissy fit, and rightly so, if we canceled. The show is live," she reminded him. "This late, she might not be able to find a replacement."

"I don't feel like doing an interview," he said.

"Life is full of challenges." Hope picked up her juice and took a sip. "Be sure and be there at half-past for your makeup."

Cameron scowled. "You know I hate that most of all. The gunk on my face is bad enough but, while I'm trapped in the chair, women working at the station just happen to drop by and leave me their phone numbers."

Hope faked a yawn. "It's tough being an idol."

He glared at her although he knew it would bounce off her like water off a duck. "You have an answer for everything."

"Hardly. Some answers are just easier than others," she said.

"Don't I know it." He slid off the stool. "But I refuse to give up on Caitlin and Joshua. I'll have my family back with me."

"If that doesn't happen?"

"It will," he said firmly. "If you can't be with me on this, perhaps I need to look for another PR rep."

Her black eyes narrowed. "You love her that much?"

"And more," he answered without hesitation.

"Then it's a good thing I happen to think of you more as family than a client, or you know what you could do with that ultimatum."

He chuckled. "Mike would wash your mouth out if he knew you talked that way."

"But you aren't going to tell him."

She was right. He wasn't. Shaking his head, he went to the door. "Russ doesn't know what he's letting himself in for."

"Why would you say that?" she asked with a frown.

Cameron backpedaled fast. "Didn't he ask you about being his PR rep?"

"Oh, that." She opened her front door. "I haven't decided if I want to take on any more clients. The ones I have keep me busy enough."

"That we do. See you later, Hope." Cameron went down the steps to his truck parked at the curb. Poor Russ. There hadn't been a spark of interest in Hope's eyes.

Opening the Silverado's door, he slid inside. Loving a woman who didn't love you back was hell on earth. "Welcome to the club, you poor bastard." Flicking the key, he started the engine and drove off.

Cameron's mood deteriorated with each passing day. He hadn't meant to give an ultimatum to Caitlin. Yet, once given, he couldn't take it back. Somehow he knew a hard line was needed this time, but he missed her even more than he had the first time she'd left. Missed Joshua.

Being aware that this time he was to blame for her not being with him didn't help.

"Cameron, you want to talk about it?" Mike asked Friday morning, his arms folded, his dark eyes pinning Cameron to the spot.

"No." Talking wouldn't help. He understood that now. He leaned against the opposite wall of the hauler and waited for Mike to continue. He didn't have to wait long.

"Tough." Mike came up from the chair he had been sitting in. He stopped a scant foot from Cameron. His crew chief might be six inches shorter, but he gave the appearance of towering over his drivers. "If you don't want this year to be a repeat of five years ago, you had better get your mind on the race."

Knowing his crew chief was right didn't make the reprimand any more palatable. He gritted his teeth to keep the words he'd regret locked inside.

"You got nothing to say?"

"What do you want me to say?" he shouted. "My son won't look at me. His mother is still running from me."

"So, life has kicked you in the teeth. But it has given you an opportunity that precious few ever get." Mike took another step into Cameron's personal space. "You're even more blessed because you're a black man in a sport that has seen damn few people of color." He pointed a thumb at himself, then a stern finger at Cameron. "You and me and precious few others beat the odds. When you do a piss-poor job of driving, some people say you're having a bad day, others say it's because the color of your skin is finally telling."

Cameron knew what Mike said was true, and it fueled his anger at his own inability to keep his family together. "I can't help what stupid people say."

"Yes you can," Mike spit out. "Win races, and for those you can't win, go down fighting. Drive like we both know you were born to do."

"Don't you think I'm trying?" Cameron shouted.

Mike's eyes narrowed. He was the only one who got to raise his voice. "Trying has never cut it for me."

A knock sounded on the door, then it opened without waiting for a response. Both Mike and Cameron knew who would walk in. Hope stepped inside, looked from her father's stern face to Cameron's angry one. "It's almost time for you to qualify. I don't need to tell you that no one has ever won this race that started in less than thirty-first position."

Cameron's laser gaze swung to Hope. "You don't have to tell me about stats."

Undisturbed by his raised voice, Hope folded her arms. "Good, then I don't have to remind you that the Texas Motor Speedway is the one track where you've never won. Odds are high that you won't Sunday, either." Her eyes gleamed. "If anyone on your team or I could bet, we'd take that and laugh all the way to the bank."

Cameron couldn't keep the surprise from his face.

"We know a winner," Mike said. "Now get your

butt out there and show those gleeful bastards that
this year you're going to own the Texas Motor Speedway."

Hope emphatically nodded her head. "I want to
see how I look in one of those black hats that are pre-
sented to the team owner and winning team. Although I'm not sure where you'll put the Beretta
six-shooters they give with the prize money." She
wrinkled her nose. "Hilliard will probably try to talk
you out of them since he has a gun collection. I'm
surprised he hasn't been hinting already."

For a brief moment, Cameron wondered how Hope
knew Hilliard collected guns. He certainly hadn't.
The question had barely registered when he realized
something far more important was going on: his team
was behind him.

Mike and Hope were leading the charge to give him
a kick in the pants. He hoped it was enough. He pulled
the black bill of his cap down on his head. "Let's go."

Caitlin had a miserable week. She missed Cameron.
It was a deep ache that never completely went away
and worsened with each passing day. She had been
tempted so many times to call him on his cell phone.
Then what? She wasn't going to change, and he was
too stubborn to back down. They were at an impasse.

With no winners.

At work in her home office Saturday morning, she
glanced down at the new story line she'd created. In
the script, Joshua had colored raw Easter eggs with
his crayons and hidden them all over the backyard

for his mother to find. He giggled as she searched the shrubbery and flower beds.

Caitlin's hand clenched on the charcoal pencil. There hadn't been many smiles from Joshua for the past couple of days. She wasn't sure if he was aware that his father would race on Sunday or he was sad because he was completely unable to push his father from his mind. Stephen's father had been out of town on a business trip when they'd returned two weeks ago. She didn't know how much his return on Wednesday had affected Joshua.

Since he traveled so much he spent as much time with Stephen as possible when he was in town. He'd taken the boys to school on Thursday and Friday. This morning they were going to a boat show. Instead of his usual enthusiasm about an outing, Joshua was subdued. She'd considered keeping him home, then decided against it.

Was she right or fair? She was making Joshua face his fears and uncertainties while she refused to do the same. How could she ask a four-and-a-half-year-old to do what his mother wouldn't?

The ringing of the doorbell startled her. It rang again almost immediately. *Cameron.* She was off the stool and running down the hall. Her heart lurched when she opened the door and saw Diana standing there holding Joshua's hand.

"What is it?" Caitlin asked, immediately squatting down to look at him. "Joshua?" When he didn't answer, she looked back up at her best friend. "Diana, what is it?"

"Joshua, why don't you go inside and wait for your mother," Diana told him.

Without a word he did as instructed, his head down. Caitlin watched him until he turned down the hall toward his room.

"Joshua hit Stephen."

"What?" Caitlin jerked her head back around. "He wouldn't do that."

Diana touched her arm. "You know I wouldn't lie to you about something this serious."

Caitlin briefly closed her eyes. "What happened?"

"They were watching cartoons until time to leave for the boat show. Unfortunately *Speed Racer* came on and Stephen asked about Cameron. When Joshua wouldn't answer, Stephen kept on asking questions."

Caitlin swallowed the lump in her throat. She'd confided in Diana why they had returned. *Speed Racer* was a cartoon character who fought crime while racing around the world.

"Bill was in the family room with them, reading the newspaper. He said he was about to tell Stephen to stop when Joshua hit Stephen in the chest. Stephen hit him back. Bill pulled them apart before much else happened. By then both were crying."

Caitlin felt horrible. The boys had been close ever since they'd met. "I'm sorry, Diana."

"I know. I wish there was something I could do to help."

If Dr. Grayson was right, only I can do that. "Thank you. I'm sorry about Stephen."

"He'll be all right. His feelings were hurt more

than anything," Diana said. "He'll be willing to forgive and forget in a couple of hours."

But Joshua wouldn't. "I better go check on Joshua.
Thanks for understanding."

Diana hugged Caitlin and stepped back. "Call me
if you want to talk."

Caitlin closed the door and went down the hall to
Joshua's room. The sight of her son sitting on the side
of his bed, his head bowed, his hands held loosely in
his lap, tore at her heart.

Praying she'd find the right words, she crossed the
room. Sitting beside him, she drew his small body to
hers. "I love you, Joshua."

He leaned against her, but he didn't say anything.

"I know that things haven't been easy the last couple of weeks. Mrs. Howard understands that, too. So
will Stephen."

"He won't want to play with me anymore," Joshua
said, his voice teary.

She hugged him tighter. "Yes he will, but you have
to apologize and promise not to hit him again."

Joshua snuggled closer.

"Do you want to tell me what happened?

Joshua stiffened and shook his head.

Caitlin plunged ahead. Not talking certainly hadn't
helped. "It was about Stephen asking about your father."

Joshua abruptly pulled away to stare down at his
feet. "May I have some water, please?"

Gently she took his arms and turned him to her.
How do you reason with a frightened four-year-old?

"Your father loves you and misses you very much. He wants us to visit."

Joshua's eyes filled with tears. "No. No."

"Baby," Caitlin cried, picking him up and hugging him to her. "It's all right. It's all right," she crooned, well aware that it wasn't, and the answer lay with her.

Chapter 19

Cameron had two of the worst days he'd ever had in racing—and that was saying a lot, he thought as he left the garage for the night and headed for his motor coach. First, number 23 had been cited by the NASCAR officials for being too low to the ground and sent back to the garage. Then, once the car returned, it had to be inspected all over again. He'd just made it in time to qualify. His problems weren't over.

Number 23 had been sloppy in the corners, drifting. He'd come in thirty-second and been glad to do that well. The problem—the tie-rod—had been adjusted for tomorrow's race, but that didn't make him or his team any less anxious about the outcome. The saying that bad things came in threes wasn't always wrong.

Passing though the security gate where his motor coach was parked, he absently spoke to the security guard, his mind still on the race. As Hope had pointed out, no car had ever won at Texas Motor Speedway who had qualified past thirty-first. He wanted to be the first. He wouldn't if he and his car weren't at their best. While he had driven his best, racing on a track by yourself to qualify was vastly different than going against forty-two other cars with the same goal of coming in first.

Bounding up the steps, he opened the door and came to a dead stop. He couldn't believe his eyes.

A wide grin transformed his face until he realized that while Caitlin tried to smile it kept slipping. Beside her, Joshua hadn't lifted his head. He closed his door.

Looked like the prophetic bad-luck number three wasn't going to wait until the race tomorrow.

"Hello, Cameron. I hope you don't mind us waiting," Caitlin said brightly, her arm around Joshua's stooped shoulders.

"No. Not at all." He didn't know what to do, what to say. Obviously Joshua's feelings hadn't changed. "Have you eaten?"

"Yes, thank you. We got something on the way from the airport. The driver of the car Hope sent for us was kind enough to stop," she explained.

He'd been about to sit on the edge of the chair farthest away, but straightened abruptly. "Hope knew you were coming?" He couldn't keep the accusation from his voice.

"I asked her not to tell you." Caitlin brushed her hand over Joshua's head. "I didn't want to distract you."

He still didn't understand. "I'm glad you're here, but I have a feeling there is something else going on."

Taking Joshua's hand, she came to her feet. "It's time for me to help our son get over his fear, and we need your assistance."

Cameron could see the fear and uncertainty in her face. He wondered what had happened to change her mind, but sensed finding out would have to wait. "Anything."

"We'd like to see your car, if you don't mind."

Cameron couldn't keep the mixture of surprise, hope, and worry from his face. His concerned gaze flicked to Joshua's bowed head. "Are you sure?"

"Yes."

Cameron opened the door. "She's in the garage. Security will let us pass."

Caitlin picked up Joshua. His small arms clamped tightly around her neck. She swept her hand up and down his back in reassurance, then went down the motor coach's steps. "Mommy's here, and so is Daddy."

Cameron followed, closing the door after them. Laughter, conversation, and music drifted out from the other motor coaches. A few golf carts rumbled by, ferrying individuals around the infield. They didn't talk as they walked.

He had so many questions buzzing around in his head, but knew they wouldn't be answered until he and Caitlin were alone. However, most of all he wanted to touch her, reassure her. Yet he didn't want to frighten Joshua. He had to content himself with a quick swipe of his hand down her back. "I'm glad you're here," he whispered. Then aloud, "This way."

He led her back to the garage. A few people still mingled outside the haulers parked directly in front of the bay for their car, but it was quiet compared to the earlier noise of the engines being readied for the race tomorrow.

For a brief moment he wished the area wasn't so well lit. His gut ached at seeing the fear on Caitlin's face she so desperately was trying to conquer. He had to touch her again, just a brush of his finger down her cheek.

"You can do this," he told her.

Her smile wobbled, then firmed. Gently she withdrew Joshua's arms from around her neck and turned him to the car, holding him so he couldn't turn away. "This is Daddy's car. It keeps him safe while he does something he loves."

"Mommy, I wanna go home."

She kissed him on the cheek. "Soon." Without giving either a chance to object, she handed him to Cameron, then awkwardly holstered herself into number 23.

"No!" Joshua cried, reaching for her.

"I'm safe, Joshua," she said, her heart beating so fast she felt light-headed. "Just as your daddy is safe." She went over the safety features, her heart steadying as she explained each one just as Cameron had done on the film. Finished, she climbed out, finding it more difficult than getting in.

As soon as she was on her feet, Joshua cried out for her. Taking him, she kissed him, stroked him. "See, Mommy is fine. Just like Daddy will be tomorrow."

"Everything all right, Mr. McBride?" a security guard asked.

"Yes, thanks," Cameron told him.

"Good luck tomorrow," the man said,

"Thanks. Things are certainly looking up."

The man looked at Caitlin and Joshua, and smiled.

"Anytime." Tipping his hat, the guard returned to his golf cart and drove away.

"Let's go see the track." She started walking in that direction, and felt Cameron's arm around her waist. She wanted desperately to lean against him. She couldn't. Not yet.

They went up the incline leading to the pit road where tomorrow the pit crews would be lined up in preparation for the driver. She didn't stop until they were off the grassy infield of the track and on the 1.5-mile track. She set Joshua on his feet and took his hand again.

"Tomorrow Daddy and number twenty-three will compete against forty-two other cars doing what he enjoys, like you enjoy playing on the monkey bars." She pointed to the grandstands. "People will fill the bleachers and cheer their favorite drivers. Many of them will be cheering for your daddy, just as I'll be."

Cameron, walking beside her, caught her hand and squeezed. "Thank you."

"It's time," she repeated. She stopped and squatted in front of Joshua. "It's all right to be scared. I'm scared, but Daddy isn't. He likes racing and has been racing since he was a few years older than you are now. He told you about it."

Joshua tucked in his head.

Caitlin refused to give up. "You remember how afraid I was when you wanted to roller-skate or go higher on the swing, but I let you anyway because I knew how much you wanted to." She swept her hand up and down his arm. "We have to be the same when your father races."

Joshua kept his head lowered. Caitlin bit her lip, looked up at Cameron. He came down in front of Joshua. His large hand reached out, then he clenched it into a fist and placed it on his thigh.

"I love you, Joshua. I never want you to be scared of what I do."

Joshua finally lifted his head. "I don't want you to get hurt."

"Joshua." Cameron held his son tightly to him, then away so he could see his face. "I know, but remember how good it felt flying high in that swing? That's how I feel when I drive. It's what I've always wanted to do as long as I can remember, but not if it makes you not want to be with me."

Caitlin gaped. He meant it. He'd give up racing. It was what she wanted or so she had thought. Cameron would never be content doing anything else. Joshua leaned against his father, but didn't say anything.

Picking up his son, Cameron curved his free arm around Caitlin's waist and started toward the motor coach. It felt good to hold them, and he planned to keep on holding them every day from now on. And tonight Caitlin had given him the chance to do just that.

Once they returned to the motor coach, Cameron released her and searched with one hand through a stack of DVDs. He put one into the player and turned it on. The cartoon movie *Happy Feet* came on. Joshua turned his head toward the sound, but he remained against his father's chest.

Curving his arm back around Caitlin's waist,

Cameron pulled her down on the sofa beside him. "I'm not ready to let either of you go."

Caitlin smiled and placed her head on his shoulder. "Good, because we aren't, either."

Less than thirty minutes into the movie, Joshua was asleep in his father's arms, his face toward Caitlin's, not the television. The heavy weight on her heart lifted. She hadn't been sure he would ever willingly want to be held by his father again. "He's asleep."

Cameron twisted his head until their gazes met. "Thank you for giving my son back to me," Cameron said, his voice thick with emotion.

"You gave him to me," she said with a smile.

He blinked, then laughed softly, then sobered. "I'm glad you're both here with me."

"So am I." She stood. "Let's get Joshua to bed."

Cameron went with her to the room Joshua had slept in before he left. The night-light that had remained plugged in softly illuminated the small room. Caitlin stepped around him and pulled the covers of the twin bed down.

"All of his things are still here," Cameron told her.

Caitlin went to a built-in dresser for a pair of pajamas. Together they got Joshua ready for bed and under the covers.

With Cameron's arm around Caitlin's waist, they watched their son sleeping peacefully. She had made the right decision to come.

"I wasn't sure I'd ever see him in that bed again," Cameron confessed.

"Neither was I."

Joshua kicked off the covers, rolled from his back to his stomach. His parents reached to tuck the covers at the same time, then smiled at each other before Caitlin adjusted them.

"I guess this means we can go to bed," Cameron said, his meaning all too clear.

"I'll say good night then." Smiling, she left the room.

Stunned, Cameron walked into the hall in time to see her enter the other guest bedroom where she had once stayed. He thought that since Joshua was going to be all right, they would pick up where they had left off—sleeping together.

Cameron went to the partially opened door. Maybe she expected him to come get her like he had the first time. Indecision held him still, and then he heard the shower running.

His forehead rested against the door frame. He could imagine Caitlin, naked and wet, beneath the spray. And he was in the hallway.

"Cameron."

His head snapped up. Was he imagining things or had Caitlin called him?

"Cameron."

He was inside the room in an instant. He leaned his head against the bathroom door. "Yes."

"I seem to have forgotten to get soap or a washcloth. Would you mind?"

"I'll be right back." Cameron quickly went to his bathroom and grabbed the things Caitlin had requested, then he returned. He was about to knock and tell her he was back, but then had a much better idea.

Quickly undressing, he picked up the items. The tempting outline of Caitlin's body showed through the steamed enclosure. His body hardened. "I have the soap and towel."

The door opened. Caitlin's gaze swept from his face to the blatant arousal he didn't even think of trying to hide with the towel, then back up to his face. "I guess this means you're joining me?"

"Caitlin." He breathed her name and entered the shower. He had just enough presence of mind to put the soap in the dish before pulling Caitlin into his arms. Her skin was wet and felt like warm silk.

His mouth devoured hers as his hand swept over her, but it wasn't enough. He lifted her, his mouth fastened on her nipple. She moaned, her fingers clutching his head closer. He suckled one, then the other, loving the taste of her, the cries of pleasure.

His head lifted. "Wrap you arms and legs around me."

As soon as she complied, he pulled his hips away enough to find her center and entered. The fit was perfect. His hips began to move, pumping, grinding. The cries of release came simultaneously.

Breathing hard, Cameron steadied Caitlin as she stood on her own. Moving them both under the spray, he grabbed the soap, then lathered and bathed them both with his hands before shutting off the water.

"You're much better than a washcloth," Caitlin murmured.

He kissed her, then reached for the large bath towel

on a ledge and dried them off. Finished, he stared down at her. "I'm glad you're here."

Her hand splayed on his broad chest and she stared up at him. "So am I. Now."

"We'll check on Joshua, and then you can tell me." Cameron went to his room to pull on a pair of jeans while Caitlin opened her suitcase and put on a gown. Hand in hand they went to Joshua's room.

"He hasn't moved," Caitlin murmured.

Cameron looked down at her. "You sound surprised and relieved."

"I am." Taking his hand, she went to his bedroom. She climbed onto the bed, still holding his hand. "I need to tell you some things."

Sitting with his legs under him, the same way she was, their knees almost touching, Cameron caught her other hand. "Then tell me."

She did, ending by telling him about Joshua hitting Stephen. "He was miserable and so scared. I knew I had to stop being frightened if I wanted Joshua to have a normal life with his father."

His hand cupped her cheek. "You did it."

"I realized something else. I had become my mother. I knew how it ruined her life and mine. I didn't want that for Joshua or me," she said softly.

"You were brave enough to ensure that it won't. I knew you had it in you," he told her.

"It just took a while for me to realize it."

"The important thing is that you did."

"What if Joshua can't get past his fears?" she asked. "You can't quit racing. You'd never be happy doing anything else."

"Maybe it won't come to that," he said, his face troubled. "We'll just have to see how Joshua feels in the morning. In the meantime, you better get some rest." Reaching over, he pulled the covers back enough for her to climb over, then he slid beneath the bedding beside her, pulling her against his chest.

She didn't think she would go to sleep. She was too worried about what would happen if Joshua remained afraid. She might not be able to reunite her family after all.

Chapter 20

"Get up! Get Up!"

Caitlin was abruptly awakened by Joshua's voice, and his bouncing on the bed. Frightened, she sprang up. She must have finally dozed off that morning with Cameron holding her as he had all night, both of them too aware that their time together might be limited.

"Joshua, what it is?" Cameron rushed from the bathroom with a towel wrapped around his waist, shaving cream on one side of his face.

"Daddy!" Joshua shrieked, scrambling from the bed and running to his father. "I thought you were gone. I wanted to tell you to make sure you wore your helmet and buckle up."

Tears welled in Caitlin's eyes, but thank goodness she was able to see the happiness in Cameron's face, see him scooping up Joshua to hold him high in the air, hear the delighted giggles of their son. Joshua was giving his father permission to race.

"I will, son. I will." Sitting on the bed, Cameron stared at Caitlin. "I'll have Hope bring you down to the opening ceremonies so you can see me when I get into my car."

"Thanks, and then we can stay for the race," Caitlin said, and waited until his gaze met hers. "Joshua and I plan to be there every second to cheer you on."

Sheer happiness spread across his face. "I'd like that."

"You're going to win, Daddy," Joshua said with complete conviction.

"I'm going to do my best," he said. "I have two more very important reasons to race the best of my life. My family will be watching."

Caitlin's heart lurched. Did he want more from their relationship? She prayed so. "Whatever happens, we'll be proud of you, Cam," Caitlin told him. "Hope told me you had a problem with number twenty-three during the qualifying trials."

He grinned, cocky and sure. "It will just make the race more interesting. I have only thirty-one cars ahead of me, but I'm in a much better position than the eleven behind me."

"You gotta get in your suit first, Daddy," Joshua reminded him.

Setting Joshua on his feet, Cameron stood. "You're right, son. You and your mother get dressed. After breakfast we'll walk over to the hauler and the garage."

"Come on, Mommy. We don't want Daddy to be late." Joshua grabbed his mother's hand and pulled her from the bed.

Grinning over her shoulder, she allowed her son to lead her out of the room.

*   *   *

Race days were always filled with excitement and an overload of adrenaline, but Cameron couldn't recall one that compared to this day. The saying that "they did things bigger in Texas" was certainly proving to be true.

There was a buzz in the air created by the more than 180,000 fans—the largest attended single-day sporting event in the state and among the largest in the country. In terms of vastness, the speedway was large enough to fit eight Texas Stadiums, home of the famed Dallas Cowboys, inside of it.

Carrying Joshua, with Caitlin beside him, Cameron headed for the garage. Once they arrived, he saw the avid fans armed with cameras and Sharpies, on the hunt for their racing favorites. Media from around the country carried long-lens cameras or video cameras. In the mix were the tours provided to employees or associates by the major sponsors. There was a constant swarm of people in and out of the area.

Dozens of campers were on the grounds across from the garage and behind the secured infields of the drivers' motor coaches. Some of the campers had been there since Tuesday to stake out their spot. In the air was the mouthwatering smell of meat cooked on the open grill in front of several haulers, and from the campsites.

And always the loud roar of the engines split the air, while others were silent as they were pushed to and from the fueling area before inspection. Cars were weighed, fueled, then pushed out of the bay and later onto the grassy infield inside the racetrack. The engine wouldn't ignite until the driver flicked the switch at the signal from the grand marshal, the mayor of Fort Worth.

"Wow! Joshua said, his eyes wide as he tried to take everything in.

Cameron laughed. "I pretty much said the same thing at my first NASCAR race."

"I was the same way," Caitlin replied. "Once the fans catch sight of your father, they'll swarm him. Joshua, I want you to hold my hand tight."

"I remember," Joshua said. "They wanted your picture and autograph at the airport, and when you signed autographs."

"Smart boy." Cameron set Joshua on his feet at the side door of the hauler. "Only on race day the fans tend to be more intense. So keep close to your mother. I have to check in with Hope and do a commercial for one of my sponsors."

"I wanna go!" cried Joshua.

Caitlin tensed until she realized Joshua wasn't afraid; he just wanted to follow his father. She caught his hand. "We can watch."

"Is that your fan club?" a snide voice asked.

Cameron's smile faded as he turned to see Burt Haskell, a sneer on his hard face. It was Cameron's bad luck that Haskell's hauler was next to his. He'd never liked the egotistical man who thought winning was everything, and who was known to drive aggressively on the track, bumping cars out of his way. "Hello, Haskell."

Haskell's gaze stayed on Caitlin. "Don't I know you?"

"I don't think so," Caitlin said.

His smile was just short of a leer. "Then I'd like to correct my oversight."

Cameron stepped in front of Caitlin. NASCAR would suspend him if he threw the punch he wanted to throw. "Was there something you wanted?"

Haskell folded his arms across his chest and grunted. "I got what I want. The pole, and I'm going to stay in front. You'll be eating my smoke all afternoon."

Cameron flexed his fingers. "Big words. It remains to be seen if you can back them up."

"I'll win this race and then, later, maybe I'll take something else from you." Grinning, he turned away.

Cameron took a step after him, felt Caitlin's fingers clench on his arm.

"Show him on the track," she said. "Don't give him an easy win."

His head snapped around. That was the last thing he expected to hear from her.

"Put a smile on your face, Cameron. People are watching," Hope told him as she joined them. "Caitlin, don't tell me I was wrong to help you."

"Not her. Haskell," Cameron spat.

"Then show him where it will count the most. On the track," Hope told him.

"Caitlin said the same thing," Cameron said.

"Smart women think alike." Hope smiled down at Joshua. "Hi, Joshua. I've got a special seat waiting for you in the Speedway Club to watch your daddy the first part of the race. Then later you and your mother can come down here for the final laps."

"Wow!" Joshua cried.

"Thank you, Hope." Caitlin smiled. "I appreciate all you've done for us."

"All part of the service." Her dark eyes narrowed on Cameron. "I know it won't go unrewarded."

"Haskell is dead meat," Cameron said.

Hope grinned. "Now that's what I'm talking about. Let's get this commercial over. I'm ready for the race to begin."

"Gentlemen, start your engines."

The loud, earsplitting roar of the engines filled the arena. Caitlin pressed her hands to Joshua's headset to make sure they were in place. "How do your ears feel?"

Her answer was a quick up-and-down bob of his head, and a struggle to turn around to see the cars on the track. They hadn't made it to the Speedway Club. The club was above the stands and thus too far away from the track. She needed to be close to the action, close to Cameron. It was important to her that she be there, even though he wouldn't know it. They ended up on the lookout tower in front of the pit stop with the crew chief, Mike.

"Cameron," Mike said into the mic linked to Cameron. "You know what you have to do. Conserve gas and easy on the tires. We've studied the track and mapped out strategy. This one is going to come down to who can stay in the longest."

"Got it," came Cameron's calm reply.

Caitlin bit her lip. Mike had given her a set of

earphones, but had warned her that if she said one word he'd take them back. He didn't appear to be the type to bluff.

"You've already mapped out the point to hit to get the fastest lap time," Mike went on to say. "It saved you during qualifying time; it will win the race today."

Caitlin jerked her gaze to Mike, but his face was a study in concentration as he watched number 23 in a double-file circle on the track behind the other cars.

"When the green flag comes out, you know what you need to do," Mike said.

"Win the race," Cameron answered without missing a beat.

"The pace car is leaving the track, ladies and gentlemen," the announcer said, excitement in his voice. "This race is going to be a hotly contested one. Burt Haskell and rookie Russ Simpson are looking for their second win to tie Cameron McBride, who starts today in thirty-second place. No driver has ever won at TMS who qualified that far back."

"The flag is out and there they go!" shouted another announcer. "McBride in twenty-three will have to race like he's never done before if he expects to win after starting so far back today."

"The way he's been racing lately, I'd say the odds aren't in his favor."

Wondering if Joshua fully understood what they were saying, Caitlin hugged him tighter to her chest, then cut the mic off and whispered into her son's ear what she'd always told him. "Winning isn't as important as always doing your best."

Through the roar of the engines, she heard Joshua whisper, "We'll still make Daddy the posters."

Pleased and proud, she kissed his cheek. "We certainly will."

Cameron raced smart. With forty laps to go, he was in sixth place; with nine laps left, he took the inside and passed number 90 on the front stretch to gain third place. His hands were clamped on the steering wheel, his eyes were focused on the two cars in front of his. One was Haskell's car. He'd had the devil's own luck today.

There'd been two yellow flags so far, allowing Haskell to pit for gas the first time and tires the second. He'd lost his lead down to ninth in the thirty-seventh lap, but had steadily worked his way back to the front. He clearly intended to remain in the lead as his car stayed in front of car number 07.

Somehow Cameron had to get past him. He concentrated, waiting for the opportunity. Patience was needed in racing as well as skill. Haskell couldn't keep both of them pinned, and he knew it. Cameron's chance was coming.

"Fans are on their feet, and I don't blame them," the announcer said. "This is a race that won't be soon forgotten."

"You bet," agreed the other announcer. "Cameron McBride in number twenty-three has beaten the odds and now is in third place. He's driving like the man who won his first Daytona this year, and won two weeks later at the Las Vegas Speedway."

"You're right," took up his cohost. "He's been smart, patiently waiting his turn to move up, not taking chances. His crew chief, Mike Alvarado, deserves credit as well, but that might cost him. At the last yellow flag, McBride didn't come into the pit stop. Haskell has an edge and plans to keep it."

With the last 3 laps of the 334 to go, Haskell went high on the third turn as he had done all afternoon to give himself the slingshot effect. Number 07 followed, and was on Haskell's bumper.

"Now!" Mike shouted in his ear, but Cameron had already gunned his car, taking the inside. It was a risky maneuver. He had to be out of Haskell's way when his car came down and out of the turn.

Out of the corner of Cameron's eye, he saw the orange of Haskell's car and then the open track ahead. He'd done it, but he had to keep ahead. Haskell wouldn't go down easy.

Caitlin was on her feet, clinging to Joshua's hand, yelling at the top of her lungs with the standing 180,000-plus crowd. "Go, Cameron! Go!"

"Go, Daddy!" Joshua took up the cry.

Then it happened. Haskell's front bumper banged into Cameron's back bumper. Her heart thudded.

Mike hissed. "Hold, Cameron. Hold."

Cameron held, but Caitlin's hands were sweaty. Her throat was dry.

"Is Daddy all right?" Joshua asked, his face worried.

"He sure is," Hope said. "And he's going to be better when he beats Haskell. Isn't that right, Caitlin?"

Caitlin looked down at Joshua. His eyes were glued to hers, waiting. "Yes. We're going to make that poster."

"The white flag is out, Cameron. Let's make history today," Mike said.

Smiling, Joshua turned back to the race. "Daddy's in the lead."

Caitlin looked, but Haskell had shortened the lead by a quarter of a car length. One mistake, and Cameron would lose the race. She wasn't sure she could watch.

"This might be a photo finish, ladies and gentlemen," the announcer boomed. "Here they come! Here they come, going all out! Haskell's car with his fresh tires is getting more traction on the track and gaining. Number twenty-three might pay the price for not taking on tires back at the yellow flag."

Caitlin glanced at Mike. His face was stoic, his eyes hard, his lips moving. She wondered if he were praying.

"Mommy! Mommy!"

She jerked her head around. Her eyes widened. The checkered flag came out with number 23 shooting across the finish line and still in the lead.

Joshua's cheers were drowned out by the crowd and Cameron's crew. Grinning, Caitlin watched Cameron waving his arm, pumping his fist out of his window in victory. She could only imagine the joy and triumph he felt. She shot her arm in the air. "Yeah, Cameron!!"

* * *

"Ladies and gentlemen, you've just seen history made. McBride in twenty-three is the first driver ever to win who started lower than in thirty-first place, and what a way to do it. That was some driving. With the win today at the Texas Motor Speedway, he's had three wins, more than any other driver in the NASCAR Sprint Series."

"McBride is going around the track in his traditional salute to the crowd, his arm upraised," the coannouncer said. "He's pulling off the track. His crew chief and team are waiting for him."

"They pulled off an upset today. His crew chief made the right call. Wonder what Haskell and his crew chief are thinking? One thing I can guarantee, there'll be a shoot-out when these two meet next Sunday at the Phoenix International Raceway."

Cameron flicked the switch to kill the engine and climbed out of his car. He was immediately hoisted into the air by his pit crew. Over their heads, he saw Caitlin and Joshua standing nearby. Their proud smiles made the grin on his face bigger.

Realizing he only had a few seconds before the media would descend on him for an interview, he waved her over. Smiling, she and Joshua came running.

Placing him on his feet, his team surrounded him. He pulled Caitlin into his arms, his mouth finding hers. The kiss was far too brief, but he knew longer might have proved embarrassing for her since there wasn't a doubt that they were being filmed.

He had seconds. He took her hand. "I love you. Marry me."

Her eyes widened. Tears pooled in her eyes.

A mic was stuck in his face, the glare of the camera lights hit him in the eyes. "What are you thoughts after such a phenomenal race?" the reporter asked.

He had to bite his lip to keep the sharp reprimand locked inside. NASCAR had been good to him.

"Speechless with thanksgiving," Hope said, handing Cameron a bottle of Gatorade and his cap.

Cameron frowned. It wasn't like Hope to interfere with an interview unless it was going badly. Then he looked inside the band of the cap. *Yes.*

He shot a fist into the air and put the cap on. He strained his neck, searching for Caitlin in the crowd, but couldn't find her.

"Looking for your team owner, Mr. Hilliard?"

"Someone much more important," Cameron answered.

The reporter didn't see Hope elbow Cameron. "He's kidding. He's still on a natural high."

"Yeah," Cameron said. "I'm thankful to be a member of the Hilliard Motorsports Team, and to have a crew chief like Mike Alvarado."

"This is his victory as well," the reporter said. "You all must be so proud."

"There aren't words to tell you how I feel. Today is definitely going to go down as one of the best of my life."

"You made history today," the interviewer said.

Cameron took a sip of his drink, and finally caught sight of Caitlin and Joshua. His family. His life. "Yes, I did. I have everything I've ever wanted."

Epilogue

"You're supposed to be nervous," Brandon teased from his place beside Cameron.

"You weren't," Cameron said, a broad smile on his face. "When it's the right woman, it's right."

Brandon slapped his best friend on the back and laughed. "Who would have thought we'd end up this way?"

Cameron shook his head, and stared past the assembled guests to the flower-draped terrace door where Caitlin stood, a radiant smile on her beautiful face. Joshua was beside her in a tux with a white rosebud in his lapel.

Cameron slipped his hand into the pocket of his tux and fingered the handwritten notes, delivered every hour by their son with a giggle and a hug. Cameron's mother, Faith, and Diana had managed to keep Caitlin out of sight until now.

Last night when he'd kissed her good night at her door, knowing people would descend on them early the next morning, she'd promised this time there would be no doubt that she'd show up. He'd cherish each note that counted the hours until this moment, when she'd pledge her love forever.

The wedding march began and his world, his family, started walking toward him. Caitlin was a vision of loveliness in her off-white wedding dress. She looked like a princess in the full-length gown. Her eyes sparkled with love and happiness.

Caitlin and Joshua didn't stop until they were in front of him. He reached for her hand, allowing Joshua to step in front of them and to the side. They both wanted him to be a part of the wedding.

"Who gives this woman?" the minister asked.

"I do," Joshua said proudly, and without the giggles of last night's rehearsal.

Diana moved forward and lifted the half-veil, then stepped back.

This was it, Cameron thought as he faced the minister with the woman he'd always love.

"Don't forget to say yes," Joshua instructed in a whisper loud enough for the wedding party and probably the guests on the lawn in the front row to hear.

"We won't," Cameron and Caitlin said, then they smiled at each other.

"Ladies and gentlemen, we're gathered here today in the sight of God to unite Cameron McBride and Caitlin Lawrence in holy matrimony."

Duncan McBride listened to the minister with a smile on his face. Cameron had overcome the odds. Again. It just wasn't winning his second straight NASCAR Sprint Cup Series championship a week ago; he'd won in life, too—the woman he loved and the son he adored.

He'd beat the McBride curse.

Duncan didn't hold out much hope for himself. Faith was happy with Brandon. Cameron was on top of the world with Caitlin and Joshua. The odds weren't in Duncan's favor that Lady Luck would strike a third time. All he had to do was look at the misery on his parents' faces to know that sometimes you had to play the hand you were dealt—even if it sucked.

"You may kiss the bride."

Neither Cameron nor Caitlin needed any urging. Duncan whistled, applauding with their family and friends. If he had to live without love, at least Cameron and Faith didn't have to.

"I present to you Mr. and Mrs. Cameron McBride, and their son, Joshua McBride."

More applause. The legal papers were finalized six weeks after Caitlin accepted Cameron's proposal.

Cameron picked up Joshua for the photographer to take a picture, then set him on his feet and curved his arm around Caitlin's waist for a photograph of just them. Then he and Caitlin were going down the aisle, hand in hand, heart to heart. Diana, Caitlin's matron of honor, caught Joshua's hand and pulled him beside Stephen, his best friend and the ring bearer.

"Man, I'm happy for them," Brandon said from beside Duncan. "Just goes to show that love conquers everything."

Duncan didn't answer. He didn't want to disillusion Brandon. Love didn't conquer all. He knew and regretted that more than anyone.

Read on for an excerpt from Francis Ray's upcoming book

AND MISTRESS MAKES THREE

Coming soon in trade paperback from St. Martin's Griffin

Max kept the pleasant smile on his face as he led the travel agent and her party through the kitchen, the separate living room, and then up the polished oak stairs, pointing out as they went the various improvements to update the house that he had completed in the past two years.

It was in the best interests of Journey's End for him to be cordial, even when it wasn't deserved. Besides, he had been around his friends' teenagers and knew their brains often lagged behind their mouths.

"This place was in pretty bad shape when first I saw it. It took a lot of hard work to bring it back to its former glory, but it was worth it," Max said as he walked down the hallway with Gina. "The pine flooring beneath our feet is original. This is the first of four guest bedrooms." He paused to let them enter the open door, watching Gina's face closely.

Neither he nor his aunt were decorators, but they had both decided that all the guest rooms should have a complete suite of furniture. He tried to see from an outsider's point of view. The queen-sized bed was covered with a bedspread splashed with small pink and red roses. The topper over the single window—at least that was the name he thought was on the package—was in solid pink. It wasn't so overly feminine that a man would go "yuck" if he had to spend the night there.

Gina went in, looked around, glanced at the friend beside her, then, wearing the same placid smile on her face, came back out. The teenager, Gabrielle, didn't bother going inside. She just kept the bored expression on her face.

He'd expected more of a reaction from the women and began to worry. He led them to the next room. "This is the largest of the rooms. As you can see, all have antique furniture and adjoining baths," he said, hoping to get some reaction out of the two women as he opened the door to the bathroom.

Gina peered into the rectangular mirror over the new, upright basin and ran her hand over the stack of freshly laundered white towels on a shelf next to the white commode. "The claw-foot tub is nice. Does the other bathroom have a shower?"

"Yes. It even has a bench." *Finally, some interest*, Max thought. Perhaps he should have hired a decorator, but he had wanted to do it himself. It had been important to Sharon's memory that he do this on his own, just as they had planned. But Sharon had been great with colors and design.

Worry creeping through him, he followed Gina and her friend back into the hallway and watched them enter the next bedroom. He hung back a bit to let them have a better view of the room.

"Do you have your first booking?" Celeste asked, looking at him over her shoulder.

"Yes," Max answered, watching Gina out of the corner of his eye as she opened the armoire, her son stepping in front of her to peer inside. The space for the TV contained an extra pillow and a down comforter. Max figured people on vacation would want to be out sightseeing and not watching television. He had put a small alarm clock radio on each nightstand. "Some of my friends from Memphis are coming up."

Gina closed the doors. "What is your official opening date?"

"October second," he answered. "A month from now. I wanted to give travel agents, such as yourself, and potential clients a chance to see Journey's End and book."

"You must be excited," Gina said, her hand on her son's shoulder.

"A bit." Max was buoyed by the warm smile on her face. "There's another bedroom, and then you can tell me what you think," he said, watching Gina's eyes widen, her gaze dart toward Celeste. Max knew that look couldn't be good. "Or perhaps you'd like to tell me now."

"I, er—"

"Mama thinks it needs work," the little boy blurted.

Gina gasped, her eyes widened with embarrassment. "Ashton!"

"Can we go home now?" Gabrielle asked with a loud sigh. "This is boring."

Gina whirled on her daughter, then took her arm.

"I—" She turned, her gaze stopping in the middle of Max's chest. "Forgive me. I'm sorry." With her daughter's arm clasped tightly, she hurried from the room with her son close behind them.

"He's sorry. Thank you for the tour, and good luck," Celeste said, then followed.

"Well, that went dismally," Max muttered.

Gina didn't release Gabrielle's arm until they were by Celeste's car. "What is wrong with you? How could you be so rude?"

Gabrielle absently rubbed her hand over the upper forearm where her mother had held her. "It was boring."

"The world does not revolve around you, Gabrielle Evette Rawlings. This was business, and you knew it."

"If Daddy—"

Gina held up her hand. "No. Do not go there. I've tried being patient with you, but today is it. When we get home, there'll be no phone for a week and you're grounded."

"But I'm supposed to go with the gang for pizza Friday night!" Gabrielle wailed

"You should have thought of that before you embarrassed all of us by your thoughtlessness."

Flouncing around, Gabrielle opened the car door and got into the backseat. Gina glanced at her son slowly making his way toward her. He had his head down as if he knew he was next to be reprimanded. Ashton was a loving, giving child. He wouldn't hurt anyone's feelings intentionally. Besides, he'd only been repeating what he'd heard her say, so Gina shared the blame.

"You mad at me, too?" he asked as he reached her, his head still down.

Her hand on his shoulder, Gina squatted down to eye level with him and lifted his head. "No, but I wish you hadn't repeated what I'd said in confidence to Celeste. It made Mr. Broussard sad. How would you feel if no one liked one of your drawings you worked so hard to complete?"

Next to soccer, Ashton loved drawing with crayons best. Her refrigerator was covered with his "masterpieces."

Ashton momentarily tucked his head again, then glanced up and said, "It would make me sad, too. I'm sorry."

She smiled at him. "I know. Now, let's go to lunch."

Ashton looked back at the house. "Maybe I should go tell Mr. Broussard I'm sorry."

"I already told him for you, Ashton." Celeste opened the driver's door. "Now, what do you say we go get some food, with apple cobbler and ice cream for dessert? My treat."

As she knew it would, that got Ashton moving. Happily he climbed into the backseat next to a sulking Gabrielle, who had her arms crossed tightly across her chest, her gaze fixed pointedly out of the window.

Shaking her head, Gina slid inside and buckled her seat belt. Not only had she failed in her marriage; she also had failed one of her children. Gabrielle was

too big to turn over her knee, as Celeste advised.
Gina just wished she knew what to do.

Closing the back door after the caterers left, Max
looked around the kitchen. Had he missed the mark?

"Everything went well, so why do you have that
worried look on your face?" Aunt Sophia asked in
her usual straightforward way.

Max walked over to the island, leaned his hip
again it, and folded his arms. "Probably half the people here came for the free food and had absolutely no
intention of staying here; the other half were support-
ive friends."

"The newspaper sent a reporter and that travel
agent came," Aunt Sophia pointed out.

"She thought the place needed work." His arms
came to his sides. "At least that's what her little boy
blurted out when I asked her what she thought of the
place."

"Some children," Sophia said, and the way she said
it wasn't a compliment. "Most of them are a joy to
teach. Seeing students blossom when they suddenly
get it is one of the greatest joys of teaching. However,
the day they took prayer out of the school system was
a sad day for the country and the schools."

Max had heard the sentiment before. "I thought
the place looked pretty good."

Lines radiated across Sophia's broad forehead. "I
don't guess she said what concerned her?"

"Nope, she didn't," Max told his aunt. "She had
barely turned to her son before the daughter said
she was bored. She apologized and hustled her chil-

dren out of the room. You could tell she was embarrassed."

"As well she should have been," Sophia said. "Children need a strong hand."

Max smiled. His aunt might love all of her nieces and nephews, but they had never been able to get over on her as they had with their parents. But she was fair and loving, as she'd proven by hunting him down in Chicago and getting him to turn his life around. "Everyone should be blessed to have someone like you in their lives."

A pleased smile crossed her plain face. "The same goes for you. You rescued me from a monotonous life in Memphis. With helping you, there is something new each day." Her smile faded. "Although, if the travel agent was right, I wasn't that much help."

He went to her. "Nonsense. You helped me bring Sharon's dream to fruition. Kept me strong when I wanted to give up. Without you, there would be no Journey's End."

"Sharon loved you so much and would be so proud that you didn't forget the dream you shared together," Sophia said.

"I loved her, too," he said, his voice hoarse. "I'll do whatever it takes to make this place a success."

"I haven't a doubt in the world."

His aunt always believed in him, just as Sharon had. "That means a lot." He turned toward the back stairs leading up to the second floor, where the guest quarters were located. His and Sophia's bedrooms and two other bedrooms were on the third floor. "I'm going upstairs to see if I can visualize what's missing."

"You do that. I'm going to call your mother and the rest of the family to tell them how it went."

Nodding, Max took the stairs two at a time. He'd worried about his aunt climbing the stairs, but they'd actually been good for both of them to keep in shape. He recalled the first time. They'd both been out of breath when they reached the top. They had looked at each other and laughed. It had been good to laugh again, to share with someone you cared about.

A few minutes later, Max stood in the middle of the fourth and last bedroom. He couldn't see anything missing. All the furniture pieces made the room a little tight to maneuver, but it couldn't be helped. The antique store wouldn't break up the sets.

Sharon had wanted the B & B to have period pieces and to be as comfortable and as charming as possible. But was it?

Frowning, he pulled the travel agent's card from his pant pocket. He'd failed Sharon in life; he didn't want to fail her in this as well. If Gina Rawlings could help him, he'd find a way to convince her to do so. Perhaps when they met again, her two rude children would be nowhere around.